Death
of a
Diplomat

SUSAN COLLINS

A Detective Crime Novel

Published by Birch Tree Publishing

Printed in the United Kingdom
Available at all off-line and on-line bookstores

Amazon.com and other retail outlets

ISBN: 978-1-990089-71-8

www.Birchtreepublishing.com

First Printing Edition, 2024

Table of contents

Chapter 1..6

Chapter 2 The 20th and 21st July.....................................16

Chapter 3 Tragedy at the Villa...30

Chapter 4 Mr. Reeves Giallo..38

Chapter 5 The Testimonies...50

Chapter 6 Intermission 58

Chapter 7 The Inquest..71

Chapter 8 Unforeseen Occurrences..................................92

Chapter 9 Diplomatic Relations.....................................104

Chapter 10 Revelations 111

Chapter 11 The Grapple with Death................................123

Chapter 12 The Missing Link..133

Chapter 13 To Part and to Love......................................140

Chapter 14 Epilogue..185

SUSAN COLLINS

Introduction

Throughout the many years of my friendship with Reeves Giallo, I have detailed many of his cases in which I took part of; the first of which was the Birmingham case in the summer of 1917. In that account, I mentioned briefly that I had met him in France prior to the Great War and that he had made such an impression on me that he remained at the forefront of my mind until our chance reunion in that small, unassuming village of Birmingham Kitts Green. Much of the world believes that the Birmingham case was our first collaboration together; this is in fact quite untrue. The Birmingham case was merely the first case we encountered on English soil and, in reality; Giallo and I had found ourselves under extraordinary circumstances working as, if you will pardon the phrase, partners in crime in Paris four summers previously.The case Giallo encountered there while he was still a detective in the French Police is admittedly lacking in comparison to the cases he encountered later in private practice; the death of a diplomat in Paris seems almost ludicrously commonplace with, for example, his life and death struggles with these murders. However, despite the humble and unusual beginning of our partnership, this one case affected me not only on a professional level regarding crime and detection, but more importantly, on a personal and emotional one. In that warm summer in France in 1913, my eyes were opened in more ways than I had ever possibly imagined, and it is because of the events which transpired during that fateful summer, twenty-three years later, I am still very much at the Paris' side.

St.Louise

London, October 1936

Chapter 1

Paris here I come

I found myself in Paris 1913 July visiting my old friend from
school. I had just been given a month's leave from my work
at Christie's and had been at a loss as to how I could best use
my time when I had received a letter from Larry Stokes who
generously offered me to stay at his father's villa in the Paris
capital. It had been many years since we had crossed paths since
leaving Haney and I took up the offer at once, packing a suitcase
and the necessary items required for a visit to the Continent.

Having crossed the Channels, I then headed for Paris by train.
I arrived in Paris in the early evening and was soon greeted by
Larry, who welcomed me warmly at the station. Although it had
been in fact at least eight years since we had last met, Larry
Stokes was very much his jovial old self and his grey eyes shone
with obvious delight upon seeing a familiar face in the crowd.
St. Louie,' he cried, grasping my hand and shaking it firmly.

'Awfully pleased that you could make it. I wasn't sure
whether you'd take up my offer seeing that it was on such short
notice.'

'My dear fellow, I wouldn't have missed the chance to meet
up for the world.'

It was at this moment that I looked hard at my old friend. He
had hardly aged at all. Dark-haired, urbane and infinitely
charming, Larry Stokes suited very much the role of an
ambassador's secretary; the ambassador being none other than
his own father, Sir Charles Stow, the British Ambassador to
France.

But I saw the years had given him a quality which he had lacked during our Haney years; seriousness which I had hardly seen before and which I saw now in his matured countenance. There was a certain gravity about his person, which conveyed immediately that his line of work involved matters on an international scale, and I marvelled inwardly at the change. Perhaps I showed my surprise too plainly, for Larry caught my expression and gave a brief grin. 'Almost didn't recognise me, eh?'

Not at all,' I replied as we made our way to the car waiting outside the station, my suitcase in hand.

'You've hardly changed at all, my man. I was only noting how serious you look now.'

To my surprise, a slight shadow came over his face at that moment and he murmured lowly, 'To tell the truth, I wouldn't be surprised if I did look rather grim these days, St. Louie.'

'Is something the matter?' I asked instinctively.

The grey eyes turned to look at me for a moment before diverting their attention to the driver who now held the car door open for us. He shook his head and said in a lighter voice, 'Don't mind me, St. Louie. I wouldn't want to spoil your visit when you've only just arrived.' He smiled, gesturing to me to enter the car. I obeyed obediently, and we soon set off.

Once we were safely on our way, Larry's dark mood at the station vanished and he was soon pointing out various attractions and important buildings as we drove through the city. Having never been to the capital, I listened to him attentively, occasionally commenting or replying to something he had said or drawn attention to.

They adorned the streets with decorations; streaming satin ribbons of red, black and gold and fluttered in the warm summer night from lampposts and Paris flags of all sizes were displayed proudly out of windows along the streets.

Several photographs of a sturdy looking, dark-haired man with sharp features was also to be found almost everywhere in the city and whom I quickly recognised as the Paris king.

Paris National Day coming up next week,' explained Larry, catching my curious gaze. 'No matter how many disagreements they have, the Jodus and the Hallonds at least love their king and country, that's for certain. It's probably the only day when they're actually united and not at each other's throats, thank God!' He chuckled a little.

'But your father doesn't have any problems with the French, I hope.'

'Father? Not in the least. The French, despite their disagreements, are very agreeable chaps. No, he's actually had a spot of trouble with the Germans at the Embassy.' His face darkened again, and I feared he would once again retreat into himself and we would then descend into an awkward silence. Thankfully, this time he went on and added: 'At least we think it was the Germans.'

'What happened?' I asked, my voice jolting a little as the car traversed a rocky section of the road. My eyes momentarily glanced outside, and I noticed we were no longer in the heart of the city but heading toward the suburbs.

'Some of Father's Embassy papers went missing during the night last month. Things like this sometimes happen – papers being accidentally misplaced, that sort of thing…but unlike those other occasions, the papers in question were of a highly sensitive nature, if you understand my meaning.'
I nodded.

It was common knowledge that tensions in Europe were reaching a critical level and that any misunderstanding or mishap, however small, could stoke the already dangerous fire even higher. The only outcome of such tensions, of course, would be a war on a massive scale.

'Of course, Father went into a complete rage when he found out. It didn't help at all that I was not only his son but also his secretary,' he sighed, wincing visibly at the memory. 'I was certain that I had locked them up in the Embassy safe that evening before we left and Stancliff the sentry saw me locking it as well. Can't figure out at all how the safe was broken into the next morning.'

'Was anything else taken? Other papers, I mean.'

'No, only the ones I've told you about. Which narrows it down really…this was no ordinary break-in. The thieves knew exactly what they wanted since they didn't have a need for the rest. That's why we suspect the Germans and that wily fellow Cliffberg.'

'Cliffberg?'

'Oh, Vondick vann Cliffberg. He's the German Ambassador in Paris. Brilliant man – got a doctorate from Oxford or Cambridge, so I've heard, but he's a clever old devil. Always coming up with new ways to learn what we at the Foreign Office are up to so that he can inform his superiors in Berlin. Ah, here we are.'

The car stopped, and we stepped out onto the gravel drive. I looked about, noting the neatly kept gardens, the white-painted garden tables and chairs laid out on the terrace around the corner and, moreover, the distinctly English atmosphere which surrounded us. This was only increased by the appearance of the house itself, a solidly built redbrick villa covered in ivy which seemed peculiarly out of the place in the flat surroundings of the Paris landscape.

An elderly man who I immediately recognised as the butler came out of the oak front door and greeted us in sombre English tones. I realized Sir Charles Stow would spare no expense in keeping his private sanctuary in the country absolutely English despite it being in the heart of another country.

'Ah, Stanford,' said Larry as I retrieved my suitcase from the car. 'This is my old friend, Nicolas St. Louie.'
Stanford's usually impassive face gave a faint glimmer of a smile as he set his dark eyes on me. 'I remember you well, Mr St. Louie.'

'And I you, Stanford,' I replied, recalling those wonderful school holidays I had spent at the Wiggins' summer retreat in Birmingham, where Stanford too had been the butler. 'I expect you can hardly recognise me now.'

'You have indeed grown much taller, Mr St. Louie, but one could still recognise you. May I ask whether your family is faring well, sir?'

'You may indeed,' I smiled. 'They're all faring splendidly, Stanford.'

'I am glad to hear that, sir.' Here, he gave a small bow of the head and returned his attention to his master.

'Mr St. Louie's room has been prepared as you requested, Master Larry. Supper will be in half an hour.'

'What? So early in the evening, Stanford? It's only half-past six now,' cried Larry, glancing at his watch.

'Your father has returned earlier than usual today, sir, and requested that supper be served earlier at seven o'clock,' came the butler's voice in calm monotones before he politely picked up my suitcase and carried it into the house.

Larry gave a small sigh next to me. 'Didn't expect him to come back so early today...Samantha must be out of her mind with nerves!'

'Samantha?' I asked, not recognizing the name.

Before he could reply, a woman had emerged from the house and was rapidly making her way towards us. She was a young woman with brown hair, an elegant tall creature whose slim figure was only accentuated by the pale blue evening dress she wore. Her oval face too was extremely pretty and there was an air of coquettishness about her, which I found quite attractive.

My overall impression, however, was that though I was certain that I had never seen her in my life, I was sure that I had seen her somewhere before.

'Oh, thank goodness you're here, Larry' she said when she had reached us. 'I was having the most awful time – oh!' Here she stopped abruptly when she saw he was not alone. She looked up at me curiously (despite her considerable height, I still managed to be an inch or two taller than her) and I noticed that her dress complimented her eyes, which were of the same colour.

'Hello, Samantha,' said Larry easily. 'This is –'

'No, no, no...let me guess,' the woman replied, waving her hands to silence him. There was a theatrical brief pause during which those blue eyes scrutinized me closely.

'If I'm correct, you must be Nicolas St. Louie.'

'You've guessed correctly,' I agreed warmly.

'However, I'm afraid I can't say who you are, though, and forgive me if I'm wrong. I know I've seen you somewhere before.'

'You probably have,' she replied with a note of triumph in her voice. 'I'm Samantha Milton.'

'But of course!' I exclaimed, realization finally dawning on me as I shook the hand which was proffered gracefully to me.

'You're the stage actress.' I marveled at the fact that here before me in the middle of France was one of the rising stars of the West End who had delighted audiences with her comical and dramatic roles in various plays, some of which I had seen in London.

I turned to Larry reproachfully. 'I didn't know you were acquainted with Miss Milton Larry.'

'Oh, we're more than acquaintances,' cut in Samantha happily before Larry could say a word. 'We're engaged to be married, Mr St. Louie.'

Now this piece of news was quite unexpected, and I immediately offered my hearty congratulations, which the couple accepted in varying ways; with Samantha looking the very picture of happiness while Larry looked as if he was half-delighted and half-embarrassed at receiving them.

'Well, I'm very glad you're both here,' she said, flashing us a smile of genuine relief. 'Larry, your father has been most horrid to me.'

'What? Has he said something unkind to you?' he replied with a start.

'Nothing as bad as that, but he's made the afternoon quite unpleasant for me today. So unpleasant that I was compelled to spend most of my afternoon in the garden just to avoid him. Not that I dislike the garden, I actually prefer strolling about it to being shut up in the house all day but there's just something dreadful about not being allowed to do as one pleases...' She glanced at me, her manner one of slight embarrassment. 'I'm afraid to say that Sir Charles and I don't quite get along, Mr St. Louie.'

'I'm sorry to hear that, Miss Milton,' I replied with sympathy. Larry's frequent complaints about his father had informed me of the latter's difficult character. Though the man was a brilliant diplomat, it was well known that when it came to conversing with people, his social skills could be quite lacking and he could even become extremely unpleasant when he was in a bad mood.

'When did he arrive home?' asked Larry.

'Around half past four.'

'It must be something important then,' concluded Larry with a sigh. There was a sudden crash from within, which sounded like a piece of expensive china being dashed to pieces onto the floor.

Glancing at each other with concern clearly written on our faces, the three of us decided that now would be a good time to enter the house.

As I let Samantha through the front door, Larry pulled me aside, his face anxious.

'I wonder whether you could do me a bit of a good turn, old fellow.'

'Of course. What is it?'

'I wonder if you wouldn't mind keeping news of our engagement to yourself for a while. Well…my father doesn't know about it and I'm not very keen to let him learn of it either. For all intents and purposes, Samantha's merely a guest of mine staying with us for the summer.'

Catching his drift immediately, I said: 'Secret engagement then, Larry?'

'For the meantime, yes.'

I assured him I would keep mum about the entire subject, and he thanked me gratefully before we passed into the entrance hall and into the inner sanctum of the villa.

Inside, the house differed little from its exterior in the sense that it was completely devoid of Paris influence. In contrast to the numerous photographs of the Paris king in the streets of Paris, a giant portrait of King George V dominated the center of the entrance hall. Although I confess I am proud of being an Englishman and have even fought for King and Country in the War, I found Sir Charles's extreme patriotism a little alarming if not slightly in bad taste, especially when we found ourselves in the heart of the Paris countryside.

What thoughts must have gone through the minds of the two local housemaids as they went about their work with the bearded face of the British King staring impassively over them?

An angry, booming voice alerted us of Sir Charles's presence in the drawing room and we quickly directed ourselves in the latter's direction.

Samantha was nowhere in sight and I thought it wise of her to have retreated somewhere in the house in view of the storm that was brewing up in the drawing room.

As we stood at the doorway, we were greeted with the sight of the ambassador rebuking one maid, who looked quite beside herself with misery. She had upset a vase while transferring a new batch of flowers in the presence of her master, who was now scowling over the top of his newspaper. Sir Charles had not even risen from the depths of his comfortable armchair and yet the power of his voice which had heard from the hall had already informed me that this was a man not to be reckoned with.

'And mind where you're going, girl! I can't have you breaking vases every time you come in here. Do you have any idea how much these antiques cost?'

'Je suis desolé, Sir Charles,' said the girl in terrified tones, and continued to offer distressing apologies in French.

The Englishman dismissed her with a curt wave of the hand.

'That's enough as it is, Camie. C'est fini. I'm sure you've other duties to attend to – jump to it!' he barked brusquely and my heart went out to the poor girl who swiftly made her exit past us, her eyes welling up with tears.

Meanwhile, the dissatisfied master of the house tossed his newspaper violently onto the floor and grumbled audibly: 'Girls like those should be abolished.'

Larry passed me a fleeting look of despair before entering the room.

'Father, my friend St. Louie has arrived from London.'

Up to that point, I had never had the chance to meet Larry's father in person seeing that though I had been invited numerous times to spend the summer at the family's summer retreat, Sir Charles had always been abroad, apparently on some diplomatic duty or other and had been rarely present in the upbringing of his two children.

Though Larry never talked of her as I could feel that this was a painful topic for him, I had a feeling that his mother, the late Lady Elizabeth, had met a premature death partly because of her husband's cold and unsympathetic nature. Larry had taken the death of his mother hard when she passed away during our last year at Haney but I believe it was mostly because of her entreaties before her death that he followed in the footsteps of his father who he clearly regarded with a mixture of fear and respect.

That same feeling of fear and respect somewhat permeated my impression of the man when he finally deigned to rise from his chair. He was not a tall man, but his solidly built frame and his piercing blue eyes in a hard dark face were the epitome of the strict and unyielding disciplinarian, the image of which was only emphasized by his greying beard. It appeared very much that Sir Charles had been a navy man in his youth and, as my vision subconsciously wandered about the room, my deduction was proved correct by the various pieces of naval memorabilia adorning the mantelpiece and walls. But what impressed me most was the contrast between this sullen-looking fellow and his son, who looked and acted quite the opposite from his father. Sir Charles extended a hand towards me in a gruff acknowledgement of my presence.

'So you're Larry's friend St. Louie, eh?' he said shortly. His telegraphic style of talking complemented his character superbly. 'He's talked quite a lot about you.'
His eyes travelled up and down my person and I shifted a little in discomfort. 'I've heard you work at Christie's, Mr St. Louie.'

'Yes,' I replied. 'My father is one of the directors of the company and offered me a post as his secretary hoping I'll follow in his footsteps one day.'

'Same case with Larry here. Though being honest, I'd rather like to see him in the navy than in the diplomatic service. The Royal Navy builds up a man's character.
It teaches him discipline and the meaning of duty, Mr St. Louie. Not at all like those pencil-pushing types you find in the Foreign Office. Laziest people I've ever come across in my entire career. I think they've hardly done an honest day's work in their entire lives,' he said contemptuously.

'Father,' coughed Larry in obvious embarrassment.

'And I know you've heard about the fiasco we encountered at the Embassy the other day?' his father continued, not noticing Larry.

'The theft of your papers, you mean, Sir Charles?'
I answered quickly, as I had no wish of incurring Sir Charles's wrath when I knew he was quite passionate on the subject.

'Scandalous business,' he growled with feeling.

'This sort of thing would have never happened in the Navy. Utterly unthinkable. But it's sheer laziness and irresponsibility.' The implication of his words was not lost upon Larry, who I could see biting his lip in an effort to keep his feelings in check.

'However, young Tom is in the Navy – so that's a sort of compensation, thank God,' said Sir Charles with a sigh.

'I suppose you've already met him, Mr St. Louie?'

This 'Young Tom' was Tom Mc Cloud, a cousin of Larry's who I had briefly met during a visit to London during Christmas a couple of years ago, and I nodded.

'He's a Lieutenant now – you'll probably meet him at supper. He's come down to visit us for the summer on a month-long leave. Marvelous boy, as well. If only all the young men in England could follow his example.'

'Oh, are there more guests staying here, Sir Charles?' I asked, to steer him away from what was an uncomfortable subject for Larry.

'What? Oh yes, all of them are friends or relations of the family,' replied Sir Charles distractedly. 'There's Janett Thompson, another one of my nieces and Luke Grimms, my daughter's Ella's fiancé.' He paused and then added scathingly:

'And then, of course, there's that actress Samantha Milton...'

It was clear from his tone that Samantha Milton was not the type of woman that the exceedingly conservative Sir Charles approved of and I could only imagine the stress which the young lady underwent every time she and Sir Charles found themselves in the same room. I was therefore not surprised that Larry had pleaded with me to keep quiet about their engagement, since I suspected that his father would have flatly refused to give his consent had even a whisper of this possibility reached his ears.

Our conversation stalled at this point and I wondered, a small sense of panic coming over me, how on earth was I able to extract myself from this difficult situation.

Fortunately, it was at this exact moment that the gong sounded from the hallway, announcing the start of supper. Larry and I snatched our opportunity to retreat from the drawing room, muttering that we had to dash upstairs to quickly change for supper.

Running up the staircase two steps at a time, we nearly crashed into a young woman descending the stairs when we reached the first landing. She gave a startled cry, and I immediately attempted to offer my apologies when Larry said...

'Ella!'

Ella St. Cloud was Larry's sister, who was older than him by two years. She was a blonde-haired, ethereal sort of woman who I remember being fascinated by when I was growing up and as she stood there a step or two above us like a Greek goddess, I could sense that my adolescent fascination I had had with her had not quite released its hold of me. Currently, she was wearing a cream-coloured evening dress and was gazing at the both of us with an air of profound irritation.

'Met Father, have you?' said Ella to no one in particular. 'I'm surprised that the entire country didn't hear him from the drawing room.'

'Hullo, Ella,' I said as pleasantly as I could.

Ella's stony expression gradually warmed, and she smiled at me.

'Hullo.

Nicolas Sorry for being so cross but Father does sometimes annoy me. You've caught us at a bad time, I think.'

'Yes, I've heard it all from Larry on the way here. I hope everything is all right.'

'We' Ella was all she said. She cast a glance at our flushed faces.

'But we can talk much later…you look absolutely travel-worn, Nicolas. I'll let you both change for supper,' she said, moving aside to the other side of the stairs. She turned her head towards the top of the stairs and called with a distinctly disgruntled expression on her face: 'Are you coming, Luke?'

We followed her gaze and heard hasty footsteps from above us before they were followed by the sight of a bespectacled young man who halted in his tracks when he saw the group of people assembled in front of him.

'Oh, good evening, Larry,' he said awkwardly as he descended the stairs before joining Ella at her side. His eyes then focused on me with intense curiosity and also, to my surprise, what seemed to be a faint suspicion.

'Nicolas St. Louie,' I said, offering my hand, which he shook cautiously. 'I'm one of Larry's friends. Came to stay for a month.'

The uneasy look on his thin face dissipated, and he smiled.

'Ah, I see. Larry mentioned you. It's a pleasure to meet you, Mr St. Louie. I'm Luke Grimms.'

Remembering that this was the man whom Ella was now engaged to, I offered my second round of congratulations on another impending marriage which caused, like the last time, varying degrees of happiness. Grimms's smile to me had expanded into a grin while Ella smiled enigmatically, with little visible emotion on her part. In fact, her fiancé looked very much as if he desired to talk further about their engagement when Ella quickly cut in that her brother and I needed to change for supper. Abashed, Grimms nodded his head and led his betrothed downstairs while we ascended.

'Your room's in the west wing, St. Louie. Second farthest on the left. Stanford's probably already prepared your things by now, good fellow. I'll meet you here in ten minutes.' He dashed off to the other wing, and I obediently followed his directions, finding my clothes, as he had said, already prepared and laid out on my bed. Changing as quickly as I could and after taking a momentary glance in the mirror to check that my appearance was in good order, I soon joined Larry at the top of the stairs and we made our way down to the dining room.

The rest of the family was already at the table and along with Sir Charles, Samantha, Ella and Luke Grimms, two other familiar faces were also to be seen. In naval evening dress and sitting on the right of his uncle was the aforementioned Tom Mc Cloud, who indeed suited the part of the naval officer with his tanned, handsome face and dark beard, which was very much the vogue in the Royal Navy.

Sitting rather self-consciously next to him was another cousin of Larry and Ella's, Janett Thompson, who I recognised with some surprise. For Janett had really been only a girl of twelve when I had last seen her eight years ago, and she had now blossomed into a pretty young woman. She looked up as we entered, smiling shyly as I took the place opposite her.

Seeing that Larry and I had been late for supper, the beginning of the meal was a relatively quiet affair. When soup was served, it was apparent that the entire party was wholly interested in nothing else but the consumption of it. As we ate in silence, I noted the strained atmosphere in the room and wondered whether this was a normal occurrence at supper when Sir Charles was present.

Sir Charles' outburst of some quarter of an hour previously had soured the mood somewhat, but there was a certain sense of foreboding in that warm dining room which I could not quite place. Perhaps it was the strain of the past day's travelling which had influenced me to think so.

I was certainly feeling tired about halfway through supper and once the main course of thoroughly English fare had concluded could think of nothing but sleep.

Consequently, I listened rather than took part in the little conversation which petered out around the table.

I learned that Ella's fiancé was a barrister in London and a member of the King's Counsel while Tom was soon to join the naval squadron stationed in Italy, a prospect which his uncle wasted no time in giving his hearty approval.

Tom, it seemed, appeared indifferent to the matter, and I wondered whether he too had been pressured to join the navy by Sir Charles since his uncle's opinion carried much weight in the family circle.

After supper, we made our way to the drawing room where coffee was served. Though I was by now exhausted, I gratefully accepted a cup from Janett, who took a place next to me on the chaise longue. Watching me gulp my coffee down, which I found rather belatedly to be scalding hot, she commented wryly...

'Thirsty, are you?'

'No, exhausted though,' I said, leaning a little into the cushions behind me.

'Coffee might be the only thing left to keep me from nodding off here and now.'

I had always been close to Janett when we were growing up. Having grown up with sisters of my own, it had not been difficult to act as a sort of elder brother to her, especially seeing that I was six years her senior.

She was fond of confiding in me whenever we had the chance to meet, as her cousins were too impatient like Larry or too distant, like Ella. I alone seemed to understand her loneliness, seeing that I was the only son of my family. But now, when it had been eight years since our last meeting, I wondered how the situation would stand between us as she was now no longer a girl of twelve but a young woman of twenty. As I pondered this in my mind, I felt suddenly quite conscious of my age. However, I soon forgot about it when we quickly entered our familiar pattern of conversation and we talked of various things and of various people whom we were both acquainted with.

Though the years seemed to fall away as we spoke, I grew increasingly aware of the shyness in her manner, which I had noted beforehand during supper. It also seemed to increase rather than abate as we continued our discussion and it was on more than a couple of occasions during our conversation that I saw her pale cheeks flush slightly when she listened in silence as I expanded upon a certain topic.

I wondered what it meant, seeing that she had never acted like this in our previous meetings. Perhaps it was simply the usual timidity of manner which often accompanies a young woman when she speaks to a young man. Or perhaps it was a sense of glaring self-consciousness which I had also encountered when I was about the same age.

Whatever the cause, I was, as I have said, too tired to make sense of anything that evening.

Janett left me momentarily to refill her cup, and my gaze then wandered about the room. I observed with some amusement that most of the family preferred to remain in groups; Larry was conversing quietly with Samantha as they sipped their coffee, Sir Charles was in an intense discussion about naval matters with Tom while Tim Mac David was engrossed in enlightening Ella of a case he was currently working on while Ella was looking far from being amused, or at any rate, enlightened about anything.

Looking at the sadly mismatched couple, it was painfully plain to see that Sir Charles had had a considerable role in arranging his daughter's engagement if not being the sole person who had orchestrated the entire matter himself and without I knew, soliciting Ella's own feelings on the subject. It was little wonder then that I had encountered that strange, strained atmosphere at the dining table; it was probably one which prevailed constantly at the house.

It was about half an hour later that Sir Charles retired early that evening and the party took this as a sign that we, too, should follow suit and retire to our rooms. I received this news with a sense of intense relief and I gratefully dragged myself up to my chamber, my mind once again thinking of nothing but sleep. After wishing the others a tired good night and heading towards my room, I encountered a tall, fair-haired man returning from the other end of the corridor.

He was dressed in a waistcoat, shirt and tie, but I could see from his tanned face he was not a member of the family. He started a little upon seeing me but recovered and hastily nodded his head, muttering a 'Good night, sir', and quickly made his way downstairs. My curiosity suddenly piqued, I watched his descent distractedly before I gave into my now constant yawns and finally went to bed.

Chapter 2

The 20th and 21st July

The following few days after my arrival were uneventful. A downpour of continuous rain meant that most of us were forced to remain indoors, except for Larry and his father, who habitually arose early and were at their desks in Paris by nine in the morning. The rest of us whiled away the time as best as we could. Samantha, who was not only an accomplished actress but also I found to be a highly talented water-colourist, spent most of her time painting in the conservatory, which was attached to the house. She and Janett seemed to have bonded well before my arrival and Janett was often found accompanying her while reading a book, which she invariably carried everywhere. They also joined both Tom and I in our games of badminton.

Tom was initially annoyed with Janett's company which I thought rather hard-hearted but after a few games in which both of them beat Samantha and me three games in a row, they soon got along with each other extremely well, even laughing at our exasperated expressions when Tom scored against us thus defeating us for the fourth time running.

Tim Mac David, who I soon found to be of a relatively aloof character, rarely joined in our pursuits, leisurely or otherwise. Instead, he was often to be found in the library perusing the morning and evening editions of the local and English newspapers, the latter of which I too read daily to inform myself of the latest cricket scores.

'Luke is such a tiresome bore,' sighed Ella as she saw me emerging from the library one morning. 'Is he still in there, Nicolas?'

'I believe he is. You can go in, if you like – he's just finished reading The Times.'

'Oh no, I'll wait until he remembers that we have to visit one of Father's friends at noon. Besides, it's always Luke' habit to read the local Paris papers once he's finished with The Times. I doubt he'll be out before eleven-thirty.'

'Oh, are you both going out this afternoon?' I glanced at one of the nearby windows and I could see that although it had stopped raining, the clouds still looked dreary and uninviting.

'The weather's still rather awful, isn't it?'
Ella shook her head. 'I'm afraid we've already postponed our visit last week. Father's friend is a bit of an invalid and is returning to England for the summer. I doubt we can see him later on in the year since by that time Luke and I would already be married. And besides, Garvious's driving us in the car.' She heaved another weary sigh. 'I do despise these social conventions…making everyone visit you or vice versa when the only thing that's happened is that you've become engaged.'
I chuckled. 'You were never one for formalities, Ella.'

'No, I never was, was I?' she agreed, letting a small smile light up her somewhat gloomy countenance. She looked up at me and said brightly: 'It's so good to see you again, Nicolas. Goodness knows how long it's been since I've seen another friendly face.'

'You make it sound like as if this place is the end of the world,' I said with some amusement.
To my alarm, some of the cheerfulness in her face disappeared as I said this.

'Sometimes, to tell the truth, I think it actually is,' she whispered.

Up to that point, I had never seen Ella so grave. Her personality of old as I knew it was an odd mixture of haughtiness, unconventionality and a certain recklessness of temper which was more suited to perhaps a woman living ten or twenty years after the events of this account. She was simply too modern for her time and in the past; she had flaunted her open disdain for social convention quite daringly, which had often resulted in monumental rows between father and daughter.

She was fond of cigarettes and was not afraid to be seen drinking with the gentlemen after supper, which had caused quite a scandal when her younger brother was still at Haney and barely eighteen.

Her bohemian habits had perhaps sobered a little after the death of their mother, which came very much of a shock to them, but I did not know that the years had worn her character down as much as it appeared now. In fact, I realized she looked very much like Larry when I met him at the train station a couple of nights previously and a grim thought passed through my mind about whether this had all been Sir Charles's doing.

She passed her eyes back and forth along the deserted corridor and without preamble, took my arm.

'Do you mind accompanying an old friend to the conservatory?' she asked, recovering herself.

'Not at all.'

'Good. I could do with a bit of a walk.'

As we made our way towards the stairs leading downstairs, we passed the library and I could see Grimms staring out of the slightly open doors and the expression of displeasure on his sallow face informed me he had recognised that his fiancée had been conversing with me in the corridor.

He hastily lifted his newspaper to his face as I caught sight of him and I realised that despite his intelligence, Tim Mac David was an extremely jealous and insecure man.

Once we arrived at the conservatory, which was deserted this rather chilly morning, Ella immediately reached for a cigarette from a box on one of the tables, which evidently belonged to her father.

'I hope you don't mind.'

'Of course not. No – not for me, thanks,' I added quickly as she proffered the box to me.

'Still very much the naïve Nicolas St. Louie,' she teased, lighting her cigarette airily. 'I doubt you've ever tried one.'

'Well, I have to confess I had a bit of a try once. In fact, Larry was the one who egged me on. It was a couple of weeks before the end of our last term at Haney, I think.'

'And?'

'The experience proved disagreeable to me.'

She laughed then and her light peals of laughter echoed around the glass windowed room. I stared at her with some surprise, unaware that I had said anything amusing.

'Oh dear, I've offended you,' she said, sitting down next to me on the wicker couch. 'It's just that you sounded like Luke just now. Always speaking in those dry Victorian tones when a simple word or phrase really could suffice. "The experience proved disagreeable to me." You should hear Luke giving me a reply when I ask about what happens in the courts when he's there. He turns even the most exciting court cases into something out of an old history book.'

'Well, if you find me rather dull,' I said a little stiffly, finding it difficult not to feel a little annoyed at such an unflattering comparison.

'No, no, no, Nicolas! My goodness, how on earth can you even think so?' she cried soothingly and patting my hand affectionately.

'You're much too endearing to allow me to entertain a moment's thought that you're dull. True...you can be a little old-fashioned but that's only bias colouring my opinions. You mustn't take my silly talk too seriously.'
Convinced of her sincerity, I gave a small smile.

'In fact, I wouldn't have minded much if Father asked me to marry you instead of Luke really,' she said musingly, deeply inhaling on her cigarette. Again she took me by surprise by talking about this matter in so blunt a fashion, but I pushed away my bewilderment and asked lightly:

'When did your father ask you to become engaged?'

'Last December, during the time we spent in London for Christmas. We were having tea with Luke's family; I thought it was just a social call when Father suddenly excused himself and asked me to come along with him into the study. Then he informed me what I was about to be proposed to and that I should on no account refuse Luke's offer or he'd take away Larry's inheritance.'

'The utter cad!' I cried despite myself, knowing that Ella was always one to protect her younger brother, more so after their mother had passed away.

She cast an admiring glance at me as I flushed a little, aware of my less than gentlemanly outburst.

'So Mr St. Louie has some fire in him,' she murmured with a mischievous grin, to which I laughed rather sheepishly. 'Well, yes…Father knew I didn't care for Smithe about my inheritance and so he threatened to take away Larry's instead, which he knew I would never allow if I could help it. And so, in what you would call a highly uncharacteristic move, I accepted Luke's 'proposal.'

'Luke seems rather pleased with himself on this point.'

'He indeed would be. Marrying the daughter of a baronet was perhaps one goal that his parents taught him to pursue in life,' she said scornfully. 'From the very cradle, perhaps. I've heard that Luke's family wasn't wealthy to begin with, but his father made a fortune in coal just a few years before he married. Oh, you mustn't misunderstand me, Nicolas.

I have a lot of healthy respect for the meritocracy, but not when your son ends up being like Mr Luke Grimms, MT, who simply looks for ways in which to raise his status in society with no attention whatsoever to the feelings of other people. Everything he ever talks about is really all about himself. Or at least it ends up relating to him in some way – it's quite revolting, really.'

Here she stubbed out her cigarette, and I regarded her sympathetically.

'Don't feel sorry for me, Nicolas,' she said, catching my pitying look. 'If there's one thing I can't stand, it's someone feeling sorry for me. And if there's one thing you'd have to feel sorry about is that I happen to be the daughter of one of the callous men in England.'

She paused.

'But then again…I do thank the fact that I am his daughter or where would my poor brother be?'

Although our characters and beliefs were so different, my heart warmed at her words.

'Larry's jolly fortunate to have a sister like you.'

'You're much too kind. I sometimes wonder whether he'd be better off without me.'

There was a sudden clap of thunder, and we instinctively turned our gazes outside. The clouds, which had been grey and dreary only half an hour before, were now pouring with rain. A storm was brewing, and I was glad that I was currently indoors; I would not have been tempted for all the gold in England to venture outside at the present moment. Then I saw a blurred outline of a man hastily making his way from across the garden in the conservatory's direction. Not noticing us, he threw open the door and cannoned inside, dropping what appeared to be a pair of garden shears noisily onto the floor. As he removed his soaked peaked cap, I recognised him as the man I saw in the corridor outside my room the night of my arrival.

Suddenly realising that he was not alone, he let out a torrent of curses, which I will not recount here. Shocked by his language, I was about to reprimand him when Ella said sharply, rising from her seat,

'What are you doing here, Mallon?'

'I beg your pardon, Miss.'

'I thought you were given express orders by my father to never enter through the conservatory doors. There is a servant's entrance on the other side of the house,' she said, her voice unusually high and tense. She had transformed into the role of the master's daughter marvelously, I thought.

Mallon bowed his head apologetically. 'Forgive me.

I forgot about it in my haste to get inside. I will remember to use it the next time it rains.' His dark eyes focused themselves upon her and though there was nothing offensive in his manner now, there was something in his expression which I did not like. He was not a bad-looking fellow, and he even reminded me of a certain acquaintance of mine in the past who at the moment I could not quite place but the over-earnestness of his manner signaled a man who was highly attractive and also dangerous to women.

Ella cast a doubtful look towards him but said nothing more and returned to her seat. Having been wordlessly dismissed, Mallon left the room, picking up his shears as he went.

I looked after him disapprovingly.

'Good Lord, what an impudent fellow! Who is he?'

'Mallon's the gardener here.'

I raised a brow. 'Odd that a gardener would wander around the corridors late at night,' I mused, more to myself than anyone in particular.

'A gardener? Mallon?'

'Yes, I ran into him the night I got here. He was coming from the other end of the corridor near my room, if I remember correctly.'

'Ah,' said Ella in comprehension. 'He must have been repairing the electric lights in the other guest bedroom. They've been giving us no end of trouble these past few months. Mallon's a sort of modern day Figaro.'

'Who?'

Ella sighed in what was clearly mock exasperation.

'Larry and I must take you to the opera one day, Nicolas.' I quickly but politely fended off the offer, seeing that opera was far from being one of my favourite pieces of entertainment. Childhood recollections of my various aunts dragging a young boy of ten into the opera house at Covent Garden is certainly an experience I hope never again to repeat. The mere idea of people singing and acting in such an unnecessarily exaggerated fashion and how people could get any sort of entertainment from that was beyond me.

'He's a jack-of-all-trades,' she explained. 'Father's really a miser. Why get over one man, he says, when one man can clearly do the job. But so far, he seems to take to his duties well, although his manner, as you can see, requires a little getting used to.'

'I dare say,' I replied, taking an instant dislike to the gardener, who seemed much too at ease with himself.

A polite cough from the door leading into the house alerted us to Stanford's presence.

'I beg your pardon, Miss Ella, but Lord Carlton has just telephoned. He begs both you and Mr Grimms to stay indoors in on account of the storm and would like to cancel the luncheon scheduled for this afternoon.'

'Oh, really. Lord Carlton's much too kind – and we've already postponed our visit once before.'

Ella turned to me darkly, lowering her voice.

'And Father is going to have a fit when he hears we haven't paid a visit to him yet again.'

'He would also like to inform you that he has already telephoned your father' said Stanford a little louder, evidently catching his mistress' words, 'and that he has fully explained the matter to him.'

I smiled a little to myself; despite his outward appearance, Stanford clearly knew the inner workings of both Larry and Ella's minds intimately.

'Thank you, Stanford,' said Ella, also unable to repress a brief grin of amusement as the butler left us.

'And thank God for him as well!' she added in relief.

'Well, your wish of not seeing this illustrious Lord Carlton has been granted too,' I reminded her.

'Yes – if only my other wishes could be fulfilled in that way as well, I'd be perfectly content.' She shrugged her shoulders wearily before rising once more to her feet.

'I should inform Luke that the luncheon has been cancelled…and goodness knows how we'll spend the day now! Really, Nicolas, I'm half tempted to ring up Lord Carlton and beg him to let us visit regardless of the weather.'

'Out of the frying pan and into the fire?' I remarked sympathetically.

'Very much so,' sighed Ella sadly.

Though the 20th of July proved dismally uninviting in terms of the weather, we were greeted with a welcome change of mild sunshine on the 21st and the effect it had on us was instantaneous.

'The gods must have known it was Paris National Day,' quipped Larry, peering out of the dining-room window after we had finished breakfast. Seeing that it was a national holiday, he had taken the day off from his duties at the Embassy and keep the rest of us company.

'The grass doesn't look quite dry yet, but there isn't a cloud in sight, thank God.'

'The weather looks simply divine,' agreed Samantha.

'It would be terrible of us not to venture outside after all these days of being cooped up indoors.'

'Tell you what, why don't we head into town, then?' suggested Larry. 'You haven't seen the city in daylight yet, St. Louie. And seeing the French and especially the Hallonds celebrate is quite a sight. All this Carnival thing and tradition and all that. Not that you'll see much of that today…it is more formal around this time, but never mind that. What do you say, old chap? Think you're up to it?'

'Certainly Larry,' I replied eagerly, folding my napkin and setting it aside on the table. Like Samantha, I was feeling the inevitable sense of tedium after being stuck inside for so long despite the company of the others and was keen to stretch my legs a little outdoors.

The rest of the party enthusiastically welcomed the idea of leaving the villa for a journey into town and after finishing our various pieces of business, Garvious and the car were called for at about half-past eleven to take us into Paris. Only Tim Mac David put up some opposition, muttering that he still had important matters to attend to and, as a result, Ella had to remain at the house, though she promised to join us later in the day.

As the car could only accommodate three people at a time; Larry, Samantha and I were to be driven into town first, while Tom and Janett were to follow afterwards once Garvious returned to the villa. Samantha and Larry occupied the passengers' seat while I sat up front with Garvious, who was a jovial chap and was more than obliging when I quizzed him interestedly upon the various mechanics and features of the car. We arrived in the city in due course and the inhabitants of Paris were making their presence known to us. The shops, apart from a few restaurants and cafés, which were already quite full with customers, were closed.

'Where are we going to meet Tom and Janett later on?' I asked as Larry led the way with Samantha at his side.

'Not sure, St. Louie. Garvious says that he'll drop them off in front of the Hôtel de Ville in the Grand Place in about half an hour. We might have a spot of luncheon when they arrive. While we wait for them, let Samantha and I show you round the place.'

I was then duly thrust into their care and I was brought hither and thither to various landmarks nearby. Paris, though much smaller than other cities like London or Paris, was indeed a splendid-looking place and its fine architectural masterpieces impressed me very much, though I admit I hadn't the faintest idea of the logic behind them. This impromptu tour was not without its difficulties; the city was packed with what seemed the entire populace and I soon became disengaged from my surroundings as I struggled to keep up with Larry and Samantha's frantic pace through the crowd.

As the minutes went by, so too did the amount of people as they increased in number, evidently hoping to catch sight of their beloved monarch as the cortege passed through the streets in a quarter of an hour's time. I observed they were all smartly dressed in their Sunday best and many of them were chattering in various Walloon and Jodus dialects, which I found incomprehensible, prompting me to worry somewhat as to how

I could communicate with the locals if I encountered any difficulties.

Wishing very much I had brought my Baedeker with me, it was at this precise moment that I found myself politely but firmly asked with hand gestures to make way for the approaching advance guard of the royal family. I did so admiring the cavalrymen resplendent in their full dress uniform on their noble steeds as they passed before realizing with a jolt that I had lost sight of Larry and Samantha amongst the teeming crowd.

After a few minutes of frantic searching, I knew I was indeed hopelessly lost for Larry and Samantha had seemed to disappear into thin air. Fortunately, I recalled we were to meet Tom and Janett at the Town Hall and glancing at my watch. It was only five minutes until they were expected to arrive. Judging perhaps that it would be best for me to retrace my steps and make my way there, hoping they would all be waiting there for me, I wove my way through the packed streets.

As I was repeatedly noting the street signs around me, I paid little attention to where I was going and I cannoned heavily into a short man who gave an exclamation as the parcel he was carrying dropped onto the ground.

Apologizing profusely on both sides, we immediately stooped to retrieve it, but being the taller one between us, I got to it first and straightened myself and he too did the same. As we did so, I was acutely aware of myself looking into a pair of very brown eyes in a round cherub-like face which glowed appreciatively as I handed back the now slightly dusty and dented parcel.

'Merci, monsieur,' he said, smiling up at me and it was then that I noticed his extraordinary sharp jaw which looked more pronounced importantly as he spoke.

'I'm afraid it's got a little dusty– ' I started before realizing that the man might not understand English. I paused and was about to repeat what I had said in my halting schoolboy French when he cried in perfect English.

'Ah you, I presume, are the mysterious St. Louie, are you not?'

I stared at him, my mind momentarily uncomprehending. 'Why yes…but how did you –?' I started, extremely taken aback by the stranger's words. Was the fellow able to read minds as well as speak English, which I noted was rare amongst the French in the city?

The little man gave a small knowing smile, and he turned, pointing with a leather encased finger towards none other than Larry and Samantha, who seemed to have magically reappeared outside a nearby tobacconist and who were anxiously craning their necks over the crowd.

'Your friends have been looking for you,' the man said simply as a way of explanation.

'Come, I will lead you to them.'

Dazed and at a loss for what to do, I followed my newly made acquaintance through the crowd. Though he was a small man of perhaps only five feet in height, he carried himself with great dignity in his smartly cut suit and it was with great politeness but authoritative firmness that he asked various people to allow us to pass through.

Clearly here was a man who had experience in dealing with people, I thought, and I wondered briefly whether he was a politician of some sort.

'There you are, St. Louie!' cried Larry, looking relieved when we eventually emerged from the crowd. 'We've been looking everywhere for you.'

'Sorry, Larry…I got stuck in the crowd a little way back. Part of the royal guard was coming through and had to make way for them.'

'It's all right,' came Samantha's soothing tones, smiling at me.

'At least we've found you at last.' She turned to my companion. 'Thank you so much, monsieur…we wouldn't have found him without your help.'

The man bowed gracefully and touched a hand to his hat.

'Pas du tout, mademoiselle. I was happy to be of help.'

He took out a pocket watch from his waistcoat pocket and, upon reading the time, frowned a little.

'But my apologies – the time it marches on and I shall have to take my leave or I will be late in meeting my sister...'

'Oh, but yes, don't let us detain you any longer,' said Larry sympathetically, knowing all too well the plight of running late for an appointment.

'You are too amiable,' the other man smiled. 'Mademoiselle, messieurs,' he said, touching his hat again and taking his leave of us. I looked after his little figure as it quickly disappeared into the teeming populace, my mind transfixed by the man's remarkable personality. And it was not only his personality which had caught our attention.

'Extraordinary look the man has,' commented Larry a while later as the three of us made our way towards the Grand Place. Entering the square, I was at once impressed with its size and its collection of fine Gothic buildings and guildhouses. We saw Tom and Janett already waiting for us there outside the Town Hall and they waved at us as we approached. 'Seemed almost too big for him but I'll bet you he'll give the men back in Whitehall a run for their money.'

'He's a nice chap,' I said. 'How on earth did you get him to help you?'

'Oh, he overheard us shouting over the crowd. I think he was just passing by when he heard us. He suddenly came forward and offered his help – very nice of him,' replied Samantha.

'You know, I've only realized that I didn't ask him his name...oh, what a pity. We could have invited him to the villa later on Larry.'

'And you always being the sociable one of us,' laughed Larry. 'Losing your touch Samantha.'

'Stop it, Larry,' warned Samantha sternly, though there was a glint of playfulness in her blue eyes.

'At last, you're all here,' said Tom, looking at us reproachfully with his green eyes and looking very much the authoritative naval officer who I knew from experience couldn't abide unpunctuality.

'Thought you said half-past twelve Larry?'

'Sorry Tom,' I said. 'It's my fault that we're late. I – er – got lost in the crowd.'

Tom cast a somewhat disapproving look at me but nodded mutely in acceptance. Beside him, I saw Janett attempting to repress a small smile in vain and which she hid quickly behind her gloved hand.

'Well, I think that's too much adventure for one day,' remarked Larry diplomatically. 'Shall we find a place to have lunch?'

'Shall we go to the gallery at the Rue de Vangus?' asked Janett, seizing my arm.

'You haven't been there yet, Nicolas. It's quite a beautiful place.'

'Yes,' said Samantha. 'Janett's quite right; it really is. And I suspect, too, that it'll be less crowded there.'

A short walk from the town hall soon placed ourselves at the Galeries Royales Saint-Helga, which as both Janett and Samantha had already described beforehand as exquisite. As we sat down at a small outdoor café, I looked around at the surrounding shops stretched along the long arcades and observed aloud.

'I say, it reminds one of Italy, doesn't it?'

'The arcade here was the first of its kind,' said Larry, taking the menu from the waiter, who was now giving us recommendations in rapid French.

'The French can probably take credit for those later built in Milan or similar.'

Our orders taken. The server disappeared inside and Larry turned to me, the corners of his thin mouth curling into a grin.

'So it was the Royal Escort who you had to let pass, eh, St. Louie? Are you certain it wasn't a group of les femmes jolies who strayed along your path?'

'Larry you know you're talking nonsense,' I said, flushing a little, seeing clearly what he was hinting at. Janett looked somewhat confused while Tom sighed and opened the front pages of a local newspaper he had bought on the way here.

Being one of my closest friends, Larry knew far too well of the certain difficulties I had encountered when coming across the gentler sex, which had caused me no end of trouble when we were growing up. He was especially fond of recounting the time I once apparently got tongue-tied when a pretty cousin of his had addressed me and inquired how old I was during a visit. I had overcome my boyhood shyness soon afterwards, but then again, I had always noticed that I seemed more at ease in the company of fellow boys during my adolescence. Thankfully, by now at twenty-six I had trained myself to be more relaxed in the presence of women and to the best of my ability, to at least enjoy their company. However, this one and, dare I say it, trivial childhood incident gave Larry no end of amusement throughout the years and it would always invariably emerge as a subtle joke or other when he was in one of his more jesting moods.

Noticing my embarrassment, his fiancée chided him soundly and Larry obediently composed himself and turned his attention to the dishes and pots of coffee which were now being placed in front of us. We then enjoyed a delightful lunch, our conversation turning to the itinerary for the rest of the day and forgetting the little man we had met earlier in the street.

Little did we know we would soon re-encounter our newly made acquaintance under less enjoyable circumstances.

Chapter 3

Tragedy at the Villa

After our enjoyable excursion to the capital on Paris National Day, I remember the subsequent days as ones of great turbulence and discord and which ultimately ended in tragedy. One reason for this unpleasant turn of events was the fact that Sir Charles had somehow got wind of his son's engagement to Samantha. This had caused a very unpleasant scene during supper one evening, which was then continued in the library where both father and son had argued, their voices muffled but audible behind the closed door.

The rest of us remained in the drawing room, where the prevailing mood was one of mingled embarrassment and gloom and memories of an enjoyable day spent in Paris only two days previously were as far away from our minds as possible. Samantha had sat a little apart from us, gazing wordlessly into the fire. I could see that she was painfully aware of the situation and had even offered to leave the house during supper. Larry would have none of it and had openly said so in front of Sir Charles, which had only enraged the latter more.

Understandably out of sorts, Samantha retired to her room a little while later, at around half-past nine. Janett appeared rather pale and upset; I surmised she was of a rather sensitive disposition and I attempted to comfort her a little by assuring her that everything would soon be all right.

'Nonsense,' said Ella coldly as soon as I said the words.

'Father would never budge from his position. He's a stubborn bastard.'

Her unreserved use of language sent a slight ripple of shock across the room and we stared at her.

'Ella,' warned Tom, glancing up from the cup of coffee, which was cold and undrunk in his hand.

'Defending him, are you Tom?' she retorted angrily.

'I wouldn't be surprised seeing that you epitomize almost everything that he stands for.'

'I'm not defending him. I find his behavior as repulsive as you all do. But someone has to understand the situation from his perspective. Larry's his only son, Ella, and that usually means that he can't be free to marry where he chooses.'

Ella appeared as if she wanted to disagree with him on this point, but then seemed to think the better of it and instead shot him a look of great disdain. Personally, I thought it rather dreadful to have even more discord amongst the family when there was already a row between father and son and I was inwardly grateful when I heard Ella and the rest of the party announce their intention to retire ten minutes later. I stayed behind, intending to wait for Larry. However, when it appeared that neither Sir Charles nor his son would leave the library in the next few hours, I too made my way to my room at about half past ten.

I was already in my nightshirt and dressing gown when there was a knock at my door. Opening it, I saw Larry framed in the doorway. Far from his usual urbane self, he looked upset and unusually pale, but he made to move away when he saw I was preparing to turn in for the night.

'Sorry, St. Louie. Perhaps I'll come talk to you tomorrow,' he murmured apologetically.

I protested vigorously, assuring him he was causing no inconvenience to me and invited him inside. Sitting down on the chair near the fireplace, he nodded gratefully as I pressed a large glass of whisky into his hand.

'Thanks,' he said, and he gulped the entire contents of his glass down as if attempting to draw strength from it.

'God above, did I need that?'

I moved away from the sideboard and stood opposite him, waiting to see whether he would broach the subject which the both of us knew was at the forefront of our minds.

He did not disappoint. Words soon tumbled from his mouth, aided it appeared by drink and I soon learned that the outcome of their furious row had resulted in an ultimatum Samantha would have to leave the house by the morning or Larry himself would have to leave, disinherited and unrecognized by his own father.

'But that's not the point. Damn his money. I don't need any of it. And neither do I need his patronage. People usually think Ella's the one who's got the nerve to stand up to him, but I'll prove that I'm just as self-sufficient as she is.'

I glanced at him, feeling unconvinced. Though Larry was a decent chap, I knew he had expensive tastes and that a life without his father's support and patronage would be difficult and would be made even more so when supporting a wife and, perhaps, in the near future, children. Also, the chances of him having any career in the Foreign Office would be made impossible once he turned his back on his father and follow his own ambitions through. I hardly liked Sir Charles personally, but I could easily see how much Larry's welfare depended upon him, especially at such an early stage in my friend's career.

You don't think I'm being serious, do you?' Larry pronounced, gazing at me with open suspicion.

I am taking you seriously. I'm merely thinking whether this would be the best thing to do for your sake.'

'You think I'm a coward, don't you? You don't think I have the nerve.' There was an edge in his voice which I recognized as anger and I hazarded a guess that the alcohol was now playing havoc with his emotions, which had been put under enormous strain during the evening. Although I wanted very much to admit that it was simply the whisky that was causing such a violent change of temper in him, I took up the mantle of mediator.

'Larry, it's been a long night…for all of us. You're tired and worn out. Take some rest and see how you feel in the morning,' I advised.

'Good heavens, who could have told him about our engagement?' Larry blurted out suddenly, ignoring me.

'My dear fellow, you know I would never have dreamed of –'
He cut me off with a curt gesture, the empty glass nearly flying out of his hand.

'Of course not. I didn't mean you, St. Louie.'
I was rather pleased by this show of his confidence in me, despite his current state of mind.

'Perhaps word got out of it somehow,' I suggested.

'It happens, Larry. Perhaps at the Embassy or –'

'Impossible. I've only told a few people and none of them are from the Embassy. You, Ella, Tom, Janett…and Stanford, of course.'
I contemplated this.

'Yes, it doesn't seem likely that any of them would have told your father.'

'But someone must have done. That's the only way this whole thing would make any sense at all to me.'
He shook his head.

'It makes me ill, St. Louie…to even think that one of my family would have told my father. It's just revolting – there's no other word for it.'
My thoughts flew to Tom and his close ties to Sir Charles because of his position in the navy. After all, he had been the one who had tentatively risen to his uncle's defense after dinner and had subsequently incurred Ella's wrath.
It certainly wasn't like Tom's character to break his word to anyone, much less his own cousin. The remaining suspects weren't much promising either; Janett was much too afraid to even talk with her uncle, while I suspected that Ella would rather die than discuss anything with her father. The only remaining person was the butler, Stanford. But he was a trusted member of the household, and I knew he was extremely close to both his young master and mistress.
It was indeed an entirely unpromising list of suspects, but that wasn't the point now; what mattered now was the dilemma which Larry and Samantha now had to face because of this terrible betrayal of trust.

'Sleep on it, Larry,' I said, opening the door and standing by it. From my vantage point there, I could hear the clock chiming midnight from downstairs. It must be much later than I imagined.

As if I'd get any rest at this rate. God, what a night.'
There was a momentary silence.
  'St. Louie?'
  'Yes?'
  'Do you still have your grandfather's old revolver with you?'
  'Why yes. As a matter of fact, it's in that drawer there,' I said
with some surprise, gesturing towards it.
  'Why do you ask?'
  'I know I sound mad, but I'm half tempted to take it to his
room and blow his brains out there and then.'
  'Now calm yourself. You're talking nonsense,' I said sternly,
though immediately alarmed by his outburst.
I removed the glass from his hand and pulled him to his feet.
As soon as I did so, it was quite clear to me that the glass of
whisky I had given him had not been the first one he had had
this evening. He had probably taken some downstairs before
coming up to my room, and the smell of alcohol upon him was
now quite overpowering. Knowing instinctively that it would be
best for me to see him in his room, I led him outside into the
now darkened and deserted corridor.
Upon reaching his room, I helped my half-drunk friend inside.
Larry eased himself wearily upon his bed, still in his dinner
jacket, appearing on the verge of collapse. It would certainly not
be long before he passed out, I thought privately, and what a
good thing it would be too. At least that way I could be sure that
he wouldn't be able to do anything foolish during the night.
I was about to say good night when he whispered, his voice a
little indistinct and slurred: 'I say, old chap, I spoke out of turn
just now. I hope you didn't take any offence, St. Louie.'
Peering into the dim light afforded by the single lamp by his
bedside, I could see that his face was now suddenly alert and
that he was indeed in earnest.
I shook my head.
  'Of course not, Larry. It was probably the alcohol talking just
now.'
  'What? Oh, yes..Quite.' He stared glumly into the darkness.
  'But damn it, St. Louie. What am I to do? What on earth can I
tell Samantha?'

'Leave it all until the morning, Larry. And I'm certain that whatever you decide to do, Samantha will always stand behind you.'

I left him sitting in the darkness and it was with a sense of relief that I heard him finally lie down a moment later when I shut his door. Returning to my room, I checked the drawer containing my revolver, assuring myself that it was still there.

I rarely made it a rule to travel with a gun in my luggage, but my father had insisted that I take it in case war should break out during my time on the Continent. I hardly thought it would come to that, but had taken it with me to humor him. It was still there, tucked neatly under a pile of shirts. I was tempted to lock the drawer but then decided that Larry's talk of killing his father had only been on the spur of the moment and left it as it was.

I returned to bed and soon fell into a fitful slumber; my mind troubled by the developments of what had been quite a dreadful evening. Tossing and turning, I heard the clock downstairs distantly striking one, which was followed by a faint popping noise from somewhere close by. Too tired to investigate, I threw the bedcovers over my head and finally fell asleep.

The assembled group I encountered at breakfast the next morning was grim and ashen-faced, though I was pleased that Samantha was still among our party. Larry looked rather worse for wear, but had risen to his feet and appeared calmly defiant when I entered the dining room, perhaps expecting his father. His expression softened considerably when he saw it was me.

'Oh. Morning, St. Louie,' he said, his voice shaking a little in what I assumed was relief.

Taking my plate of bacon and eggs and seating myself at the table, I noted that the rest of them had already finished breakfast. I glanced at the clock on the mantelpiece; it was nearly nine o'clock.

'You're not heading to the Embassy this morning, Larry?'

'He's been up since six this morning waiting for Sir Charles,' said Tom, putting down his newspaper. He was avoiding eye contact with Ella, who was sitting opposite him and who had obviously not forgiven him for rising to her father's defense the previous evening.

'It's rather late, though. Shouldn't the both of you be at the Embassy by now?'

'Yes, that's what I thought,' said Tom again, cutting over his cousin.

'I've told you already,' he said, now directing his attention to everyone else at the table.

'Someone has to go upstairs and check if he's all right.'

'How wonderfully gallant of you, Tom,' said Ella coldly. He ignored her and went on: 'I'll just ask Stanford if he's heard anything.' Tom left the room and reappeared with the butler a few minutes later.

'No sir,' Stanford was saying. 'Sir Charles didn't ring for his tea this morning. But then again sir, I must inform you that per your instructions, I have checked his bedroom and found it to be empty.'

'What?' cried Larry, looking surprised.

'You mean he's already left the house?'

'But that's impossible,' rejoined Samantha.

'Larry's been up since six o'clock; he can't possibly have missed him.'

'He might have left earlier,' I suggested, taking a sip of my tea.

Rather abruptly, my naïve suggestion was shot down as soon as it left my lips, and I then threw myself into finishing my breakfast, feeling unwanted. The driver was then called for and Garvious confirmed that Sir Charles had not called for the car that morning.

'Well, he can't have walked to Paris. He's probably still in the house,' said Tom.

The atmosphere in the room was becoming increasingly frantic and Stanford cleared his throat politely during all the excited flurry of conversation. We all quietened down at once.

'If I might be so bold, I might suggest checking the study, Lieutenant Mc Cloud. Sir Charles sometimes spends his mornings there.'

Larry immediately volunteered to go upstairs. I could see from his expression that he had decided on a course of action over the night and was prepared to go through with it. Tom and I joined him and we left the ladies downstairs with Grimms.

Sir Charles's study was unusually on the second floor, opposite his bedchamber in the west wing and just a few rooms away from my own. I assumed he had done so for convenience to save him the trouble of going upstairs after a long night in his study. We approached the double doors gingerly, Larry suddenly looking as if his nerve had failed him.

'Come on, Larry,' said Tom impatiently.

Larry did as he was told and knocked. 'Father?'

There was only silence. When there was no reply, he knocked again with more force but with the same result of receiving nothing but resounding silence.

'Are you sure he went to his study after you argued?' asked Tom.

'Well, I'm quite certain he didn't leave the house,' replied Larry somewhat shortly. 'We parted, and he went upstairs. I followed up a while later. He's probably decided not to speak to me ever again,' he added darkly.

'Tom, you try calling him.'

Tom's authoritative voice rang out along the corridor, but even the sound of his favorite nephew's voice seemed to have no effect on the man inside.

'Try opening it,' I said, feeling strangely unnerved by the silence from within the room.

'It's locked,' said Larry, trying the handle. He made way for us as both Tom and I took turns in trying to wrench the door open but to no avail.

'Do any of you have a key?' I asked. They shook their heads.

'Father, let no one but himself have a key. He might have given one to Stanford –'

'There's no time for that, Larry,' interrupted Tom.

'He might be in trouble for all we know. There's only one thing for it then. St. Louie, help me with this door.'

Larry gave a small cry of protest, possibly fearing his father's reaction at having his doors unceremoniously broken down, but we ignored him. Choosing what appeared to be the weaker one of the two doors, we threw ourselves against it. The doors were made of solid oak and it was with an aching shoulder that Tom and I finally smashed them open on our third attempt.

Disregarding the various splinters of wood on the carpeted floor, we stepped cautiously inside.

The room was dark, as the curtains had not been drawn. From what I could see in the near pitch-black darkness, Sir Charles was nowhere to be seen.

'Should we turn on the lights?'

'There aren't any – Uncle Charles refused to have them installed in his rooms. Here, take this.'

Tom tossed a box of matches from his jacket pocket towards me and I quickly lit a candle, which was sitting on a nearby table. Taking it in my hand, the light from it reassured me somewhat, and I called out....

'Sir Charles?'

When we received no answer, we made our way inside.

By the light afforded by the candle, I could see that the room was Spartan in design and neatly arranged.

Two armchairs were by the fireplace while bookshelves made from mahogany surrounded us. I suspected, too, that Sir Charles's study would also look quite similar to the drawing room downstairs, full of naval memorabilia and other miscellaneous items.

Three windows faced outwards into the garden down below and a large desk occupied the space in front of the middle window, facing towards the entrance of the room.

Tom suddenly caught me by the wrist. He too, had apparently fixed his attention on the desk at the same moment as I had.

'Do you smell that, St. Louie?'

'Gunpowder,' I said, familiar with the scent due to numerous occasions of hunting in the country with my father and uncles. Tom no doubt knew the smell well because of his naval experience, and he nodded in agreement.

We both immediately darted towards the desk and Tom gave a cry of surprise as the candle illuminated the slumped and motionless figure of Sir Charles Stow, a small amount of blood trickling from a single gunshot to his grey-haired head.

'Good God, he's been shot!'

Larry rushed into the room, hearing his cousin's exclamation.

'What?'

Tom stretched out his hand and felt for a pulse in the diplomat's neck.

'Nothing. He's dead, Larry.'

'He can't be,' said Larry sharply, waving us to move out of the way. 'Let me see.'

We stepped aside, allowing him to see for himself.

I saw Larry's already worn out expression take on yet another layer of mental anguish. Pity overwhelmed me at once, but it was combined with the uncomfortable sensation of a feeling much more sinister and cold-hearted suspicion. Despite my attempts at shutting them out as I stared at his grim profile, Larry's words of last night were now playing repeatedly like a gramophone record in my head: 'I know I sound mad but I'm half tempted to take it to his room and blow his brains out there and then.'

My train of thought was interrupted by Tom, who was reaching for something on the floor near Sir Charles's left hand.

'St. Louie, the candle…quick!'

I passed it to him.

'Wait!' I said as he reached forwards.

'Use a handkerchief…it might have fingerprints on it.' Retrieving one from his pocket, Tom wrapped it around a revolver and my heart skipped a beat as I immediately recognized it as my own and I stared at it in disbelief.

'He's shot himself,' said Larry faintly before I could say anything.

'My God, what have I done?'

A doctor was soon called for as well as the police, but we all knew it was wishful thinking to believe that anything would bring back the man from the dead. Sir Charles Stow was dead and now we were left with the task of finding out why.

Chapter 4

Mr. Reeves Giallo

The villa which had been originally envisioned as a relaxing retreat was now the scene of a suicide. A local doctor arrived half an hour after we had discovered Sir Charles and had ascertained that the man had been dead for at least eight hours. This was then supported by the opinion of the police surgeon, who soon arrived after him.

Stanford's call to the police in the capital had sent a shock wave through the Paris government and this had resulted in floods of police officers descending upon the house only two hours after the call had been received. Within moments of their arrival, we were politely asked to remain in the drawing room until further notice to the outrage of Tim Mac David, who did not take kindly to being treated like a suspect.

It's obvious that it's suicide,' he complained.

'He locked himself in his room, shot himself in the head and Tom Mc Cloud found the gun near his hand – how much more proof do you need? I hardly think your treating us in this manner is justified.'

'I am deeply sorry, mesdames and messsieurs, for any inconvenience this has caused you,' said a burly, plain-clothes officer who we immediately assumed to be the detective assigned to the case.

'However, it is in the interests of both your and our countries to confirm that there was no foul play involved in the death of such an important man as Sir Charles Stow.
I hope you understand the situation.'

'Damn impertinence,' murmured Grimms angrily as he returned to his place near Ella's side. Ella had taken the news of her father's death calmly, but I could see that despite her long-standing hatred towards her father, the way in which he had died had a serious effect on her and she was unusually silent.

'But surely it'll be only his rooms you'll be checking, Inspector?' asked Larry.
The man gave a sudden laugh, as if finding his query amusing.

'Me, an inspector? No, you are much mistaken, monsieur. I am merely the sergeant here.
We are all waiting for Monsieur Giallo; it is under his orders that no one is to be allowed upstairs.'

'And when is this Monsieur Giallo going to arrive?' asked Tom with a hint of impatience, unimpressed with the sergeant's apparent lack of seriousness. 'Shouldn't he be on the case at this very moment, seeing that he is apparently in charge of this investigation?'

'He is on his way, monsieur. He has merely been detained by the Commissaire, who has given him direct instructions of his own.'

'Isn't the Commissaire the equivalent of the Chief of Police in this country?' said Grimms, a slight air of surprise in his voice.

'The very same, monsieur,' replied the sergeant with a hint of obvious pride. It seemed that this Monsieur Giallo was much admired by the sergeant, who appeared quite honored to have been given the responsibility of holding the castle as it was until his arrival.
A constable descended the stairs and whispered something into the man's ear. Excusing himself, the sergeant left the room, delegating another constable to guard the door until he returned.

'It's awful,' breathed Janett to me as soon as we were left to our own devices. 'Why would Uncle Charles ever want to kill himself?'
I found myself unable to answer and merely shook my head. The shock of finding my revolver in Sir Charles's study had not worn off. I consoled myself with the possibility that the gun Tom had

found was merely a copy of the exact model and that my revolver was still in my chest of drawers but with access to our rooms restricted until the arrival of Monsieur Giallo; I had no way of finding out.

On the other side of the room, Larry was being comforted by Samantha, the former appearing as if he had aged ten years since the morning. They said nothing as they sat there on the couch, hand in hand, but I could see the feeling in Samantha's eyes. It was apparent that despite all the ugly scenes we had endured last night; she was not above feeling sorry for Sir Charles's sudden death.

We sat there in silence, each of us in a state of surreal consciousness of the world outside which seemed quite indifferent to the tragedy which had occurred inside the house. All seemed to go on as if nothing had happened and I was suddenly very aware of the sense of my mortality, a haunting sensation re-experienced far too often later in my years at the front.

So engrossed was I in my pensive state of mind that I nearly didn't hear the clock strike twelve and the sound of a car pulling up in the driveway outside. Out of the corner of my eye, I saw the others around me stir a little at the sound and Janett turned to me, laying a hand on my arm and murmuring a little.

'That must be the detective.'
There was the sound of footsteps in the corridor outside the drawing room and a hasty flurry of conversation in French. The sergeant, returning from his inspections upstairs, stopped at the doorway and said respectfully.

'Monsieur Giallo!'
He made way for his superior and looking up; I was astonished to see the man I had met in Paris walk hurriedly into the room. For a fleeting moment, I thought of myself in a bizarre dream where memory and reality seemed to be surreally indivisible. But when I noted the same look of astonishment on Larry's face, which undoubtedly reflected my own, I understood that the man before us was not a figment of our imagination. He was now dressed in a police uniform, no doubt because of his meeting with the Commissaire, but he was very much the same person. Indeed, with such extraordinary features, it was exceedingly difficult to forget him.

'I apologise for the delay, mesdames and messieurs,' he said, bowing a little. 'I am Reeves Giallo, Chief Detective Inspector of the Paris Police. I –'

'And about time too,' snapped Grimms, his anger returning and proceeding to complain to the little man who, to his credit, merely looked calmly at the Englishman who towered above him.

When it was clear that the barrister had quite finished, Giallo asked quite amiably.

'And will that be all, monsieur?'

Grimms looked taken aback.

'I – I believe so,' he stammered a little, finding the shorter man's complete composure in the face of his tirade rather disarming. I could see why Ella found him to be an immensely unlikable young man. Insecurity had made him irrationally aggressive when his reputation or dignity was threatened.

'Bon!' said the detective. 'Your words are well noted and I will apologize once again for, as you have termed it, monsieur, the "appalling treatment" that Sergeant Flexthure and my officers have subjected to you all.'

'No, Monsieur Giallo,' said Samantha quickly, trying to patch up what had been a less than successful introduction.

'We haven't been treated appallingly at all…I'm sure that Mr Grimms here is understandably upset for Ella's sake.'

Almost instantly, the brown eyes lit up upon recognizing a familiar face, his air of officially lessening somewhat.

'Ah, mademoiselle, pardon but did not I meet you and two other gentlemen the other day in Paris?'

'Quite so,' replied Samantha with a small smile. 'I believe you've already met Mr Larry Stokes…' Larry unsteadily rose from the couch and shook the detective's hand, '…and Mr Nicolas St. Louie.'

He stepped forward and, to my surprise, shook my hand with the pleasure of greeting an old friend. 'But, of course, I remember you quite well, Monsieur St. Louie.'

'St. Louie will do just as well, Monsieur Giallo,' I said, slightly embarrassed as I could see the perplexed expressions of Tom, Janett and Ella staring back at me. Also, upon closer inspection, I could see that despite his high rank in the police force, Reeves Giallo was not much older than myself.

He nodded his head. 'Very well, St. Louie. And would you be so kind as to introduce the young mademoiselle?'

'Oh, this is Samantha Milton,' I said. 'She's –' I cast a questioning look at Larry, wondering whether I should reveal that she was his fiancée.

'Samantha's my fiancée,' he said, quickly picking up his cue.

'Ah, my congratulations, Monsieur Wiggins,' said Giallo.

'Thank you, Monsieur Giallo,' replied Larry. 'Though I daresay our engagement seems quite out of place now, seeing what has just happened this morning.'

'Oui, je comprends. A sad occasion, is it not?' The Paris nodded in genuine sympathy. 'Pardon, mademoiselles, but I fear I will have to return to the matter at hand,' he added apologetically, bowing a little toward the ladies.

'I understand from Sergeant Flexthure that three of you messieurs found the body earlier this morning?' Tom stood up at this.

'Yes. I'm Tom Mc Cloud, Monsieur Giallo, Sir Charles's nephew,' he said.

'Larry, St. Louie and I found him in his study.'

'I see,' he said, gazing at us contemplatively. 'Will the three of you please accompany me upstairs?' At his request, the three of us left the drawing room and followed him outside into the hall.

'At what time was this, Monsieur Mc Cloud?'

'Around nine o'clock.'

'And what made you decide to go upstairs to his study?'

'My father was the British Ambassador, and I was his secretary,' said Larry. 'We were usually expected to be at the Embassy by nine o'clock, but he didn't appear at breakfast, which was rather unusual. Tom then asked Stanford, the butler, to check his bedroom, but it was empty.'

'Why did you not look for your father earlier, Monsieur Wiggins?' Larry stopped, looking discomfited.

'To tell the truth, we had a – a quarrel the night before and I assumed that his absence at breakfast was his way of showing his displeasure with me.'

'May I ask what was the exact nature of this quarrel between you and your father?' asked Giallo inquiringly.

Tom and I were looking at Larry expectantly and he said with a small sigh: 'It was over my engagement with Samantha.'

'I take it you did not have any intention of telling your father about your engagement to Mademoiselle Samantha?' It was not a question but a statement, and Larry could do nothing but nod in agreement.

'Yes, she was merely a guest here for all intents and purposes. And I meant to keep it that way until the end of her stay here, but someone spilled the beans on me and –'

'Pardon? "Spilled the beans"?'

The detective appeared entirely mystified by this turn of phrase and I hastily explained: 'He means that someone told Sir Charles of their engagement without his knowledge.'

'Ah,' he said, giving me a small smile. 'Merci.'

We had reached the top of the stairs and he turned to Larry gravely. 'How many people did you tell of your engagement, monsieur?'

Just the same people who you saw in the drawing room. Oh, and Stanford too.'

'Do any of them wish you or your fiancée ill?'

'Not to my knowledge, no. And that's what I can't make out because that's the only way he could have known of it.'

'What exactly did your father say to you during the argument, monsieur?'

'The gist of it was that if I hadn't broken off my engagement, and that Samantha hadn't left the house by the morning, I would be out of my inheritance.'

'And seeing that both you and Mademoiselle Samantha are still here, I understand you refused to agree to your father's request.'

'Yes. I wasn't willing to let him have the last word and waited for him to come downstairs this morning so I could speak my mind.'

'At what time did you leave your father's company last night?'

'I can't say for certain, but it must have been a quarter to eleven when he went upstairs. I then heard him shouting for Stanford as he did so.'

'Did your father appear out of spirits?'

'You must remember that we had just argued, Monsieur Giallo,' replied Larry cynically.

'I do not mean it in that manner, Monsieur Wiggins. Except for last night, did it appear that your father had any reason to end his life? Were there perhaps any diplomatic matters which were troubling him?'

Shaking his head in response to the first question but agreeing to the second, Larry told him of the theft of his father's papers as he had related to me on my first arriving here. Sir Charles had been understandably furious at the development, but Larry was uncertain whether this reason alone was enough to warrant his father killing himself.

The detective nodded, and we moved into the west wing of the house. From the mutterings in French and the creaking of the floorboards under innumerable footfalls, I could hear rather than see that the second floor of the house had practically been invaded by the police. Despite the rather macabre circumstances in which we found ourselves, I felt an odd sensation of being quite fascinated by the various goings-on; it was, after all, the first time I had ever come into contract with the police and their investigations. I had always wanted to try my hand at being a detective ever since reading the tales of Sherlock Holmes in my youth, but I had never imagined that my first foray into the world of criminal investigation would be brought about because of tragedy.

Giallo led the way towards Sir Charles's study, which was now the centre of focus, and I could hear men shuffling about busily inside.

'The double doors, messieurs…who broke them open?'

'Tom and I broke them down,' I said.

'And they were locked from the inside?'

I looked at Tom inquiringly. In the confusion of the morning's events, we had forgotten to check whether they had been locked from the inside or whether there had been a key in the lock. He shook his head uncertainly.

'I don't know,' I admitted.

'I'm afraid we didn't realise. But I could say with certainty that we heard nothing falling onto the floor.'

Giallo appeared somewhat disappointed, but said nothing as he stepped inside. I got the impression that I was making a bad first show of this and sighed inwardly.

'No, I am not surprised that you heard nothing. No one would have heard anything because of this,' Giallo announced as he gestured towards the carpeted floor.

He kneeled on the carpet, examining the space behind the doors.

'Sergeant Flexthure!'

The sergeant appeared almost immediately from outside. 'Yes, Monsieur Giallo?'

'Did you find a key anywhere here?'

'No, monsieur.'

'And on Sir Charles's body?'

'No, monsieur. But we found a key under his desk.'

Here, the sergeant produced a key and handed it to Giallo, who examined it minutely.

'Merci.'

He then rose to his feet and looked about the room.

The curtains had been drawn by the police and sunlight was streaming through the windows, illuminating the interior. As I had expected earlier, the study looked very much like the drawing room downstairs. Sir Charles appeared to have been a neat man, despite his gruff exterior.

Papers were docketed and put in their various trays and pigeonholes, and this seemed to gain the detective's approval as he approached the desk. We followed suit.

Sir Charles's body had already been moved into the billiard room downstairs and all that was left to remind us of his violent death was a small pool of blood on his desk.

I shivered a little, recalling the diplomat in his prime of life only the night before.

'Nothing has been touched, I presume?' asked Giallo to Flexthure, who was now standing attentively beside us.

'Nothing. Apart from the gun which we have removed to the other room, everything has been left as we found it.'

Another flash of confusion entered my head at the mention of the revolver, and I flushed slightly. I did not have time to dwell on this when Giallo asked suddenly, after a minute's inspection of the desk.

'Your father, Monsieur Wiggins; he was left-handed, was he not?'

Larry stared at him.

'But how did you know?'

Giallo gave a small shrug. 'People who are left-handed arrange their items differently. The inkwell and the pens, you see, they are put aside to the right side of the desk. Everything of importance – they are put on the right comme ça,' he demonstrated, pushing a piece of notepaper which had been askew a tenth of an inch to the right.

'Sir Charles Stow was indeed a man of method. The gun was found in his left hand, was it not, Flexthure?' he added, turning his attention to the sergeant, who nodded vigorously.

Giallo then moved closer to the desk, picking up a cup from its saucer. The contents of the cup had already been drunk, evidently by Sir Charles before his death, and he lifted it gingerly to his nose.

'Coffee,' he said thoughtfully, returning it.

'It was Uncle Charles' habit to have a cup brought to him in his study before he turned in for the night.'

'Who usually brought it upstairs?'

'Stanford, I think.'

'Is it drugged?' I asked, failing to keep a note of excitement from my voice.

Giallo looked up at me at this, and I could have sworn that there was an amused twinkle in those eyes before they cast down again, returning to their inspection of the cup.

'It is too early to say, St. Louie. However, I will take a sample here and send it to our specialists in Paris.'

He called for a constable to bring a leather bag from which he extracted a small glass vial. Transferring the last remaining dregs into the vial and sealing it with a cork, it was handed to the constable, who then left the room after being given instructions by Sergeant Flexthure.

Finished with his examination of the desk, Giallo turned to the window nearest to him, which was slightly open, appeared interested and then looked outside.

'The windows overlook the garden.'

'Yes, Father always suspected the servants. There was an under-butler who left us in the middle of the night about a year ago and he's been keeping a lookout of sorts here ever since.'

'Ah, yes…I can see now that they overlook not only the garden below but also the front gate. A most advantageous vantage point, I must agree.
Tell me, Monsieur Mc Cloud, were the windows open when you entered the room?'

'I can't say I recall them being open.
The curtains hadn't been drawn yet at the time.'

'I see. And both you and St. Louie are certain that you smelled gunpowder?'

'Yes,' we said simultaneously.
Nodding, he questioned Larry on his whereabouts.
I listened to Larry's account, which was on the whole quite accurate. He had argued with his father for nearly three hours, had gone upstairs to talk with me in my room at eleven o'clock and had left it with my assistance just a few minutes after midnight. This latter event I vouched for and Giallo accepted my word without comment.

'And after Monsieur St. Louie left you in your room, Monsieur Wiggins…you did not leave it?'

'No. I slept like a log soon afterwards. I didn't leave my room until a quarter past six.'

'Can anyone verify that you did not leave your room at all during the night?'
It was at this point that the strain Larry had been keeping at bay tumbled over into his countenance, which reddened slightly, and when he spoke, his voice was harsh with anger.

'Well, of course no one can verify that, Giallo, but it was the middle of the night, for Heaven's sake!'

'Yes, but your father also died in the middle of the night, monsieur. Have you forgotten about that?'
There was a tense moment in which my friend glared at the detective, the latter appearing serene but steadfast in his opinion. Larry gave way and muttered tiredly: 'Yes, Yes, I can't disagree with you there.' He raised a hand to his face and rubbed it confusedly. 'Excuse me…I – I'm not quite in my right mind this morning.'

Instead of pressing his advantage when Larry appeared most vulnerable, Giallo refrained from asking any further questions, satisfied with the knowledge he had so far received. He asked Sergeant Flexthure to take Larry down to the drawing room and, in a barely discernable whisper, to give Monsieur Wiggins a glass of brandy once they reached the latter.

Once we heard their footfalls on the stairs, Giallo turned to us gravely.

'Monsieur Larry is not a man of courage, it seems.'

'He's had a rough go of it, Monsieur Giallo,' said Tom. 'These past few evenings haven't been quite easy going for him. '

'Oui, je comprends. First the secret engagement, which is later discovered somehow by his father, then the argument which inevitably arises and then this –' He gestured expressively towards the desk.

'C'est vraiment une tragédie.'

It was soon Tom's turn to be questioned, and his story was simple. He had turned in with the others at about a quarter to ten, leaving me in the drawing room. Upon reaching his room in the east wing, he had prepared for bed and read a book before turning in at about half past ten.

'Pardon, how is it that you know the time so accurately, Monsieur Mc Cloud?'

'I checked my pocket watch, which I always keep on my bedside table.'

'Thank you. Please continue.'

Having been allowed to do so, Tom continued; he had heard nothing during the night, and he rose as usual at seven this morning.

Giallo seemed quite satisfied with Tom's account and, probably having no further questions, allowed him to return downstairs just as Sergeant Flexthure came from below. Soon there was only my account left to relate, and I was about to speak when Giallo gestured for Flexthure to come inside.

'Flexthure, please bring in the gun which was found this morning.'

The sergeant did as he was told, and within a minute, the revolver was presented before us. For me, there was no need to take a second glance at it. I had long wrestled with the notion that I had mistaken the revolver found by Sir Charles with my own by the dim light of the candle, but resting as it was in Flexthure's hands and in broad daylight, there was no mistaking it. My grandfather's initials were engraved at the bottom of the grip and I could see them now quite clearly. My confusion of the morning returned.

My feelings were all too visible on my face for Giallo observed in a voice full of curiosity: 'You appear troubled, mon ami.'

It took me a short while to tear my gaze away from the weapon before directing them towards Giallo.

'I think I ought to tell you something, Giallo,' I whispered. I hesitated a little before saying: 'The revolver's mine.'

Flexthure muttered a quiet curse and appeared to be quite ready to arrest me before Giallo raised a hand to stop him.

'But Monsieur Giallo, he's admitted the weapon's his,' he said angrily in French.

'That makes him as good as guilty.'

'No, Flexthure, no. Do not you remember that what we are investigating is a suicide?'

'With all respect, Monsieur Giallo, you know as well as I do that this isn't suicide but murder!'

'I repeat, Flexthure, you do not have the right to arrest anyone unless given permission to do so.'

The sergeant backed down and, scowling at me, stepped aside.

'You suspect Sir Charles was murdered?' I asked, unable to hide the fact that I had understood what had just passed between the detective and his sergeant.

'It is not only Monsieur Larry Stokes who can play the game of giving appearances,' said Giallo. 'We can merely appear to be investigating a suicide while all the while suspecting more terrible motives at work.

To make our intentions known, St. Louie, is to foolishly give the true criminal the upper hand and time to either make their escape or hide further evidence from us.'

'And you don't believe that I did it?'

The Paris' eyes fixed intently on my face and I was grateful because I was standing in the shade as I could feel a slight blush coming onto my cheeks.

'No,' Giallo pronounced, smiling a little. 'I do not.'

While I appreciated the detective's faith in me, I realised that my admission of my owning the gun would require me to give evidence against Larry who was the only one, as far as I knew, to know both the existence and the location of my revolver.

'But I don't understand,' I said, after telling this to Giallo. 'It was there in my drawer when I returned from Larry's room.'

'Are you certain that it was indeed your own revolver which you found in your drawer?'

I floundered a little at this point. I hadn't actually picked it up when I returned since I had merely checked to see whether it was still there. And I had no reason to suspect that the revolver in my drawer wasn't my own. Giallo correctly took my silence as uncertainty and ordered one constable to check my room. Within five minutes, the man returned, reporting that no weapon was to be found anywhere in my drawers.

'But I can swear to you that –' I started in agitation.

'Calm yourself, St. Louie,' said Giallo, appearing unruffled by this piece of news. In fact, it was my impression that he had expected nothing less from the constable's report.

'Did you hear anything after you returned to your room?'

'Nothing at all. I heard nothing until that popping noise –'

'What popping noise?'

I had forgotten that I hadn't told them of my movements the previous evening and quickly did so. I told them of Larry's unfortunate and drunken intention of putting a gun to his father's head, which Giallo listened to in grave silence.

'It is a pity that he did not tell us about this himself.'

'You don't mean to say that you suspect him of murder?' I said, horrified that I had inadvertently betrayed my friend.

'All I can say is that this does not put him in a favorable position in the eyes of a court and jury. But no, please continue with your account.'

I did so.

'So you heard this noise at one o'clock?' asked Flexthure, still looking skeptical when I had finished.

'Yes, I can be sure of that since I heard the clock striking one downstairs.'

'At about the same time, which the surgeon believes that Sir Charles was shot,' added Giallo thoughtfully. 'No doubt the sound of a gun going off. The sound you heard, St. Louie, was it loud or quiet?'

'It was rather faint. You could barely hear the pop.'

'A gun which was silenced perhaps?' said Flexthure.

'Perhaps.'

'Which makes it even less likely that it was suicide, monsieur,' said Flexthure triumphantly.

'Only a person wanting to commit murder would want to use a silenced gun.'

Giallo appeared not to have heard him, for he merely said, 'This affair interests me.'

'I'm not surprised, Monsieur Giallo,' said the sergeant with a slight grin, his mood obviously improving.

Giallo took a last look at his surroundings before announcing his intention to go downstairs and speak with the rest of the party downstairs.

Flexthure led the way, gruffly making his way down the staircase. As Giallo and I reached the bottom of the stairs, I said.

'Might I ask you a favor, Giallo?'

He looked up at me. 'It would depend upon the nature of the favor, St. Louie.'

'I know this sounds rather unusual, but I'd like to ask you whether I could help with your investigations. I know you've already got more professional fellows like Sergeant Flexthure and the rest out here helping you,' I said hastily when he appeared to be ready to reject my suggestion outright, 'but I want to repay your confidence in me regarding the revolver.'

'You want to know who tried to implicate you in this affair, eh?' suggested the detective knowingly.

'That might be one part of it,' I admitted. 'Besides, I know this family, Giallo. Larry's been my good friend since our time at Haney and it troubles me to see him entangled in all this wretched business.'

There was a slight pause, in which he seemed to contemplate my offer. To tell the truth, I was preparing for the worst. I imagined it was ludicrous for a professional detective to take on a person like me as a sort of associate in a case as important as this, and I could already visualize the disapproving expression on Sergeant Flexthure's face if he ever got word of this.

At last, Giallo reached a decision which I had not been expecting. Instead of shaking his head sternly and showering me in a torrent of criticism which he had all the rights in the world to do, he smiled at me and offered his hand.

'Very well, St. Louie,' he said. 'I accept.'

'Erm…thank you,' was all I could manage before gaining enough confidence to shake his hand. 'You won't regret it, Giallo.'

'That I certainly hope not,' he replied drily.

'So, we are now, as your countrymen say, "partners in crime'?'

'Indeed we are,' I said with a laugh. 'Indeed, we are.'

Chapter 5

The Testimonies

Upon his return to the drawing room, Giallo requested to see Stanford. This came as a mild surprise, as I had presumed that the natural course of action was to interview the rest of the party. Tim Mac David looked quite incredulous, but the detective was adamant and soon the butler was summoned to the dining room across the hall.

'But why Stanford, Giallo?' I asked as we seated ourselves at the dining table, which had already been cleared after breakfast.

'Shouldn't you be speaking to the ladies and Grimms next?'

'Monsieur Giallo has his methods, Monsieur St. Louie,' said Flexthure before his superior could reply. His tone was cool and I could see that the news of my being even more personally involved in their official investigation had not gone down well with the sergeant.

Giallo seemed to correctly gauge the tension in the air and said diplomatically.

'Sergeant Flexthure has worked with me for several years, St. Louie, so yes, I have to admit that I do have my methods...inexplicable to some, as they may seem.

But I assure you I will interview the others soon enough.

I am interested in Stanford merely because he was the last person in this house to see Sir Charles alive.'

Comprehension dawned upon me and I nodded, wondering why I hadn't thought of that fact. Soon after, Stanford entered the room, looking a little paler, I thought, which I attributed to shock at his master's sudden demise. He stood to attention, casting Giallo a polite, expectant look.

'Would you care to sit, Stanford?'

'Thank you, sir, but I prefer to stand.'

'D'accord. I understand you were asked by Lieutenant Mc Cloud to check Sir Charles's rooms this morning.'

'That is correct, sir.'

'And you found both his study and his bedroom to be locked?'

'I was requested to check only Sir Charles's bedchamber, sir. I found it to be unlocked.'

Then you suggested that the gentlemen should check the study instead, yes?'

'Yes, sir.'

'Presumably because that is where you last saw your master last night?'

An expression of confusion entered the butler's face here, and it was some moments before he said slowly....

'I beg your pardon, sir – but I'm afraid you must be mistaken. I last attended Sir Charles during dinner.'

Instinctively, I turned to look at Giallo and he returned my glance of surprise before turning back to Stanford.

'But it was the same dinner at which Sir Charles and Monsieur Larry they had this quarrel at this table?'

Stanford emitted a grave sigh. 'I'm afraid so, sir. It was quite terrible to experience, if I might be so bold to say, Mr St. Louie,' he said, directing his gaze at me.

'Quite, Stanford, yes,' I agreed, feeling the butler's pain at seeing both his masters arguing at the table.

'And you did not see Sir Charles or Monsieur Larry after this argument?' continued Giallo.

'No, sir.'

'Was it unusual for you not to see your master after dinner, Stanford?'

'Rather unusual, sir. For it was Sir Charles's habit to have a cup of coffee brought to him after dinner to his study.'

'Who was the one who usually brought it up?'

'I was, sir. It was his custom to ring the bell in either his bedchamber or his study and I would bring up his coffee accordingly.'

'And did he do so last night?'
Stanford looked a little embarrassed at this question and he said quietly.

'Truth be told, sir, I have to admit that I fell asleep before I could wait for Sir Charles's summons.
I therefore have no recollection of anything that happened after nine o'clock.'

'Do you mean to say that you were sleeping on duty, monsieur?' came Flexthure's disapproving voice.
Stanford's current embarrassment quickly turned into indignation and I myself, was ready to rise to the good butler's defence.

'Now, look here, Flexthure –' I started angrily before Giallo raised a hand to stop me from continuing.

'I apologise for my sergeant's outburst, Stanford. If it gives you any consolation, you should know that I believe in the professionalism of your work. It is not a simple job, is it not, the work of a butler and especially for you, who has been the head of a household for so long?'
Again, I marveled at the detective's ability to turn a thoroughly unpleasant atmosphere into one of complete tranquility almost immediately. He had done so in his rather unfortunate first encounter with Tim Mac David in the drawing room and now he was doing the same here, for his soothing blend of charm was working on the middle-aged butler.

Thank you, sir,' he said, his countenance returning to the one of customary calm.

'I would like to make it quite clear, if I may, that I do not make it a regular habit to fall asleep during my duties, sir.'

'Mais bien sûr,' came Giallo's voice. 'Please continue.'
He shot a sharp look at Flexthure before doing so. 'It was Sir Charles's custom to ring for his coffee, sir. I was never allowed to bring it up of my own accord. I was therefore sitting at my desk in my quarters awaiting his summons until both he and Master Larry had finished their – quarrel,' he said, looking as if he wanted for a better word.

'At what time was it you were sitting in your quarters?'

'About nine o'clock, sir. I believe it was nearly midnight when Camie, one of our chambermaids, found me asleep and woke me. She had apparently been concerned by the light coming from under my door as she was on her way to fetch a glass of water from the kitchen.'

'And after this, you retired to bed?'

'Yes, sir.'

'Did you find it unusual that Sir Charles did not ring for you last night?'

Stanford thought carefully before replying.

'It was uncommon for him not to ring for his coffee, sir, but occasionally he was not in the mood to be disturbed in the evenings. I presume that the quarrel between him and Master Larry had taken away his desire for his evening coffee.'

Giallo's face was puzzled, and I too was sharing his confusion. So far, Stanford appeared to have no knowledge of the empty cup of coffee we had found on Sir Charles's desk upstairs, and Giallo too, seemed to keep his information from him to probably gauge the man's sincerity. But if the butler hadn't brought it up, then who did?

'Would it surprise you if, for example, Sir Charles had brought up a cup of coffee himself to his study?'

'I would be very much surprised, sir. Sir Charles made it a point never to enter the kitchen or the servant's quarters,' replied Stanford with an air of complete astonishment.

Giallo sat a little in silence for a while before asking, 'One last question, Stanford. Are you in the habit of taking anything in the evening before going to bed? A cup of tea, perhaps? Or some coffee?'

'I take some hot cocoa before retiring, sir.'

'Did you have some last night?'

'Yes, sir. I had some at my desk while I waited.'

There was suddenly a flash in Giallo's brown eyes.

'And do you or some of the other staff make it for you?'

I thought this an odd question and, by the bemused expression on the butler's face, I believe he was thinking along the same lines. However, he composed himself and replied,

'I used to make my own, but ever since getting arthritis in my hands, sir, I've had to ask the cook to make some for me. But she's been very obliging.'

Personally, I was at a loss as to why on earth we were quizzing the butler on his cup of cocoa instead of Sir Charles's coffee, which I thought would be of greater importance. As I was ruminating on this point, I caught sight of Flexthure's grave face and remembered his earlier remark of Giallo having his own methods and I held my tongue until the time came for me to put forward my opinions.

Satisfied with Stanford's account, the butler could return to his duties. Placing a neatly written list of the occupants of the house in front of him, I saw Giallo put a small mark next to Stanford's name besides a couple of comments, which I could not read. When he had finished, a constable was called to ask and accompany Ella to the dining room.

'I do not trust the butler, monsieur,' came the sergeant as soon as the door was closed. 'How else did the cup of coffee come to be on his desk?'

'He appears to have no knowledge of the coffee, though,' I argued. 'Looked absolutely surprised when you mentioned the possibility of Sir Charles getting it himself.'

The detective nodded in agreement.

'Yes. Either the butler is a talented actor or he is telling the truth. And I am inclined to think that he is doing the latter.'

'Here, here,' I replied fervently.

'It appears you have a great deal of confidence in Stanford, St. Louie,' said Giallo, turning to me.

'Well, I can't help it. I've known him for years, and he's treated us all very well. And surely, he's not the sort of chap who'd go round killing his own master and employer, is he?'

'Perhaps so. But beware of the bias, mon ami, and also the sentimentality. They cloud the judgment all too often,' came the detective's reply as the door opened to allow not Ella but Janett into the room.

I thought I asked for Mademoiselle Wiggins, de Burlet?'

The constable appeared apologetic but explained to himself.

'Sorry, Monsieur Giallo, but Monsieur Grimms refused to allow the mademoiselle to be interviewed without his presence. I therefore asked Mademoiselle Thompson instead.'

'Ah. Monsieur Grimms is playing the role of l'homme trop protecteur, n'est-ce pas?'

Giallo rose to his feet, gesturing courteously to Janett to take a seat.

'Very well, de Burlet, I will interview both Monsieur Grimms and Mademoiselle Wiggins after I have finished speaking with Mademoiselle Thompson.'

Having received his orders, the constable shut the door.

'My apologies, mademoiselle. I was expecting to interview Mademoiselle Wiggins first.'

'Oh, no. Not at all. In fact, I was rather hoping to speak to you as soon as I could.'

'You have something important to tell us?' asked Flexthure, mistaking, I imagine, her eagerness as a sign of a confession of some sort. I could see that Janett wanted to get the ordeal of being interviewed over and done with as soon as possible.

'I don't know, monsieur,' replied Janett, looking ill at ease, and I could see that her shy nature was showing itself. After all, I could imagine the rather intimidating sight of two detectives seated opposite her and I said gently:

'Don't be nervous, Janett. Just tell Monsieur Giallo and Sergeant Flexthure what happened last night.'

Giving me a timid smile, she reconstructed the events of last night. Like the others, she had turned in at around a quarter to ten and had fallen asleep almost instantly.

'Monsieur Giallo, I was quite tired and the mood last night was rather unpleasant, as you can imagine.'

'But of course.'

'Well, I was so tired, in fact, that despite being the light-sleeper that I am, I think I wouldn't have woken up till the morning had it not been for that crash from next door.'

'Who occupies the room next door to you, mademoiselle?'

'Ella does. I believe she had knocked over a vase or something, which was quite odd since she's rarely the type to knock over things, but I imagine one has one's share of bad days. A minute later, I heard her calling for Mallon, who I presume was doing his rounds around the house.'

'Pardon, who is this Monsieur Mallon?'

'He's technically the gardener,' I said, stepping in for Janett. 'He's more than that actually because of Sir Charles, who made him a jack-of-all-trades. Now apparently, his other duties include fixing up everything in the house.' Although I had not intended my voice to be skeptical, my tone sounded very much so once I finished speaking. Whether Giallo registered this, I do not know, for he merely nodded in comprehension and turned back to Janett.

'Do you know what time was this?'

'Yes. I glanced at my bedside clock; it was about ten to eleven. I couldn't hear what they were saying, but Ella was asking him to clear it up. Initially, I think Mallon wasn't too keen on the prospect since I heard her raising her voice at some point.'
I didn't find this latter fact at all surprising in light of the behavior I had seen Mallon displaying in front of Ella in the conservatory the other day, but I said nothing.

'Did you actually hear Mallon's voice, mademoiselle? Or what exactly what he said to Mademoiselle Wiggins?'

'No. I suppose I was half-asleep at the time, so I didn't really pay much attention to what was being said on the other side of the wall. But I was certain that Mallon was giving Ella a beastly time as usual in not doing as he was asked. Ella isn't the type to shout about, but she was certainly on the verge of getting quite cross with him by the sound of her voice last night.'
Flexthure leaned forward and asked whether she had heard anything afterwards, but she shook her head.

'I'm afraid not, monsieur. I must have fallen asleep again.' She paused, looking a little flustered. 'Oh dear, I'm not being much help, am I? I apologize...'
Giallo smiled at her kindly. 'Non, non, je comprends. The scenes that you witnessed last night were not very pleasant and a remedy for some is to perhaps, as you might say, sleep the matter off?'

'Yes, very much so,' Janett said, turning her gaze suddenly to her hands. 'Will that be all, Monsieur Giallo?'

'Oui, that will be all for the moment. I thank you very much for your help, mademoiselle.'
Appearing relieved, Janett was escorted out of the room and Giallo and Flexthure had the unenviable task of interviewing Ella in the presence of an extremely protective Tim Mac David, who insisted on being interviewed first. His mood had not improved after being cleverly put down by the Paris detective earlier in the afternoon and his expression as he entered the room and glanced at Giallo was one of the blackest I have ever seen. However, Grimms was intelligent enough not to overstep his bounds and, despite some rather tense moments in which he

complained of being unfairly treated, he answered both Giallo and Flexthure's questions without hesitation. Like Tom and Janett before him, he had retired upstairs at the same time as the others at a quarter to ten. After escorting Ella to her room in the east wing of the house and bidding her good night, he made his way to his room in the west wing.

'Ah, so you have rooms in the same wing as Monsieur St. Louie here, Monsieur Grimms?' asked Giallo.

'I do,' he replied, casting me a look which clearly conveyed his suspicion at my being suddenly involved in the investigation.

'I ask simply because I wonder whether you heard anything at all during the night,' added the detective.

'I don't believe I did, monsieur,' said Grimms bluntly. 'It is as I have told you. I returned to my room at five minutes to ten and retired to bed a quarter of an hour later.'

'And did you wake at any point afterwards?'

'Are you implying something, Monsieur Giallo?'

'I would advise that you answer the Chief Detective Inspector's question, monsieur,' said Flexthure warningly and there was suddenly a look of steel in the sergeant's dark eyes that made anyone who had the misfortune of being on the receiving end of his gaze feel considerably unnerved. Grimms backed down and replied coldly: 'I might have woken up once or twice, though for not more than a few minutes. I remember hearing voices from St. Louie' room at one point and I believe I recognized Larry's voice as being one of them.'

'Did you note the time?'

'No, I'm afraid I did not. However, it seemed rather late.'

'Did you hear anything else?'

Grimms seemed to think this question worthy of his attention and replied: 'Now that you ask, I think I heard someone passing outside my door at the same time I heard Larry's voice.'

'Really?' I asked, much intrigued since the news was new to me.

'I heard nothing. Are you sure you heard someone?'

'There's a floorboard in front of my door which creaks, St. Louie, and it creaks rather loudly,' replied Grimms sardonically. 'I hardly think I imagined it.'

'Oh, leave Nicolas alone, Luke,' snapped Ella, and I heard her voice for the first time since we had discovered her father's body. It was taut with unusual tension, but her customary air of command was rapidly returning. Grimms shot me a sharp look before scanning the surrounding room with displeasure.

'Damn place is falling apart, and no one seems to give a damn about it – much less that Mallon fellow whose job supposedly is to fix whatever's broken here.'

'You dislike Mallon, monsieur?' asked Giallo with interest.

'I detest the fellow, Giallo, if you want the truth of it,' the other snapped, appearing to forget his dislike for the detective at the mention of a person who he seemed to dislike even more.

'Always leering at the young ladies who come to the house and especially Miss Wiggins here.
The amount of times when I've heard him talking back at her is disgraceful. The man doesn't seem to know his place and by God, there have been several occasions when I could have thrashed him.'

As much as I found Grimms's character distasteful and unpleasant, it was difficult for me not to agree with him on this point.

'You appear to be a man of some violence, monsieur,' commented Flexthure.

In an instant, Grimms' face seemed to look pale, and he said quickly: 'I was speaking figuratively, Sergeant. I would of course never dreamed of – '

Out of the corner of my eye, I thought I saw a faint smile tugging at Giallo's mouth before he interrupted the barrister's train of speech: 'But of course, Monsieur Grimms. None of us consider you to be a man of violence. These feelings of rage and anger are to be expected in such cases.'

This appeared to calm Grimms somewhat, and he managed shakily: 'Yes. Quite – quite expected.'

'Mallon is in the habit of being unpleasant to you, Mademoiselle Wiggins,' said Giallo, turning his attention to Ella.

'Yes, he is a rather trying character. I do not know what he hopes to gain from being so defiant to all of us – unless he wishes to be soon out of a job. Larry made it clear to both Mallon and his father that he wished the man dismissed from service, but our father was, as usual, deaf to his entreaties.'

'But now that your brother is the new master of this house; perhaps he will put his words into action?'

'I doubt it, Monsieur Giallo. Or at least, I expect it will be a short while before we shall be able to be rid of him. Good help and especially someone English is hard to find these days. Also, our present situation of being located in France complicates the matter somewhat…which I say with no intention of causing offence.'

Giallo bowed his head. 'I assure you that none is taken, mademoiselle.'

'I suppose we'll have to cope with his presence for a little while longer, but I cannot deny that he is helpful around the house.'

'Like the case last night with the broken vase?'

Ella stared at him. 'How do you know about that?'

'Mademoiselle Thompson is a light-sleeper,' said Giallo with a smile.

'Now what's all this business about a broken vase –' started Grimms but was quickly cut off by Flexthure, who gestured brusquely for silence.

'Oh, I must have woken her up – I had no idea that I'd made such a commotion. I got up to pour myself a glass of water from the bedstand and, as I was reaching for the glass, I knocked over the vase. Since it was one of two that belonged to our mother, I was upset about it. I was about to ring for Camie to help clear up the mess, but I heard Mallon doing his rounds outside and asked him instead.' She sighed wearily. 'When I think about it now, I do not know what possessed me to call for him and when he gave me more of his awful lip, I regretted my decision at once.'

'You had to raise your voice, yes?'

'Oh God, I can't believe Janett heard me doing that as well – I'll really have to apologize to her after this.'

'I am sure that she will understand. This unfortunate scene between you and Mallon it took place at about ten minutes to eleven?'

'That should be about right. I didn't really note the time, but it was certainly nearly eleven when I finally got rid of him.'

'And afterwards?'

'I returned to bed – I also made it a point to lock my door after that; I certainly didn't want Mallon suddenly returning to my room in the middle of the night.'

'You don't mean to say that he's attempted to do so before?' asked Grimms, outraged.

'And what if he did, Luke? I hardly think that you'd be able to protect me seeing that your room is on the other side of the house.'

'Ella, you know that I only have your interests at heart,' replied her fiancé, his voice suddenly low and anguished.

'I appreciate your concern, Luke, but I've taken care of myself very well in the past and with no one's help, for that matter. Grimms was on the verge of broadening the rift between Ella and himself before Giallo politely requested to return to the matter at hand.

'I apologize if this is a delicate subject, but it is a question which must be asked in view of the circumstances.
Your father, I assume, had a will prepared in the case of his death. Do you know the contents of this will, Mademoiselle Wiggins?'

'I believe almost everyone at dinner would have known of its contents after the row last night,' said Ella darkly.

'The will and our various inheritances contained within it were always my father's tools against us if we proved to be problematic for him.'

'But this tactic did not work against you, n'est-ce pas?' Ella smiled at him, appearing deeply impressed.

'You know me uncommonly well, Monsieur Giallo. I think even most of my family don't know me as well as you seem to do.'
Giallo shrugged.

'It is my business to know people and their characters, mademoiselle. That is all.'

'Well, yes – as you say, our inheritances were always held hostage to achieve my father's aims. As Mr St. Louie will tell you if you ask him, I didn't give a tinker's damn about my inheritance, but I cared about Larry's.'

'I believe he was naturally about to inherit the bulk of his father's property and assets, seeing that he was Sir Charles' only son?'

'Yes, that's right. He's also entitled to Father's baronetcy.'

'And what of the others – of the provisions for perhaps you, Monsieur Mc Cloud and Mademoiselle Thompson?'

'My inheritance was taken away years ago but I suspect my Father must have left most of my mother's belongings to me seeing that she had always intended to pass them along the female line and to tell the truth, I couldn't be happier. Tom was always a favorite with Father, so he'll get the bulk of his naval possessions and a handsome little legacy of four hundred pounds a year. I'm uncertain of Janett's inheritance since she was never close to him, but seeing that she was his sister's daughter, Father must have given her something of a legacy as well.'

'Mais oui. It is probably because that Mademoiselle Janett is an orphan, yes?'

It was not only Ella who was startled by this pronouncement – I too gazed at the man sitting next to me with unbridled astonishment since I never recalled telling him of Janett's tragic circumstances. It was also a topic which Larry, Ella or myself ever discussed, especially when Janett was within our midst – it was simply an unspoken rule not to talk of it.

'Goodness, you are a clever fellow, Monsieur Giallo,' said Ella.

'I cannot guess how you found that out, but I have to say that I agree with you on that point. Father, as you have seen, was tight-fisted when it came to money, but I suppose the idea of duty, especially to Aunt Ursula, was sometimes important to him.'

This ended Giallo's interview with the both of them and, after checking the accuracy of details relating to times and so forth, Ella and Grimms were allowed to leave the dining room.

'How did you know about Janett being an orphan, Giallo?' was the first question to leave my mouth as the three of us were left alone.

'It was easy for the little grey cells to see Mademoiselle Janett's past in her face, St. Louie. She was keen to get our interview over and done with, her shyness and timidity of nature – and especially how she looked down at her hands after I mentioned it was a solution for some to sleep unpleasant or in her case, traumatic events off.

Her being a light-sleeper also tells me that despite her youth, she has suffered through something which has caused her to be so. Young people, you comprehend, sleep more deeply.

Also, I suspect she omitted the fact that she attempted not only to sleep to rid herself of unpleasant memories; she cried herself to sleep – and this is not the first time that she has done so.'

'Good Lord,' I breathed, my mind reeling from the barrage of information.

'You're really quite remarkable. Janett's father was a missionary in China, and both Janett and her mother accompanied him during his travels. Unfortunately, they got caught up in all that horrible business with the Boxer Rebellion when it broke out. It was simply a case of being at the wrong place at the wrong time. That's the most awful part of it. Both her parents perished. Janett was only seven, but she got out of the place with the help of one of Thompson's Chinese colleagues. Since then, she's been brought up by her father's sisters in Shropshire.'

'La pauvre petite,' said Giallo softly.

'However, it is pleasing to see that she has turned out so well despite everything which has happened to her.'

I nodded in agreement before my thoughts returned to dwell upon what we had learned so far. I thought we can construct a timeline of sorts of the events last night.

There was still nothing strong enough to point towards the suggestion that Sir Charles Stow had been murdered.

Of course, we ourselves knew it was murder, but everyone who had a motive for killing Sir Charles seemed, at least for the moment, accounted for.

'You forget that we have not spoken with the housemaids or Mallon, mon ami,' said Giallo when I told him of this.

His mentioning of the gardener set me off.

'I think Mallon's got something to do with this entire business, Giallo. From what we've heard and seen of him, I'd wager there's something not quite right about him.'

'That may be so, but I prefer – what is it you say – to not count my hens before they are hatched? For a crime to be committed, there must always be a motive…and that I cannot see with Mallon.'

'Do you wish to interview them here, Monsieur Giallo?' asked Flexthure.

Giallo took out his pocket watch and consulted it.

'It is now half-past one – and I suspect that Stanford and the maids would be pleased to see us vacate this room so they may be allowed to prepare lunch.'

'I doubt anyone would be in a mood to eat anything after all that's happened,' I said.

'I think I would like to speak with the housemaids and the gardener in their natural settings, so to speak,' he said, rising from his chair. Flexthure and I followed suit, and we left the dining room. Once we were in the corridor, Giallo informed the butler that lunch could now be prepared, though he would be much obliged to have a word or two with Camie and the other maid after the meal had finished.

'I see no problem with that, sir. I shall ask Camie and Estrella to wait for you in the library after lunch.'

Thanking him, Giallo made his way outside, and we followed him to the grounds which were now almost deserted as the majority of the police officers who had descended upon the house in the morning had either returned with evidence to be examined in Paris or were still upstairs checking our rooms. However, there were at least three or four men outside, two of whom were trying to calm an irate Mallon who appeared incensed at not being able to continue with his work in peace.

'Now look here, Inspector, I'm not all too happy about these fellows following me about,' he growled when he saw the three of us approaching.

'There has been a death at the house, monsieur, if you haven't noticed,' said Flexthure.

Mallon shoved his mud-stained hands into his pockets. 'That may be, sir, but last time I heard, Sir Charles killed himself.'

'And what if he was murdered instead?' continued Flexthure.

'Would that change things for you at all?'

The gardener shrugged in obvious indifference; his expression unchanged.

'Whether the old man got himself shot or the other way round is no concern of mine.

As long as I'm able to work and get paid for, it is all I care about.'

His eyes narrowed as he glanced at the two police officers standing behind him.

'And my work isn't made any easier by these two trailing me about, so if you don't mind, Inspector, I'd like us to part company.'

'I'm afraid you will have to endure their company a little longer, Mallon – that is until you have answered my questions,' said Giallo.

'Well, I haven't been bumping anyone off, that's for certain,' replied the man flippantly, which only increased my dislike for him.

'Fire away, sir.'

Giallo did so, and the various details and accounts gleaned from Ella and Janett were confirmed by the gardener.

Yes, he had been doing his nightly rounds about the house and the gardens as usual, but no; he had been nowhere near the rooms in the west wing at midnight since he had already retired to his small cottage, at the back of the villa and which was at least a five-minute walk from the main house. When asked about the incident in Ella's room concerning the broken vase and, to my disgust, he did not deny that he was causing any offence. In fact, he was proud of being able to 'put the young mistress of the house ill at ease'.

'Women like Miss Wiggins need a bit of rough talking back,' said Mallon, smirking and looking revoltingly smug. 'Gets them off their high horse and makes them realize that not all the world revolves around them. And I'll wager that with that snob of a fiancé she's got, she's actually welcoming the prospect of getting a bit of rough and tumble with a chap like me, if you take my meaning...'

The implication was disgustingly clear, and despite myself, I took a step forward.

'You swine!' I cried and I believe I would have hit the man had it not been for Giallo's restraining hand suddenly on my arm.

'St. Louie, calm yourself! We are here to ask questions not to fight duels – exertions of the mind and not the body is required at the moment,' he reasoned though he too was looking at Mallon with an expression of complete disapproval.

Breathing deeply, I composed myself and after a while, Giallo released his grasp on my arm.

'I see that Miss Wiggins has another admirer,' commented Mallon, gazing at me in amusement.

'Not an admirer – merely a fellow who knows how to respect a lady. Something which I believe you know nothing about, Mallon.'

Giallo threw a warning look in my direction and I held my tongue, albeit with great difficulty. I paid little attention to the rest of the interview, feeling that the longer I spent near the wretched gardener, the more incensed I would become. Instead, I detached myself a little from the others and allowed my gaze to wander up and down the expanse of the garden and its finely cut lawn and pristine-looking flowerbeds. The sun was now at its highest point in the cloudless sky above us, and I lifted a hand to my eyes to give me some respite from the dazzling light. It was at that moment that I saw a glimmer reflected off something embedded in the grass. Ascertaining that what I had seen wasn't merely a trick of the light, I moved forward. Locating the object and reaching out towards it, handkerchief in hand, I extracted what I instantly recognized to be a bullet. I imagine I was a little bewildered upon seeing such an unexpected object in my hand that it took me some time to realize that Giallo and Flexthure had concluded their interrogation and had joined me.

'Have you found something, Monsieur St. Louie?' asked Flexthure.

In reply, I simply passed the handkerchief to the sergeant who examined the item enfolded within it carefully.

'Another bullet?' he exclaimed, his voice one of surprise and handing it to Giallo.

'But why on earth should we find it out here?'

We turned to look at Giallo, half expecting an answer, but his attention was instead fixed on a point behind us.

I eagerly followed his gaze but was disappointed to find nothing of interest, seeing that it was merely the villa he was looking at. I was about to speak, only to be prevented from doing so when he murmured softly.

'C'est curieux. C'est vraiment curieux.'

Chapter 6

Intermission

After our unexpected discovery in the garden, I naturally had expected Giallo to enlighten us on his thoughts on the matter but to my disappointment, he did not make any attempt to elaborate as we stood there in the afternoon sun. Instead, his only words to me were that I should join the others for lunch. This suggestion I immediately declined, protesting that I was not hungry in the least and I would much prefer to stay and help with the investigation.

He thanked me but said there was nothing left to do until lunch was concluded, since he had only the housemaids to interview after the meal was over. Thus, with great reluctance, I made my way back to the house and left Giallo and Flexthure to converse in the garden. As I entered the front door, Stanford spotted me and said:

Ah, Mr St. Louie. I am afraid that lunch started fifteen minutes ago and that the soup has already been served, but I asked the maid to keep yours warm, sir, until you came.'

'Thanks, Stanford,' I replied gratefully, feeling quite affectionate towards the elderly butler. He bowed slightly and disappeared into the library.

As I had expected, lunch was a dismal affair with plates either left untouched or at least half of what had been served still remaining on them.

I fear that the events of the morning and the subsequent feelings of shock, fear and bewilderment inspired by them had unfortunately had their effect on me and though I had not been feeling hungry as I took my seat at the table, the sight of food being presented before me proved too much and I was suddenly ravenous. However, to maintain decorum and avoid appearing utterly insensitive, I left a third of my plate uneaten.

I had the impression sitting there in that eerily quiet room that it was only after their interviews with Giallo that the enormity of the situation had sunk deep into the family's consciousness. The faces and people I saw now differed greatly from the ones I encountered at breakfast that morning. The air had been grim and tense. It was quite subtle and intangible and I must confess it is only after years of experience that I have recognized the mood which pervaded that room: one of overt fear and suspicion. I did not pay particular attention to anyone specifically but I was aware of numerous pairs of eyes flitting guardedly from face to face and casting sideways glances as the various courses were served. The mood in that room became so stiflingly uncomfortable, in fact, that I was nearly rejoiced when finally we rose to our feet and shuffled silently out of the room.

As I stepped outside into the corridor, there was a light touch on my shoulder, and I turned to see Larry looking intently into my face. He motioned towards a nearby alcove and we pulled quietly away from the others, who seemed not to notice us.

'Grimms tells us you've joined forces with that Giallo chap,' Larry said in a low voice.

'I haven't 'joined forces' with him, Larry,' I replied, disliking the phrase immensely. 'I'm only trying to help you all out of this horrid mess – you understand that.'

'Trust Grimms to bring a bit of dramatic exaggeration into the picture,' said Larry with a laugh. He was returning to his usual good spirits, but having known him for so long, I could immediately detect the nervousness belying his smiling visage, and it was clear that he was quite terrified of something.

'Come now, Larry,' I said gravely. 'There's no use beating about the bush. You're afraid of something, aren't you?'
He gave a slight start but composed himself.

'What makes you say that?' he plunged on in a nonchalant manner.

'You forget that we've been friends for years, old chap.'
Ah yes. Well, there's no denying that, St. Louie.
And you've always been a damn good one to me, too.'
He hesitated. 'Tell me then –'
'Tell you –?' I said when he did not continue.
'Oh, damn it all. Inevitable really how this was going to crop up some time but tell me and tell me truthfully: Giallo's suspecting me of murdering my father, isn't he?'
It was my turn to hesitate.
'Well, I can't say that things are entirely going in your favour,' I replied, choosing my words carefully, afraid that I would give something inadvertently away. But as so often in these cases, my attempt at sounding ambiguous was taken rather badly and Larry's face paled and instead of appearing panic-stricken, he gave the impression of a man resigned to his fate, lowering his eyes to the floor.
'I knew it,' he murmured. He suddenly looked up, his grey eyes looking quite lost in disbelief. 'Does he know of my outburst last night? The one where I said that I would take your revolver and –'
An expression of pained guilt entered his face, and he could not speak further.
'I'm afraid so,' I answered.
'Thought as much.'
He appeared to be on the verge of becoming more morose but surprised me when he suddenly said in a very forcible tone: 'But I swear to you, St. Louie. I didn't kill him. Yes, yes,' he said impatiently when I made to say something, 'I know everything seems to be against me – I had a motive and perhaps the opportunity but I swear on my mother's grave – on my mother's grave, you understand, that I didn't murder my father.'
'Larry –'
'I think someone's trying to frame me, St. Louie,' he continued in a lower voice and cutting me off.
'I don't know who and God only knows why they're doing this blasted thing, but I feel it in my bones. They have it out for me, I just know it.'

I was now painfully aware that he was gripping me by the arms in his anxiety to get his point across and the thought of him presently overcome by a fit of madness briefly passed through my head. I had never seen my friend in such a terrible, anguished state and I was saved by the sound of footsteps coming from the staircase above us. The sight of Giallo and Flexthure soon followed and their appearance jolted Larry back into a more composed state of mind, and he hastily released me, much to my relief.

'Monsieur Giallo,' he said shakily as Giallo bowed his head as both he and Flexthure approached us.

'Have you met with any success so far in your investigations?'

'Success can be many things, Monsieur Wiggins. I have been successful in finding some very interesting features of this case but as to finding out what actually occurred last night; I am, as you might say, still piecing the puzzle together. Also, I am glad to see that you look much better than in the morning.'

'Samantha's a wonder in reviving my spirits, Monsieur Giallo. Lord only knows where I'd be without her.'

At this, Larry cleared his throat a little in embarrassment, as if wondering whether he had said too much.

'Have you finished interviewing everyone of interest?'

'I have only the maids left to question.'

'Oh good, good. But surely, Camie and Estrella will have nothing to do with the matter? They were nowhere near the rooms upstairs.'

'In my experience, Monsieur Wiggins, it is best to be thorough. Oh, and I would also like to speak to Mademoiselle Milton.'

'Whatever for?' said Larry, his voice sharp.

'I have not yet had the chance to interview her.'

'You don't need to. She's feeling terrible enough as it is and I would appreciate it if you'd be kind enough to leave her alone – at least for today. She retired early at around half-past nine last night and didn't leave her room until a quarter to eight this morning.'

'How do you know this?' asked Flexthure.

'Samantha – Miss Milton told me so herself.'

'You can vouch for this?' said Giallo.

'Of course I can. I'd even swear on it if you like.'

Giallo waved his hand politely.

'Non, that will not be necessary. Thank you, monsieur.'
Larry then took this opportunity to leave us, mumbling that he had to find Samantha and wishing Giallo every success in his investigation.

'I thought that you'd finished looking upstairs,' I said to Giallo as soon as Larry had disappeared outside.
I realised I sounded faintly accusatory, but I had really believed that Giallo's investigations had concluded before my departure for lunch.

'But yes, that was the case, St. Louie. Or so I thought until I made a closer examination of one or two various little points of interest. Even Reeves Giallo, you must understand, cannot foresee everything!'
His earnestness reassured me, and I smiled a little.

'One or two points of interest?' I asked eagerly.
'Such as?'
I was prevented from receiving a reply by the appearance of Stanford, who quietly informed us that the two maids were now ready to speak with Giallo in the library. We were duly led to the room in question and as we entered, the two young ladies who had been exchanging words in rapid French stopped their conversation and fixed their eyes upon Giallo with noticeable nervousness.

I had seen Camie countless times around the house during my stay so far – the first time being was that rather awkward night when she had knocked over a vase in Sir Charles's presence. She was much calmer now but clearly quite upset with the whole business of her master, having met an untimely end.

My impression was that she was a timid young lady, capable and reliable, but not exceptionally pretty. Beside her was the other maid, Estrella, who I had never seen before and was quite another personality altogether. Coquettish and petite, she appeared to be the younger of the two maids, but seemed to know much more about the world. She was also with her dark chestnut-coloured hair and large brown eyes unbelievably attractive. Stanford explained that the duties between the two maids were shared; with Camie being the one mainly responsible for tending to the needs of the ladies and gentlemen 'upstairs' while Estrella stayed 'downstairs' in the servants' quarters and helping the cook with the meals.

I could sense too that another reason she had been delegated to duties downstairs was that either Sir Charles or Stanford had decided that her presence upstairs would cause too much unwanted attention, particularly from gentlemen visiting the house.

As Stanford left the room, Giallo greeted them politely and offered them to take a seat.

'Thank you, monsieur. You are much too kind,' said Camie as they both sat down.

'Not at all. I trust that you have not been too upset over this tragedy.'

'It is not always nice to have someone die in a house where one is living but Estrella and I, we have both seen our parents leave this good earth and meet the bon Dieu so we have not been affected too much.'

'Ah, you and Estrella are sisters, Mademoiselle Camie?'

I hardly believed that such a thing was possible, but apparently these two ladies who were so very unlike each other were indeed sisters and they nodded in confirmation.

What followed next was not very interesting. Camie confirmed Stanford's account of her finding him asleep at his desk the previous evening and was opposed to the suggestion put forward by Flexthure that he would have gone upstairs and murdered his master.

'The whole idea – even the notion of Monsieur Stanford killing the master is absurd. I have not worked in this house long, monsieur, but I can be sure that he was devoted to Sir Charles.'

'And to Monsieur Wiggins and his sister as well?' asked Giallo with interest.

'Them even more so.'

Giallo nodded, and they continued on the topic of Stanford. In response to Giallo's question about whether the butler's behavior had changed recently, Estrella remembered she had sometimes seen him taking walks about the grounds late at night from her bedroom window. She had no idea as to the purpose of these nocturnal wanderings, but she thought once or twice that he was heading in the general direction of Mallon's cottage.

'Once Monsieur Stanford even forgot where his own room was!' Estrella cried, evidently keen to go on about what she deemed as the increasing follies and faults of old age. Young people usually have either no patience or understanding of those much older and experienced than them.

'It was about a month ago, monsieur. It was nearly two in the morning, and I remembered I had forgotten to switch off the electric light in the larder. So I went there, switched it off, but on my way back, I crashed into him. The corridor was dark, so I suppose he wasn't aware that there was another person coming his way. But imagine my surprise, monsieur, when he suddenly asked me where his room was! For a moment, I thought he was drunk, but I couldn't smell any drink on him.'

'He appeared genuinely confused, mademoiselle?'

'Confused and bewildered? Yes, monsieur. I said to myself, "Estrella, you know too well that Monsieur Stanford never touches a drop of alcohol."

Oui, monsieur, not a single drop. So I'm guessing to myself that he suddenly had a fit of forgetfulness or something. He even said sorry for giving me trouble and after I had led him to his door, he thanked me and I went back to my room. And imagine my surprise when I ask him for a day's leave the next morning. He instantly refuses to give it to me. I don't think he even took one moment to consider it.' She threw up her hands expressively.

'The English, monsieur. What can I say? They are quite insane.'

I felt the urge to protest at this unfair remark. Giallo, however, appeared to throw me an amused look, and I stopped myself at the last minute.

Camie appeared to know nothing of this matter and therefore could not elaborate on it. But when returning to the events of last night, she firmly stated that she had seen nothing out of the ordinary when she had come across Stanford in his rooms and the same applied to her sister who had spent the entire evening in her room as she had been feeling unwell.

The migraine, monsieur,' explained Estrella sadly, with an exaggerated air of melancholy when Giallo inquired after her malady.

'It often strikes me at the most inconvenient of times.'

Though her answer was more or less straightforward, I detected that besides her attempts to seek sympathy from the men standing before her; she was also attempting to make eyes at us. Her attention was drawn to Giallo, who I imagine was of special interest to her because of his obvious rank and seniority. Personally, I thought her behavior was ridiculously inappropriate. Whether or not Giallo noticed her – after years of experience, I am led to believe that nothing ever escapes those sharp eyes of his – I do not know. He did however, hold her in his gaze for quite a while and suddenly, I felt a vague sense of irritation coming over me. It gripped me quite out of the blue and without warning and I suspect that it would have gone for much longer had Flexthure dismissed the maids at that moment.

'Well, that ends our investigations for the moment, Monsieur Giallo,' said Flexthure.

'So it seems, Flexthure.' He looked up at me.

'St. Louie, are you unwell?'

'What?' I started. 'Oh, it's nothing.'

I realised I had been staring at the door through which Camie and Estrella had departed and I coughed self-consciously.

'Attractive young girl,' said Flexthure suddenly.

'That Estrella, I mean.'

To this, Giallo gave a slow nod of the head. 'Though I am not in the habit of noting women's appearances in investigations such as these, I would have to agree with you there, Flexthure. There are probably few men in this world who could ignore such a girl as that one.'

I coughed even louder and Flexthure looked at me irritably.

'Caught a cold, Monsieur St. Louie?'

'Sorry. Cursed hay fever, I imagine,' I lied, eager for a change of topic. I knew deep down that both Giallo and Flexthure were right about Estrella; I had been quite struck by her appearance upon setting eyes on her, but I was suddenly quite unwilling to admit to it, especially in front of Giallo, whose interest in her annoyed me inexplicably.

'Are you returning to Paris soon, Giallo?' I asked.

'Yes. This instant, in fact. I have checked everything of interest upstairs, including Sir Charles' body, which has already been sent down.'

'I suppose that means we'll be saying farewell then,' said Flexthure, shaking my hand. His tone was unusually jolly, and I got the impression that he was extremely keen to be rid of my company as soon as possible.

'Seeing that we've concluded our investigations here, I doubt we'll need your opinions any longer, monsieur. Monsieur Giallo, with your permission, I will go outside and order the men to return to headquarters.'

With a curt nod of the head in my direction, the sergeant exited the room, and I looked after him indignantly.

'Have I done anything to upset him, Giallo?'

Giallo gave a faint smile and said consolingly.

'Non, non. Flexthure, though he is a more than capable officer, has a deplorable lack of what one could call the social graces. But in his defense, I should add that those are not necessarily required in an officer of la police belge.

Not only that, he is fanatically devoted to his duty and is therefore understandably against those not of the police to meddle in our affairs.'

'And you? What do you think of these meddlers such as myself?'

'Ah, pardon,' he said, catching the hurt expression on my face.

'Perhaps the word 'meddle' was not the best choice.

I should have said 'take part'. But returning to your question, St. Louie; as for myself, I am more open than our Sergeant Flexthure. Therefore, while the Sergeant has stated that he no longer needs your opinions, I'm very interested in receiving them.'

Giallo's continued faith in me cheered me up to no end, and I grinned.

'Thanks, old chap.'

'Pas du tout,' he replied. 'But tell me, St. Louie. Before Flexthure and I came downstairs, you were speaking with Monsieur Wiggins, yes?'

There was no point in denying this; Giallo, with his keen powers of observation, had obviously overheard us. I then told him about my awkward exchange with Larry.

He listened in attentive silence and gave a nod when I had finished.

'Well?' I demanded. 'Do you think there's any truth in what he's saying, Giallo? Is someone really trying to frame him?'

'It is possible, bien sûr. What is more interesting is to learn that Larry Stokes seems more than aware of the case building up against him – and it is a strong case indeed.'

I paled a little.

'Good Lord, I hope I'm not sinking him deeper and deeper into the mud by helping you with your investigations.'

He looked at me gravely as I said this and said sharply: 'I hope you are not getting the cold feet, mon ami. You have offered to help me, St. Louie, to solve this case, and I have accepted. Playing the role of detective is not only about deduction and catching the one responsible; it is above all about obtaining justice – and moreover, the truth. Without truth, without justice, people like myself are merely playing the farce in this already farcical world. And playing the farce is a pastime I like not.'

He fixed upon my face those brown eyes which were now blazing with a fire I had never seen before, and I felt myself in danger of getting singed by the metaphorical flames.

'So, St. Louie – what is it to be? To keep your loyalty to your friend? Or to be objective and to seek the ultimate goal; the truth?'

I swallowed nervously; my throat suddenly parched. Here I knew I was standing at a crossroads and that my choice now would irrecoverably set the course of my friendship with the little man.

'The truth, Giallo,' I said finally, after an excruciating silence.

'Regardless of how it might turn out to be? Remember, mon ami, the truth does not always reveal itself to be the one we often desire.'

'The truth,' I repeated firmly. 'And nothing but the truth, old fellow.' I breathed a small sigh of relief. 'There……
I've decided…for better or worse, and I won't waver from it.'

And it was apparent that I had decided which Giallo was hoping for. The fire in his eyes softened, and he looked at me with an expression of warm affection.

'Thank you, St. Louie. It is not a simple choice to make, but it was the right one.' He put one of his square hands on my shoulder and I flushed a little, half-embarrassed and half-touched by his gesture.

'Not at all, Giallo,' I managed. 'Well, I've told you of my conversation with Larry outside the dining room. Now, what are these one or two points of interest upstairs you mentioned?'

'Ah,' said Giallo with a smile and at that moment, he reminded me very much of a conjuror preparing to perform a trick.

'What would you make of these curious points? A trace of gunpowder on a window sill, a bell pull which does not ring and coffee spilling not only on the carpet but on the flowerbeds outside from a cup which has been afterwards tidily replaced in its saucer?'

I looked at him in bewilderment and I wondered briefly whether he was having a go at pulling my leg. My initial attempts at giving half-humorous responses did not go down at all well. He was apparently in complete earnest about these points.

'I hardly know. They seem so random, Giallo. Are you sure you actually see something important behind them?'

'Of course,' he replied with a hint of irritation. 'Or else I would not be asking your opinion, St. Louie.'

There was nothing I could come up with, and I shook my head.

'Another time perhaps and after you have given them some thought, you can tell me of your theories.'

He took out his pocket watch and glanced at it.

'However, now is not the time. I fear I must now return to the capital. The Commissaire will expect my report. But first, I must give you something.'

At this, he retrieved a small leather-bound notebook from his pocket and after carefully writing in it and tearing out a sheet; he passed it on to me.

'Here is the telephone number of our headquarters in Paris. The line is acceptable at best, but it should suffice. Here too is the address in case you have need of it.'

I looked at the piece of paper uncomprehendingly.

'I'm grateful, Giallo, but why would I need them?'

'What? Is it not clear to you?'

'What is?'

He gave a little exasperated sigh.

'In case you should hear or see anything, St. Louie, this is the quickest way to find me.'

'You think something's going to happen here? Another murder?' I asked, gazing at him in disbelief. The thought itself chilled me to the core. One death at the house was already quite enough.

'That I sincerely hope does not happen,' Giallo replied emphatically. 'But calm yourself, I pray for you, mon ami. I give them to you merely because I am asking whether you would like to be – what do you say in your country – my eyes and ears are here when I am not present.'

'But doesn't the Commissaire want you to be here at all times?'

'Yes and no. A case of great national, even international importance such as this requires much intensive investigation. Alas, this also entails – '

'Much intensive paperwork?' I quipped, smiling despite myself.

'Précisément,' he said, nodding in agreement.

'If only I were a private investigator, I would not need to spend the valuable time on such things. However, there is much use in it. It makes one furiously to think and thus allows me to place everything each in its proper place. Order and method, St. Louie! They are most vital.'

This was not to be the last time that Giallo would remind me constantly of the gods, as it were, of his profession, but this time being the first of my hearing them, I was duly impressed.

'Well, I'll be honored to be your eyes and ears, Giallo. I hope I'll make a good job of it,' I said as we stepped out onto the front drive.

'That I am certain you shall do,' he smiled, replacing his hat upon his pomaded head.

'Bon. Now then, we will have to part until later, perhaps. Au revoir, mon ami.'

After Giallo's departure, life at the villa seemed to return to its customary rhythm. Apart from our attire becoming more sombre and subdued and the usual customs of mourning being carried out, there was nothing to suggest from the outside that there had been a death in the house. We heard nothing from Giallo or the police, only to read in the local newspaper that investigations were currently being undertaken and that M. Reeves Giallo, Chief Detective Inspector of the Paris Police was soon due to give his first report to both the Commissaire and the Prime Minister of France.

Even a week after Sir Charles's death, a date for an inquest had not been decided upon and this resulted in the general feeling that we were currently stuck in a kind of limbo; not entirely knowing what had happened that dreadful night and yet not entirely willing to accept the consensus that the ambassador had committed suicide.

We continued our lives in relative serenity and were untouched by excitement of any kind, barring of course, the considerable attempts of the mostly British press to infiltrate the grounds to obtain the latest scoops or an interview with Larry who also had to put up with dozens of journalists literally camping out in front of the Embassy in Paris.

He never gave in to their requests and was thus dubbed Larry Stokes, soon to be Sir Larry Stokes, the aloof future baronet. However, his apparent aloofness did not stop them from publishing some positively libelous stories about the Wiggins family. These stories were more often to be seen in the Daily Express rather than The Times, it must be admitted, with the latter respectfully expressing the loss of one of His Britannic Majesty's most important diplomats in Europe and the various political consequences arising from Sir Charles's sudden passing. Papers like the Daily Express were not as philosophical about the matter and even published a deeply upsetting and disgraceful article regarding the late Lady Elizabeth Wiggins in which they claimed they had confirmed reports of her once having an affair because of her husband's unpleasant character.

As was expected, Larry took this extremely close to heart and threatened to sue the offending paper in question on grounds of slander and libel. His threat resulted in the paper immediately dropping the story from future editions and the matter was quickly dropped, but not, alas, as quickly forgotten.

'They can say what they like about me or my father, but I'll be damned if they expect me to just sit around while they sully my mother's name,' he growled as we were playing a game of chess in the library. This was approximately a week after the death of Sir Charles and my friend had returned to his former self, and that bizarre instance when he had tried to convince me he was being framed outside the dining room seemed a distant memory.

I thought carefully before asking quietly: 'You were close to her, Larry?'

I had never heretofore asked Larry about his mother, for I had always known it was a painful topic for him. If I had expected him to shut up like an oyster, he surprised me by doing the opposite and it was in a voice utterly devoid of sadness that he said:

'Close to her, St. Louie? To tell the truth, I thought she was the world to me. It's strange though that I didn't really think so at the time. Only when she died did I realize how much she meant to our lives. Funny how you don't realize you've lost something until it's truly gone.'

He paused and looked musingly at the chessboard before realizing that it was his turn.

'Did your mother and father get along while she was alive?'

'Get along?' he laughed mirthlessly.

'He hardly noticed her, even when he was at home with us in either the city or the country. But Mother always had a sense of duty instilled in her – no matter how awful Father was, she was his wife and he was her husband, and that was the end of the matter.

One could call such devotion foolish, especially when it was never returned, but you've got to admire this infallible sense of duty in her. She always said she got it from her father…you might have heard of him, he was Sir Garnet Wolseley.'

The name was familiar to me; he had been handsomely decorated for his feats and bravery in both the Zulu War and the Second Afghan War and had made a brilliant career for himself in Parliament after his retirement from the army. His experience at the front and his mingling with the infantry had given him an unusual insight into the plight of the common man and was one of the most outspoken champions regarding social reform. He had often said that it was not merely necessary to help the working classes, but also a duty of every decent Englishman.

'Father was then, of course, delighted when he was allowed to marry her. But he had to fight for her…apparently, another gentleman had asked for her hand in marriage before he came along and she had accepted.'

'Do you know anything about this other gentleman?'

'Not really. All I know was that there were concerns about his being a foreigner from my grandfather. I think he was French or something like that. Or was he Russian? I can't recall. Regardless, I believe Mother was deeply in love with him and was very much saddened when she had to marry the then Commander Charles Stow of the Royal Navy instead. Not the happiest of starts to a marriage, is it, St. Louie?'

'No,' I replied, feeling entirely sympathetic to the late Lady Wiggins's situation.

'I suppose Mother's experience, at least regarding matrimony, rubbed off on me in the end. I was determined that if I ever married, I would have to be entirely in love with her and she with me. There's no point in marrying someone if the other person isn't feeling the same way. Just spells disaster and years of unnecessary sadness.'

'Well, you've certainly found the right person then.'

'Yes,' said Larry contentedly, and by the sudden softening in his grey eyes, I knew instinctively his thoughts were revolving around Samantha.

'She's a gem, St. Louie.'

'I'm happy for the both of you.'

'Thanks, old chap. Falling in love really changes you, you know. Before I met Samantha, life seemed to just go on and on. Simply day after day of just heading off to the Embassy and repeating the same old tasks and with Father barking at me to get down his dictation or sending off a dispatch. There was no purpose in sight, but once Samantha came along, everything changed, and life had a new meaning.'
He paused.

'Now, I know I might sound preposterously sentimental, St. Louie, and you don't have to listen to me babble on,' he added, reddening a little and appearing very self-conscious. 'But love really changes everything.
It really does. And all I can tell you is that once you've found someone, regardless of what everyone thinks of the both of you, don't give that person up. Not for anything in the world. You'll have to endure some hard knocks, of course, but don't, for the love of God, give them up.'

I admit I was faintly amused by his sudden sentimentality, which was uncharacteristic of him, but instead of chuckling at him, I smiled.

'I will remember that, Larry.'

The migraine, monsieur,' explained Estrella sadly, with an exaggerated air of melancholy when Giallo inquired after her malady.

'It often strikes me at the most inconvenient of times.'

Though her answer was more or less straightforward, I detected that besides her attempts to seek sympathy from the men standing before her; she was also attempting to make eyes at us. Her attention was drawn to Giallo, who I imagine was of special interest to her because of his obvious rank and seniority. Personally, I thought her behavior was ridiculously inappropriate. Whether or not Giallo noticed her – after years of experience, I am led to believe that nothing ever escapes those sharp eyes of his – I do not know. He did however, hold her in his gaze for quite a while and suddenly, I felt a vague sense of irritation coming over me. It gripped me out of the blue and without warning and I suspect that it would have gone for much longer had Flexthure not dismissed the maids at that moment.

'Well, that ends our investigations for the moment, Monsieur Giallo,' said Flexthure.

'So it seems, Flexthure.'

He looked up at me. 'St. Louie, are you unwell?'

'What?' I started. 'Oh, it's nothing.'

I realized I had been staring at the door through which Camie and Estrella had departed and I coughed self-consciously.

'Attractive young girl,' said Flexthure suddenly.

'That Estrella, I mean.'

To this, Giallo gave a slow nod of the head. 'Though I am not in the habit of noting women's appearances in investigations such as these, I would have to agree with you there, Flexthure. There are probably few men in this world who could ignore such a girl as that one.'

I coughed even louder and Flexthure looked at me irritably.

'Caught a cold, Monsieur St. Louie?'

'Sorry. Cursed hay fever, I imagine,' I lied, eager for a change of topic. I knew deep down that both Giallo and Flexthure were right about Estrella; I had been quite struck by her appearance upon setting eyes on her, but I was suddenly quite unwilling to admit to it, especially in front of Giallo, whose interest in her annoyed me inexplicably.

'Are you returning to Paris soon, Giallo?' I asked.

'Yes. This instant, in fact. I have checked everything of interest upstairs, including Sir Charles' body, which has already been sent down.'

'I suppose that means we'll be saying farewell then,' said Flexthure, shaking my hand. His tone was unusually jolly, and I got the impression that he was extremely keen to be rid of my company as soon as possible.

'Seeing that we've concluded our investigations here, I doubt we'll need your opinions any longer, monsieur. Monsieur Giallo, with your permission, I will go outside and order the men to return to headquarters.'

With a curt nod of the head in my direction, the sergeant exited the room, and I looked after him indignantly.

'Have I done anything to upset him, Giallo?'

Giallo gave a faint smile and said consolingly:

'Non, non. Flexthure, though he is a more than capable officer, has a deplorable lack of what one could call the social graces. But in his defense, I should add that those are not necessarily required in an officer of la police belge.

Not only that, he is frantically devoted to his duty and is therefore understandably against those not of the police to meddle in our affairs.'

'And you? What do you think of these meddlers such as myself?'

'Ah, pardon,' he said, catching the hurt expression on my face.

'Perhaps the word 'meddle' was not the best choice.

I should have said 'take part'. But returning to your question, St. Louie; as for myself, I am more open than our Sergeant Flexthure. Therefore, while the Sergeant has stated that he no longer needs your opinions, I, on the other hand, will still be very interested in receiving them.'

Giallo's continued faith in me cheered me up to no end, and I grinned.

'Thanks, old chap.'

'Pas du tout,' he replied. 'But tell me, St. Louie. Before Flexthure and I came downstairs, you were speaking with Monsieur Wiggins, yes?'

There was no point in denying this; Giallo, with his keen powers of observation, had obviously overheard us.

I then told him about my awkward exchange with Larry. He listened in attentive silence and gave a nod when I had finished.

'Well?' I demanded. 'Do you think there's any truth in what he's saying, Giallo? Is someone really trying to frame him?'

'It is possible, bien sûr. What is more interesting is to learn that Larry Stokes seems more than aware of the case building up against him – and it is a strong case indeed.'

I paled a little.

'Good Lord, I hope I'm not sinking him deeper and deeper into the mud by helping you with your investigations.'

He looked at me gravely as I said this and said sharply:

'I hope you are not getting the cold feet, mon ami. You have offered to help me, St. Louie, to solve this case, and I have accepted. Playing the role of detective is not only about deduction and catching the one responsible; it is above all about obtaining justice – and moreover, the truth. Without truth, without justice, people like myself are merely playing the farce in this already farcical world.

And playing the farce is a pastime I like not.'

He fixed upon my face those brown eyes which were now blazing with a fire I had never seen before, and I felt myself in danger of getting singed by the metaphorical flames.

'So, St. Louie – what is it to be? To keep your loyalty to your friend? Or to be objective and to seek the ultimate goal; the truth?'

I swallowed nervously; my throat suddenly parched.

Here I knew I was standing at a crossroads and that my choice now would irrecoverably set the course of my friendship with the little man.

'The truth, Giallo,' I said finally, after an excruciating silence.

'Regardless of how it might turn out to be? Remember, mon ami, the truth does not always reveal itself to be the one we often desire.'

'The truth,' I repeated firmly. 'And nothing but the truth, old fellow.'

I breathed a small sigh of relief.

'There I've decided...for better or worse, and I won't waver from it.'

And it was apparent that I had decided which Giallo was hoping for. The fire in his eyes softened, and he looked at me with an expression of warm affection.

'Thank you, St. Louie. It is not a simple choice to make, but it was the right one.' He put one of his square hands on my shoulder and I flushed a little, half-embarrassed and half-touched by his gesture.

'Not at all, Giallo,' I managed.

'Well, I've told you of my conversation with Larry outside the dining room.

Now, what are these one or two points of interest upstairs you mentioned?'

'Ah,' said Giallo with a smile and at that moment, he reminded me very much of a conjuror preparing to perform a trick.

'What would you make of these curious points?

A trace of gunpowder on a window sill, a bell pull which does not ring and coffee spilling not only on the carpet but on the flowerbeds outside from a cup which has been afterwards tidily replaced in its saucer?'

I looked at him in bewilderment and I wondered briefly whether he was having a go at pulling my leg. My initial attempts at giving half-humorous responses did not go down at all well.

He was apparently in complete earnest about these points.

'I hardly know. They seem so random, Giallo. Are you sure you actually see something important behind them?'

'Of course,' he replied with a hint of irritation.

'Or else I would not be asking your opinion, St. Louie.'

There was nothing I could come up with, and I shook my head.

'Another time perhaps and after you have given them some thought, you can tell me of your theories.'

He took out his pocket watch and glanced at it.

'However, now is not the time. I fear I must now return to the capital. The Commissaire will expect my report. But first, I must give you something.'

At this, he retrieved a small leather-bound notebook from his pocket and after carefully writing in it and tearing out a sheet; he passed it on to me.

'Here is the telephone number of our headquarters in Paris. The line is acceptable at best, but it should suffice. Here too is the address in case you have need of it.'

I looked at the piece of paper uncomprehendingly.

'I'm grateful, Giallo, but why would I need them?'

'What? Is it not clear to you?'

'What is?'

He gave a little exasperated sigh.

'In case you should hear or see anything, St. Louie, this is the quickest way to find me.'

'You think something's going to happen here? Another murder?' I asked, gazing at him in disbelief.

The thought itself chilled me to the core. One death at the house was already quite enough.

'That I sincerely hope does not happen,' Giallo replied emphatically. 'But calm yourself, I pray for you, mon ami. I give them to you merely because I am asking whether you would like to be – what do you say in your country – my eyes and ears are here when I am not present.'

'But doesn't the Commissaire want you to be here at all times?'

'Yes and no. A case of great national even international importance such as this requires much intensive investigation. Alas, this also entails – '

'Much intensive paperwork?' I quipped, smiling despite myself.

'Précisément,' he said, nodding in agreement.

'If only I were a private investigator, I would not need to spend the valuable time on such things. However, there is much use in it nevertheless. It makes one furiously to think and thus allows me to place everything each in its proper place. Order and method, St. Louie! They are most vital.'

This was not to be the last time that Giallo would remind me constantly of the gods of his profession, but this time being the first of my hearing them, I was duly impressed.

'Well, I'll be honored to be your eyes and ears, Giallo.

I hope I'll make a good job of it,' I said as we stepped out onto the front drive.

'That I am certain you shall do,' he smiled, replacing his hat upon his pomaded head. 'Bon. Now then, we will have to part until later, perhaps. Au revoir, mon ami.'

After Giallo's departure, life at the villa seemed to return to its customary rhythm. Apart from our attire becoming more sombre and subdued and the usual customs of mourning being carried out, there was nothing to suggest from the outside that there had been a death in the house.

We heard nothing from Giallo or the police, only to read in the local newspaper that investigations were currently being undertaken and that M. Reeves Giallo, Chief Detective Inspector of the Paris Police was soon due to give his first report to both the Commissaire and the Prime Minister of France. Even a week after Sir Charles's death, a date for an inquest had not been decided upon and this resulted in the general feeling that we were currently stuck in a kind of limbo; not entirely knowing what had happened that dreadful night and yet not entirely willing to accept the consensus that the ambassador had committed suicide.

We continued our lives in relative serenity and were untouched by excitement of any kind, barring of course, the considerable attempts of the mostly British press to infiltrate the grounds to get the latest scoops or an interview with Larry who also had to put up with dozens of journalists literally camping out in front of the Embassy in Paris. He never gave in to their requests and was thus dubbed Larry Stokes, soon to be Sir Larry Stokes, the aloof future baronet. However, his apparent aloofness did not stop them from publishing some positively libelous stories about the Wiggins family.

These stories were more often to be seen in the Daily Express rather than The Times, it must be admitted, with the latter respectfully expressing the loss of one of His Britannic Majesty's most important diplomats in Europe and the various political consequences arising from Sir Charles's sudden passing. Papers like the Daily Express were not as philosophical about the matter and even published a deeply upsetting and disgraceful article regarding the late Lady Elizabeth Wiggins in which they claimed they had confirmed reports of her once having an affair because of her husband's unpleasant character. As was expected, Larry took this extremely close to heart and threatened to sue the offending paper in question on grounds of slander and libel. His threat resulted in the paper immediately dropping the story from future editions and the matter was quickly dropped, but not, alas, as quickly forgotten.

'They can say what they like about me or my father, but I'll be damned if they expect me to just sit around while they sully my mother's name,' he growled as we were playing a game of chess in the library. This was approximately a week after the death of Sir Charles and my friend had returned to his former self, and that bizarre instance when he had tried to convince me he was being framed outside the dining room seemed a distant memory. I thought carefully before asking quietly: 'You were close to her, Larry?'

I had never heretofore asked Larry about his mother, for I had always known it was a painful topic for him. If I had expected him to shut up like an oyster, he surprised me by doing the opposite and it was in a voice utterly devoid of sadness that he said:

'Close to her, St. Louie? To tell the truth, I thought she was the world to me. It's strange though that I didn't really think so at the time.

Only when she died did I realize how much she meant to our lives. Funny how you don't realize you've lost something until it's truly gone.' He paused and looked musingly at the chessboard before realizing that it was his turn.

'Did your mother and father get along while she was alive?'

'Get along?' he laughed mirthlessly. 'He hardly noticed her, even when he was at home with us in either the city or the country. But Mother always had a sense of duty instilled in her – no matter how awful Father was, she was his wife and he was her husband, and that was the end of the matter. One could call such devotion foolish, especially when it was never returned, but you've got to admire this infallible sense of duty in her. She always said she got it from her father...you might have heard of him, he was Sir Garnet Wolseley.'

The name was familiar to me; he had been handsomely decorated for his feats and bravery in both the Zulu War and the Second Afghan War and had made a brilliant career for himself in Parliament after his retirement from the army. His experience at the front and his mingling with the infantry had given him an unusual insight into the plight of the common man and was one of the most outspoken champions regarding social reform. He had often said that it was not merely necessary to help the working classes, but also a duty of every decent Englishman.

'Father was then, of course, delighted when he could marry her. But he did have to fight for her…apparently, another gentleman had asked for her hand in marriage before he came along and she had accepted.'

'Do you know anything of this other gentleman?'

'Not really. All I know was that there were concerns about his being a foreigner from my grandfather. I think he was French or something like that. Or was he Russian? I can't recall. Regardless, I believe Mother was deeply in love with him and was very much saddened when she had to marry the then Commander Charles Stow of the Royal Navy instead. Not the happiest of starts to a marriage, is it, St. Louie?'

'No,' I replied, feeling entirely sympathetic to the late Lady Wiggins's situation.

'I suppose Mother's experience, at least regarding matrimony, rubbed off on me in the end. I was determined that if I ever married, I would have to be entirely in love with her and she with me. There's no point in marrying someone if the other person isn't feeling the same way.
Just spells disaster and years of unnecessary sadness.'

'Well, you've certainly found the right person then.'

'Yes,' said Larry contentedly, and by the sudden softening in his grey eyes, I knew instinctively his thoughts were revolving around Samantha. 'She's a gem, St. Louie.'

'I'm happy for the both of you.'

'Thanks, old chap. Falling in love really changes you, you know. Before I met Samantha, life seemed to just go on and on. Simply day after day of just heading off to the Embassy and repeating the same old tasks and with Father barking at me to get down his dictation or sending off a dispatch. There was no

purpose in sight, but once Samantha came along, everything changed and life had a new meaning.'
He paused.

'Now, I know I might sound preposterously sentimental, St. Louie, and you don't have to listen to me babble on,' he added, reddening a little and appearing very self-conscious.

'But love really changes everything.
It really does.
And all I can tell you is that once you've found someone, regardless of what everyone thinks of the both of you, don't give that person up. Not for anything in the world.
You'll have to endure some hard knocks, of course, but don't, for the love of God, give them up.'
I admit I was faintly amused by his sudden sentimentality, which was uncharacteristic of him, but instead of chuckling at him, I smiled.

'I will remember that, Larry.'

Chapter 7

The Inquest

The inquest was to take place during the second week of August. As a result, the past two weeks of relative calm we had enjoyed came to an end. One reason it had taken unusually long for the inquest to be scheduled was that there had been rather heated debates between the British and Paris authorities over whose responsibility it was to handle the matter. In the end, it was decided that since Sir Charles had met his end in France, full rein was accordingly given to the French on the condition that the ensuing investigations were to be undertaken in the fairest and most impartial manner possible. I had smiled a little to myself when I came across this news in the paper, recalling the blazing fire in Giallo's eyes as he told me about truth and justice and I suspected that there could be no fairer or more impartial detective in the world than Reeves Giallo.

I had heard nothing from him since our last meeting at the villa, but I assumed he was terribly busy in putting together the reports he found so tiresome. It probably seems strange for followers of my friend's exploits in later years to learn that even the famous Reeves Giallo was not free from the various constraints, rules and regulations of a police hierarchy. Even I find it odd to look back upon those days when he was Giallo, the police detective rather than Giallo, the private investigator, but I suppose even the most illustrious of personalities has to start somewhere.

That being so, this has caused no end of amusement to Chief Inspector Zane, who occasionally brings up the topic when the mood takes him. But I digress.

Despite not hearing from him for nearly two weeks, he would be present at the inquest and I therefore thought about compiling a list of theories I had come up with.

This, I decided, was to compensate for the complete lack of interesting information I had picked up at the villa in my role as Giallo's eyes and ears. Apart from a few more vases being broken by Camie (who apparently didn't require her late master glaring at her to cause a mishap), nothing of interest or excitement had occurred.

The several points of interest he had shared with me before his departure from the villa had been a starting point for my list, but the results did not look at all promising.

The trace of gunpowder he had found on the window sill was obviously related to the revolver, but I couldn't imagine why it would be present there in the first place. Due to my years at the front, my knowledge of firearms is probably better than the average layman and I will therefore detail several important points on the matter.

Traces of powder are often to be found either on the person who has fired the weapon or near the place where it has been discharged. But seeing that the windows in Sir Charles's study were at least six feet behind him, the only conclusions I could draw up were that either someone had climbed up the wall from the outside and shot him from behind through the open window or someone had fired from the study window whilst being inside the room and into the garden below. The first idea I knew was preposterous.

The second was more promising since it perfectly explained the bullet embedded in the grass but it was also equally if not more baffling as I could see no reason for anyone to draw even more attention to themselves by firing out of a window, much less a murderer who in most cases I suspect would have preferred to draw no attention to their presence. I mused upon the possibility of Sir Charles perhaps being possibly aware of an attempt on his life and shooting his would-be assassin from the window.

This didn't quite explain how he had somehow got a hold of my revolver, but it was an idea.

I then moved on to the subject of the bell pull used for calling the servants, which evidently implicated Stanford or the maids but could not find any other solution other than that it had either been broken or deliberately disabled by someone in the house.

Despite myself, my suspicions immediately flew towards the gardener as I considered the latter point, but as Giallo had warned me before; there was no motive or reason to tie Mallon to the crime and so I left the matter open to suggestion, hoping to learn of Giallo's opinion when I saw him again.

The third and last point revolved around the coffee which apparently had been spilled not only on the carpet but outside. This piece of evidence, I must admit, I found quite trivial. Sir Charles might have spilled it by accident that evening and that should have been the end of the matter. Perhaps the fact that the coffee had been spilled outside too was curious but Larry had mentioned that his father often kept a lookout at his study window. Only Giallo's insistence that something important lay behind this persuaded me to think more carefully on it, but even as the day of the inquest dawned upon us, my theories had progressed no further.

Interest in Sir Charles's death had somewhat waned in the last two weeks owing to the case being overshadowed by news of a more international and political nature but it seemed to rise once again when word got out of the date for the inquest and the intense scrutiny we received as we squeezed ourselves into that hot, airless courtroom at the Hôtel de Ville in Paris was almost unbearable.

The Paris government's fear of losing its main ally in case of war because of the death of Britain's highest representative in the country had translated into masses of Paris academics, politicians and men of the professional classes crowding the public gallery and the atmosphere was not very unlike the one one encounters before the start of a play at the theatre.

'It's quite horrid,' remarked Samantha as I related this observation to her as we took our places.

'I'm certain I'll never be able to act onstage without getting the shivers after this. The comparison's far too close for comfort, in my opinion.'

Owing to the important nature of this case, all of us at the house were required to give evidence and state our various whereabouts on that fateful night. Therefore, I will not repeat what has already been recorded. The jury examined the body and Larry was called to give positive identification, after which he recalled the events of that night.

As expected, he was on the receiving end of a severe grilling from the Coroner once the latter had learned of his rash outburst regarding the revolver and the jury and the public were no less forgiving as they shook their heads or gasped with ludicrous exaggeration in response.

Sir Charles's doctor, a Dr Sam Jamison, was also called and declared that his late patient had been of sound mind and health since he had last seen him a month ago.

The rest of us followed afterwards, our testimonies being received with polite but indifferent interest from the public. This cool attitude changed a little, however, with Estrella's excited narrative about Stanford. Though not so eloquently told this time as when she had first recounted to us her bizarre encounter with the butler – she suddenly stopped midway through a sentence probably out of nerves – it had the effect of making Stanford protest vigorously when it was his turn to stand. I thought Stanford perfectly justified to argue against Estrella's story, which I thought was purely a fabrication on her part to garner more attention to herself.

That is all very well, Monsieur Stanford,' said the Coroner when Stanford had finished.

'But as we have heard from the others, there was a coffee cup on your master's desk which was found the same morning of his death. Can you explain how it got there?'

As before, Stanford was completely at a loss and I could see that he was genuinely bewildered by its presence and I thought that the court at large was also believing in the butler's innocence. He was soon allowed to return to his seat with no further questions.

Next was the police surgeon, M. Georges Darlings.

He was a short, stocky man with what appeared to be a perpetually grim expression on his countenance.

'Monsieur Darlings, I believe you were one of the first to examine the body?'

'Yes, monsieur. The family had already sent for a local doctor, Monsieur Bouilton, and whom I met when we were called to the house that morning.'

'Were Monsieur Bouilton's opinions under your own?'

'He said he was merely a doctor, but his idea that death must have occurred at least eight hours previously was very much in line with my own.'

'So you would put the time of death at about one o'clock in the morning? At around the same time as Monsieur St. Louie has already told us he heard what he supposed was a gunshot?'

'Yes. Death was unlikely to have occurred after one o'clock.'

'Monsieur Darlings, you have stated that Sir Charles's death was caused by what you have described in your report as "a single bullet to the left side of his temple."

Is that correct?' asked the Coroner.

'Yes, monsieur.'

'Can you tell us what sort of gun was used?'

'I believe a revolver was certainly used in bringing about the ambassador's death, though I have yet to discover the exact model used.'

'I believe that Monsieur Giallo requested a post-mortem to be done on the body.'

Yes, monsieur. After having received instructions and permission from Monsieur Giallo, I conducted a post-mortem once the body had been transferred to my office that afternoon.'

'What were your findings?'

'I found traces of gunpowder near Sir Charles's wound but curiously none on his fingers or his hand, the presence of which would without doubt have showed suicide.'

'Did you find any traces of foul play?'

'None whatsoever.'

At that, Darlings could leave the dock. The anticipation in the room was growing, and I observed it increased palpably when it was Giallo's turn to rise to his feet and be called to the dock. Although Reeves Giallo was not much older than myself, his opinions carried significant weight in his country and that all eyes were fixed upon him with the fullest attention, like some great actor entering onstage.

He was now dressed in the same smart dark suit I had seen him wearing on the day I bumped into him in Paris and if there were still any remaining doubts in my mind on whether the uniformed detective I had befriended at the villa and the man in Paris was the same fellow; I required no further proof.

After dispensing of the usual formalities, the Coroner said:

'Monsieur Giallo, you have been assigned to this case by the Prime Minister himself through your Commissaire, M. Clint Yearling, I understand.'

'Yes, monsieur.'

'So I am certain that you are more than aware that a great deal rests upon your findings today.'

'Very much so, monsieur.'

Nodding, the Coroner asked Giallo many questions – many of them already asked by Giallo himself during his interrogations at the villa and so I will not repeat them here. Soon, however, he was allowed to introduce his findings to the court and the subject of the revolver and the cup of coffee were brought up.

'Monsieur Giallo, do you agree with Monsieur Darlings' conclusion that death was brought about by a single shot to the left temple?'

'Entirely, monsieur.'

'And is it your opinion that the revolver found was the weapon used?'

I had expected an affirmation at this point but was completely taken by surprise when Giallo said calmly:

'No, I do not.'

Confusion flashed briefly across the Coroner's face and he consulted the notes he had written and placed before him.

'No?' he repeated, puzzled.

Aware of the stir he had just unleashed in the courtroom and the sudden flurry of whispering among the spectators, Giallo repeated firmly: 'No. The revolver found in Sir Charles's study was not the one which killed him.'

'Explain, if you please, Monsieur Giallo.'

'Bien sûr, monsieur. You see, the revolver found in Sir Charles's study is of English origin. It is a Webley, to be precise. Upon receiving Monsieur Darlings's report and the bullet extracted from Sir Charles, I ordered my men to examine the exact calibre of the bullet. It is not from a Webley but from a Nagant which all those well-acquainted with the firearms will know uses bullets of a completely different calibre from the English.'

'Do you mean to say, Monsieur Giallo, that there is a second revolver involved in this case?'

'That is correct, monsieur.'

I was utterly confounded. I remembered the complete confusion I had experienced upon beholding my revolver that morning. We had found him dead in his study.
But to now realize that it hadn't been used in the crime at all seemed fantastical. Like the others sitting around me, I stared at him, eagerly awaiting an explanation.

'And where is this second revolver? This Nagant?'
Giallo bowed his head a little in what seemed to be defeat.

'I am afraid that despite our endeavors, we unfortunately can not locate this weapon, monsieur.'

'Do you believe it has therefore been intentionally disposed of?'

'I believe so, yes, monsieur.'

There was an indistinct murmur from the jury who passed grave looks at each other.

'Monsieur Giallo, you are a man of great experience in these matters. What then do you think was the purpose of this Webley revolver if it was not used to kill the deceased?'

Giallo paused a little before saying, 'I have concluded, monsieur, is that it was placed near him intending to implicate his son, Larry Stokes, in the suspicious circumstances of his death.'

My gaze flew instantly to Larry, who was seated in front of me. His attention was focused entirely on Giallo and though I could not see his face, the relaxing of his shoulders and his posture told me he was relieved beyond belief at the latter's statement.

'That is a very serious accusation, Monsieur Giallo. Have you come to any conclusions as to who this person might be who wished to implicate Monsieur Wiggins?'

'Alas, monsieur, at this point in time, I have not.'

'And what about the cup of coffee found at Sir Charles's desk? Was the drink drugged in any way?'

Having been already been astounded by the revelation of the revolver, I was unsure of what to expect. One can never be sure with Giallo and even in the long years I have been with my friend, he still has the uncanny ability of putting one completely at a loss when you least expect it.

'The coffee was not drugged, monsieur. It was a perfectly ordinary cup of coffee.'

I admit, feeling a little disappointed at this. I was almost certain that the coffee was involved in the whole matter.

Though I would have liked Giallo to remain at the stand longer and answer the many questions now racing about in my head, the Coroner appeared to be satisfied with the information given him by the detective and politely dismissed him. I watched Giallo return to his seat and nod quickly when the man seated next to him whispered something into his ear as he sat down. From the stiff military bearing of the other man, I presumed that this was none other than his superior, the Commissaire, M. Clint Yearling.

The expression on Yearling's face appeared to be less than pleased with the outcome of the detective's testimony and I wondered what was to lie in store for Giallo, who I imagined was under tremendous pressure from all sides.

The jury then adjourned to another chamber, and it was at least a quarter of an hour before they returned, grave-faced and solemn.

'What is the verdict of the jury?' came the Coroner's sonorous tones.

A thin man, with a sharp jaw stepped forward, a piece of paper in his hands.

'The jury, monsieur, has come to the verdict of wilful murder against some person or persons unknown.'

'Thank God,' cried Larry to me as we left the courtroom, indifferent to the stares he was attracting from those around us.

'You know, St. Louie, I thought I was completely done for today.'

I was about to offer my congratulations when Tom suddenly observed:

'I say, isn't that Vondick vann Cliffberg, Larry?' followed their gaze to set eyes upon a tall, middle-aged man making his way silently through the crowd. There was a strange expression on his face, one which appeared to be caught between gloominess and relief. He caught sight of us looking after him, and he hastily averted his gaze.

I wondered what could be the source of such uneasiness, as well as his presence here at the inquest. There had been no love lost between Sir Charles and the German Ambassador while the former was alive, as they were literally diplomatic enemies and I could be sure that he was not here intending to offer his condolences to the family. He passed us without a word and disappeared down the stairs to the entrance of the building.

'He's probably here to see whether his theft of Father's papers had anything to do with his death,' commented Larry darkly.

'After all, a theft is bad enough, but combine that with a suspicious death...looks quite terrible for anyone, I'd say.'

'Fortunately, that doesn't appear to be the case – at least fortunately for him,' I added.

'Quite.' Larry turned sharply to capture Giallo's hand as the latter approached us and shook it gratefully.

'I can't thank you enough, Monsieur Giallo,' he said. 'Imagine my relief when you said you believed I was being framed – '

'Pardon, Monsieur Wiggins, but I never said that you were being framed, or at least never in those exact words. I only said that you were being implicated in your father's death,' said the Paris gravely. 'Also, I would advise you to tread carefully. We are not, as you say, out of the woods just yet.'

'Why not?'

'Even if the jury today has decided that the verdict is willful murder by some person or persons unknown, there is always the possibility of fresh evidence appearing in the meantime. Which means, therefore, that the case can be reopened at any time.'

'You don't mean to say that your investigation is going to drag on even further,' said Larry, aghast.

'I wouldn't like my family being exposed to those wretched devils from the press more than is necessary. What we've endured is already quite enough. Think about my situation, Giallo. I've a reputation to defend and keep if not for my sake, but Miss Milton's sake.'

Giallo appeared sympathetic but continued in a determined voice: 'I am afraid that it will have to, Monsieur Wiggins. Even if I wanted to leave the verdict at that, and I assure you I do not, my Commissaire has not allowed me to drop the case until I have discovered the truth of what happened that night. I believe that your government too back in London is more than keen to see the investigation being continued and brought to a proper conclusion.

They want the truth and I intend to give it to them.'

There was no use in arguing with him and Larry appeared to understand this too, for he merely nodded in grudging acceptance and walked away.

'Well, mon ami,' said Giallo wryly as he turned to me.

'What say you to my intended goal of seeking the truth? Would you prefer like your friend here to bury your head in the sand and not discover it at all?'

'You perfectly know what my answer is, Giallo. Nothing but the truth, as I've said to you two weeks ago.'

He beamed at me.

'I am glad that two weeks have not altered your opinion. Many others, I suspect, would have been persuaded to change their mind in that space of time.'

Pleased by his praise, I then congratulated him on his findings.

'I only wish that the Commissaire also thought of my findings as highly as you do. But I comprehend why he regards it as being not enough. I too think that they have been not enough, especially our being unable to locate that Nagant revolver. That has displeased me very much,' he said, shaking his head.

Being reminded of this, I expressed my astonishment on the matter.

'Ah, you did not expect it too, eh?' he asked, obviously delighted upon recalling the multitude of bewildered faces staring at him in the courtroom. 'You thought that it was your revolver which killed Sir Charles, yes?'

'I never even thought for a minute that it wasn'tmy revolver,' I admitted. 'Turns every theory I've come up with on its head, it seems.'

'Which reminds me – have you come to any conclusions upon those points of interest I related to you the other day?'

I said that I had and was more than willing to share them with him.

'Bon! But, un moment, St. Louie. This is not the place for us to talk.'

'Think we might be overheard?'

'Perhaps. Come with me.'

We apologetically excused ourselves and made our way downstairs. Upon stepping outside, I realized it was as hot here as inside the courtroom, though fortunately there was a breeze wafting through the early afternoon air, which gave us some respite from the heat. Our progress was hampered momentarily by a group of journalists who descended upon us the moment they recognized Giallo. To his credit, he politely waved and maneuvered his way out of their clutches and within minutes, we were on our way to the police station.

It was only a quarter of an hour before Giallo led me into his office, which though was much smaller than I had expected, was almost unbelievably tidy as its owner, even surpassing Sir Charles's study which I had already observed as being very organized. I gingerly sat down on the chair he offered to me, taking great care not to dislodge anything as I feared this would only incur his displeasure.

Perhaps noting my discomfited air, he called for two cups of coffee to be brought.

'I apologize. I cannot offer the tea that you English are so inexplicably fond of.'

He paused, appearing as if he wanted to offer his own opinion on the drink, but then settled on simply saying: 'It is not popular here in France.'

'Oh, not at all. Coffee will be fine,' I smiled.

After a constable had carefully placed two cups of coffee on Giallo's spotless desk, I informed him of the various ideas I had come up with over the past two weeks.

He listened in silence, his expression thoughtful and as I came to the end of my little speech, I got the impression that I had done rather well, for I had heard no word of protest or complaint from him throughout. However, I soon learned that this was quite untrue and that he saved his usually critical comments until one has finished.

To my annoyance, Giallo also made no attempt to spare me any criticism on my theories, especially regarding the gunpowder on the window sill.

'Non, St. Louie,' he said, shaking his head.

'This will not do. Your imagination, though magnificent, is not being reasonable. People climbing up villa walls? When the said walls are at least seventy feet high? And then after they have climbed this mountain of a wall, they shoot their victim from behind?'

'I think you've overlooked the note I've made next to it,' I said defensively, referring to the word 'unlikely' I had written in pencil beside it.

He appeared not to hear me and continued: 'And another suggestion is that Sir Charles might have known that he was about to be murdered and shot at his would-be attacker from his window? Mon ami, may I remind you that this is France...not the American Wild West!'

'It was only a suggestion,' I replied emphatically, feeling I was being unduly crushed into the ground.

'And then, after presumably missing his would-be attacker, he receives another bullet to the head in the confines of his study without the sound of another shot being heard. C'estincroyable.

Ah, but fortunately, what saves you from complete ignominy is your second idea, St. Louie.

The idea that someone fired a gun from inside Sir Charles's study and which perfectly explains the bullet you found in the garden.'

'Really?' My voice sounded skeptical and no doubt Giallo noted it too for he said:

'Mais oui. It is the conclusion that I have also come to.'

'But that makes little sense. Only a damn fool wanting to attract attention to himself would fire out of a window in the middle of the night.'

'Why not? It makes complete sense.'

'How so?'

'It makes complete sense, St. Louie, because our murderer – or as you call him, a damn fool – wanted to attract attention to himself.'

'What?' I cried. 'Why?'

'On that point, I am not entirely certain. But I am sure that it had a purpose. This shot out of the window. Things always happen for a reason, my friend. It is not in the human nature to do something without a meaning or a purpose. People you must understand are, alas, self-centred at heart, though of course this varies from individual to individual. But the instinct to survive and to save oneself, for example, when perhaps a battle is raging around us is inherently stronger in the majority of people than in that admirable minority which fights against this instinct and risks their lives to save those of others. But I am leading you off the point.'

An idea struck me. 'I say, Giallo. Does this shooting out of the window business have anything to do with the two revolvers?'

'I wondered whether you would come to this point eventually,' he said drily.

'Which of the two do you think fired the bullet out of the window?'

I hazarded a guess. 'The Webley?'

'Exactment..The bullet you found in the garden matches exactly with those found in your revolver.'

Despite getting the correct answer, I was still puzzled.

'But why on earth go through all that trouble taking my revolver and end up not using it at all? The fellow must have taken an awful risk doing all that. I'd understand it if someone actually stole it intending to kill Sir Charles with it and leaving it to look like suicide, but to simply take it and then to fire it out of the window is incomprehensible.'

He nodded contemplatively.

'That, I do not understand. At least not at the moment.'

'And if two revolvers were actually used,' I continued, 'why didn't I hear another shot? Surely if there were two shots fired, we would have heard two instead of one that night.'

'C'est vrai. But has it ever occurred to you, St. Louie, that perhaps one was silenced while the other was simply used to attract attention?'

'If that's the case, it makes using a silenced weapon rather redundant, I'd say.'

I tried to imagine the scene; our faceless murderer somehow entering Sir Charles's study, shooting him in cold blood with a silenced revolver and then firing my Webley out of the window apparently just for the sake of being noticed. It seemed preposterous.

I said as much to Giallo, who merely advised me: 'Do not be so quick to dismiss the possibility of such a thing, mon ami. Alors, we should move to the other points, but keep this idea in your head.'

'Oh, come now, Giallo. Do you really think this happened?'

The doubt in my voice was obvious, and he cast me a cool look.

'St. Louie, if you really desire to be of help to me, it would be wise of you to keep an open mind. In my experience, I have learned that if the fact does not fit the theory, one should let the theory go. I would advise you to do the same.'

I said nothing, feeling slightly put out. To tell the truth, I had the impression that nearly everything I had come up with was considered either ridiculous or implausible.

Giallo took in my gloomy expression and ventured to say: 'I beg of you not to enrage yourself over my words over Sir Charles shooting from the study window. I have to admit that I once had to shoot down a criminal who had taken refuge on a roof and was firing at the people below.'

'Really?' I said, utterly impressed despite myself.

'Not the greatest moment of my career, mon ami,' he replied gravely. 'But it had to be done to prevent more lives from being lost – and therefore I understand why you came up with the possibility.'

Having learned of this surprising incident in my friend's career, we moved on to the remaining pieces of evidence. On these points, Giallo seemed to be more approving of my theories.

'You are correct in assuming that the bell pull was deliberately disabled. I saw for myself that it had been tampered with when I returned upstairs for a second inspection.'

'A premeditated murder, then?'

'This is certainly not the crime passionel or the spontaneous murder of a moment. The disabling of the bell pull is proof of that, St. Louie.'

'Probably didn't want to be disturbed while he was doing the foul deed, I suppose.'

'It is interesting that you do not seem to suspect a woman,' observed Giallo with interest.

'Surely a woman wasn't involved in all this,' I argued.

I was about to continue on the subject but then, catching the chiding expression on his face, I remembered his telling me to keep an open mind and muttered half-heartedly that it could be possible but highly unlikely.

'And what about the coffee?' I asked, changing the subject.

'Now that we know it wasn't drugged at all, I cannot see the importance of it.'

He gave a groan, which I thought was quite unnecessary.

'Simply because a cup of coffee isn't drugged or poisoned or has had a multitude of things done to it, St. Louie, does not mean that it is not important,' he said wearily.

'I for one, find its presence in Sir Charles's room very curious and the spills I found on the carpet and on the flowerbeds outside even more so.'

'He might have simply brought it up himself and spilled it by accident.'

'To spill it on the carpet is one thing but to spill it so carelessly that it also manageds to drench the flowerbeds below is much more than carelessness, I think.

And we have also heard from Stanford, have we not, that Sir Charles was never the type to fetch a cup of coffee for himself, yes? Oui, I know Sir Charles's type well – always the self-important man who is keenly aware of class distinction and would never attempt to do something which he considers is below his station. Therefore, I do not think that Sir Charles brought it up himself.'

'But Stanford said that he –'

'And neither did Monsieur Stanford bring it up, mon ami.'

I stared at him, uncomprehending, for a few moments. Then I exclaimed:

'Good Lord, you don't mean to say the murderer brought up the coffee, Giallo?'

If I had expected a confirmation of this, the Paris did not disappoint.

'You have, as you English say, hit the nail right on the head.'

'But why?'

'Can you not see why?' he replied, turning my question back on me with a raised brow. I learned Giallo relished these moments where only he alone knew the answer to a particular issue, while the rest of us usually myself, were left to flounder helplessly in the dark.

I considered for a moment and reluctantly shook my head.

'I can't say. I can see why. I simply don't have the foggiest.'

'D'accord. Then allow Giallo to give a suggestion to you –'

I was however, never able to receive it as it was at that precise moment that the door was unceremoniously flung open and a red-faced constable made his abrupt entrance.

'Monsieur Giallo,' he gasped as the both of us rose to our feet in concern.

'You are wanted at the Hôtel de Ville immediately!'

'What? What has happened?'

'It is that younger housemaid at the villa,monsieur.'

'Estrella, you mean?' I cried.

'Oui, monsieur,' nodded the constable. 'She has been found dead, Monsieur Giallo – strangled, in one of the waiting rooms in the lobby.'

Giallo glanced at me, his expression shocked before reaching for his hat and cane and dashing out of the door and I followed suit, my mind dazed. A waiting car soon took us speedily back to the Hôtel de Ville where an inconsolable Camie was sobbing into a constable's shoulder as the petite figure of the late Estrella was loaded onto a stretcher, her young lips from which words had flowed only an hour before now silenced forever.

Chapter 8

Unforeseen Occurrences

While Sir Charles's death had attracted widespread public interest, the sudden demise of one of his maids almost immediately after the inquest did not appear to stir much attention in the Paris press. Only some of their British counterparts attempted to take this as an omen of sorts and put forward a ridiculous notion that the villa was haunted and that everyone living there would meet a sinister end if we remained any longer in France. All of us at the villa, however, dismissed this as a tasteless contrivance by the papers to increase their circulation.

The death of Estrella admittedly shook us all quite badly, and this included Giallo, who I now saw more often at the villa and who was entirely convinced that the maid's death had been brought about by one of those present at the inquest.

'Her murder proves it, St. Louie!' he said one morning as I accompanied him inside the villa. This was about two days after Estrella's death, and he was certainly not losing any time in relating his convictions to me.

'Remember how she suddenly stopped in the middle of her testimony?'

'I thought that was because of nerves.'

'I am certain it was not the nerves which caused her to stop. Non, I think she suddenly realized something and our murderer – oh, yes, he knew then that he was suddenly in danger and immédiatement, he dispatches her in the cruelest of ways imaginable.'

'And in public as well!'

I couldn't help but secretly admire the villain's audacity.

'Imagine the risks he was taking – what if someone had stumbled in on them and alerted the police?'

Which therefore makes him even more dangerous.'

He came to an abrupt pause and caught me by the arm and continued warningly: 'We are heading into treacherous waters, mon ami. He has killed twice so far – I imagine he will not hesitate to kill again.'

'Quite,' I replied soberly, then added: 'But if you think I'm afraid, Giallo, I'm far from being so.'

'Ah, the courage of the English, c'est magnifique,' he said, smiling at me affectionately.

'But it was not your courage, which I doubted, St. Louie. I merely say that we have to be careful from now on. He is now, how do you say, on his guard, our murderer and so as a result, we too have to watch our every move and take great care not to give our suspicions away or poof!' There was a comical flourish of hands.

'And he scurries away, never to be seen again.'

I couldn't help but smile a little at this, but quickly disguised it by nodding gravely.

'What do we do now, Giallo?'

'We search, my friend. We search for further information which might help aid us.'

'But it's been over two weeks since Sir Charles died. Surely everything which would have been of use to us would have been destroyed by now.'

Perhaps the tangible evidence, yes, which your Sherlock Holmes was so absurdly fond of. But I am not he and neither would I like to be. As for Reeves Giallo, he is more interested in the psychology. Tell me, St. Louie, what do you think of our murderer?'

I contemplated this question for a short while before replying.

'He's a daring fellow, I must admit, and with some damn cheek, too. To think that he murdered Estrella almost in plain sight of everyone – he must have nerves of steel, not to mention a pretty powerful pair of hands.'

I shuddered despite myself at the very thought of those hands strangling the maid to death in that stuffy waiting room.

'I agree with you there, mon ami. I think you will think our adversary is even more daring when I tell you of the purpose of that cup of coffee we were discussing the other afternoon.'

'So what was the purpose of the coffee, then?'

'The purpose of the cup of coffee, St. Louie, was to allow our murderer to safely enter the room where his intended victim was sitting. But here, we must stop and consider two distinct possibilities. Numéro un: Sir Charles probably recognizes this person and this same person is evidently also welcome into his study. Thus he does not make the fuss which undoubtedly he would have made had he not recognized or welcomed their presence there.'

'It couldn't have been Larry then,' I murmured.

'His father would have in all probability have thrown him out the moment he set eyes on him.'

He held up a finger. 'Attendez, St. Louie. You have not heard my other idea. You have told me, yes, that Sir Charles has not the electric light installed in his rooms?'

I furrowed my brow.

'Why yes, but I don't see –'

'St. Louie, it often seems that you never see,' he replied impatiently, and I stopped speaking. 'Now, as we all know, the electric light is much brighter than the candlelight which Sir Charles always used in his rooms. Therefore, one can expect his study to be dimly lit and with Sir Charles being in his middle age, it is quite common for men of his age to require the spectacles, a pair of which I accordingly found that afternoon we inspected his desk. Imagine then the quality of his vision in a dimly lit room and without his spectacles.'

'It'll be quite limited, I must admit. Perhaps he couldn't even see a thing.'

'And looking at the strength of his spectacles, I think that would not be far off the mark,' he said, removing them from his pocket and passing them to me. 'Sir Charles's eyesight was extremely poor.'

'Indeed,' I said, squinting instinctively in discomfort as I peered through them.

'Odd that I never saw him wearing them.'

'Vanity often makes people do the most unusual things, St. Louie.'
I handed them back to him.
'So Sir Charles's sight was limited, the room was dimly lit...' I said slowly.
'You can see where my line of theory is going, yes?'
To tell the truth, I was completely out of my depth. But having already been chided so often this morning and having no wish to repeat the experience, I simply nodded.
'Quiet,' I lied in the most confident voice I could muster.
'You impress me, mon ami. Perhaps you would also like to describe what might have happened next?'
'Er...I'd rather you did, Giallo.'
My moment of hesitation gave me away, and he gave a weary sigh.
'Really, St. Louie. I would much prefer it if you would be more forward with me rather than assuring everyone you know something when, in reality, it is quite the opposite.'
'So what's the second theory?' I said hastily.
His expression darkened a little.
'The second theory is what cost Mademoiselle Estrella her life,' pronounced Giallo gravely.
'And therefore, I do not intend to tell anyone of it until I feel the time is right.'
'What?' I cried, feeling as though I had been denied the long sought after conclusion of a thrilling story.
It is much too dangerous, St. Louie. The sort of person we are dealing with – I repeat once again that he will not hesitate to kill more people if he finds it necessary.
And I would not like to put your life in danger.'
He paused, then looked up at me intently.
'Non, I would not like that at all.'
I was moved by the sudden earnestness in both his eyes and his tone but adamantly pressed on:
'But what can be the harm in telling? –'
'A great deal of harm.'
'Well, aren't you in danger as well? Then if you know it?'
'Ah, but unlike you, I am not as well-acquainted with the family here.'

'What has being "well-acquainted" with the family got to do with anything?'

He considered for a moment.

'I hope you will not take my words to heart, St. Louie. But your unusual nature...one that is so trusting and unsuspicious and which I have heretofore rarely encountered in my work is alas quite incompatible with keeping important information from the enemy.'

A little hurt by his lack of faith in me, I argued, 'Now, Giallo, I can assure that I'm the most trustworthy chap –'

'Non, non,' he replied with a wave of his hand.

'You misunderstand me. I did not intend at all to say that you were not worthy of my trust – it is...how shall I put it...you have what I would describe as the speaking countenance. By that I mean that the emotions they appear so clearly on your face, so clearly in fact that it is unnecessary for you to speak to convey what you are currently thinking or feeling. Though such transparency is often good in other cases, it is not good when one undertakes a criminal investigation. Also, considering that you are in a position where our group of suspects converse more freely with you than they ever would with me, you are thus more exposed to risk if one of them even so much suspects that you know their secret. No, it is for the best, but I promise you you will know all in good time.'

'Oh, very well,' I sighed, barely able to conceal my disappointment. Upon seeing this, Giallo patted me gently on the arm.

'Do not fret, mon ami, the word of Reeves Giallo is never something which is lightly given.'

'I suppose,' I said a little petulantly.

'So what are we going to do now?'

'Always the man of action. We have two things on the agenda today. First, I would like to talk to Stanford again as I have a feeling that he knows something that he has not yet told us.'

'We can talk to him now; I think he's just inside here –'

'Not you, St. Louie. I would very much prefer it if I could speak with the butler alone. As for you, I would like you to do the second task for me.'

'What's the second task?'

'I would like you to take a long stroll about the grounds.'

I raised an eyebrow.

'Surely you're not being serious? You want me to take a stroll about the grounds?'

'Oui, mon ami. A very long stroll,' he nodded. 'Also, I would advise you to take as much time as you like, St. Louie. The weather it is quite admirable today, is it not?'

He added cheerfully.

'Oh, and be sure to pay a visit too to Monsieur Mallon if you pass by his cottage.'

'What the devil –' I started in exasperation, but Giallo had already darted into the library and left me standing in the middle of the hallway.

I admit to feeling a little annoyed at being delegated by what seemed to be the less important task of wandering about the grounds. Furthermore, I did not know what Giallo was trying to achieve by sending me down to see what Mallon was up to, as it had been quite clear after our last heated encounter that we were far from being on speaking terms. But I pressed on, endeavoring to prove to Giallo that I could find something of significance.

Arranging a plan of sorts in my head, I made my way first to the front gate, wondering whether I could find anything of interest there, as I remembered that Sir Charles' study window had commanded a good view of the place.

Perhaps he had seen something there which he was not supposed to have seen – and which had perhaps led to his untimely death – and my curiosity was piqued.

The cast iron gates were slightly ajar, and I squeezed my way through them only to notice that the laces on my shoes were undone.

Stooping to retie them, my eyes caught sight of a crumpled piece of paper lying under the hedge. My fingers failed to reach it and it was only by fishing it out with a fallen branch I retrieved it.

Unfolding it, I read the following:

A word to the wise; a storm's brewing at Wiggins' villa and you of all people should know what H's temper is like when the mood strikes him.

Something is going to happen tonight – you better be here by 1.00 am if you want to stop it from happening.

It was written in a rather indifferent-looking hand and, to my eyes, it was difficult to distinguish whether it had been written by a man or a woman. It was unsigned and, moreover, unaddressed, and so it would be nearly impossible to discover who had been the recipient of this foreboding missive.

Regardless, the recipient had evidently heeded the warning and had had come as summoned, dropping or discarding this when they had arrived.

The 'H' referred to in the note clearly indicated Larry, but who, apart from anyone in his immediate family who were all at the villa that night, would have an interest in him?

Perplexed, I tucked it into my pocket but was rather pleased with myself seeing that I would have something of importance to show to Giallo on my return to the house.

Further investigation at the present time, however, was made impossible. The morning was wretchedly hot, and it was only after about fifteen minutes in the sun that I sought the sanctuary of a small glasshouse located halfway between the villa and the gardener's cottage. It had clearly been a fine piece of architecture in its day, probably when Lady Wiggins was still alive, but now it had fallen into decay and instead of people, it contained only various gardening tools which were strewn haphazardly about the place. I was making my way gingerly around these objects, hoping to wait out the sun for a while, when a voice startled me.

'Oh, hello Nicolas.'

Turning my head sharply in the speaker's direction, I saw Janett appearing from behind a clump of tall potted plants at the other end of the glasshouse.

'Dear me, Janett. I nearly didn't notice you there.'

'Well, that was sort of the point really,' she replied drily.

'Don't you want people to see you?' I asked, walking towards her.

'Lately no. To be honest, I'd much rather spend my time here.'

'It might get a little lonely here, wouldn't you say?

'Oh no, with a good book, the hours can simply fly by.'

I noted the small leather bound volume she had just placed aside and nodded.

'Yes. I suppose with all that's happened, I wouldn't feel like talking much with anyone either.'

She shivered a little and said, 'Please don't remind me of that. It's just ghastly. Terribly so. I thought Uncle Charles'dying bad enough, but with Estrella's death the other day and her being str' She stopped and appeared as if the sheer horridness of the maid's death had deprived her of speech.

'I know, I know,' I said sympathetically. I put out a hand and gave her a brief pat on the back.

'But you can rest assured that Giallo and I are both determined to get to the bottom of this.'

'There won't be any more...more murders, will there?'

'Not while Monsieur Giallo and I are around,' I reiterated firmly.

She did not reply but cast me a shy smile and though there was no change in her appearance; I observed that there was something quite different about the expression in her eyes, which were fixed wholly on my face.

'I'm relieved to hear that. One can always depend on you, Nicolas. You're so –' She faltered a little.

'So constant, so dependable.'

Oh,' I said.

'Well, I'm glad you think so.'

I was pleased, but a little perplexed by her praise.

'My father though, would disagree with you on that score.' I winced at the mere thought; being the only son of the family certainly had had its advantages but also its disadvantages and, to my father's future disappointment, I could never fulfil his rather exacting expectations in various ways.

I turned to Janett, but she evidently hadn't heard me for she was fidgeting and her face was unexpectedly pale with what appeared to be apprehension.

'Janett, are you feeling all right?' I asked, in concern.

'Would you like to sit down?'

I looked about and saw that because of the clutter about the place, my suggestion, though well-meant, was rather impractical. The only place where anyone could sit was the rather suspect-looking marble bench Janett had just vacated, but looked as if it was on the verge of collapsing at any given moment.

'Oh, I'm quite all right –' she said a little breathlessly.

'Would you like me to fetch a glass of water?'

I was already moving towards the front door.

'No! I mean, please don't go,' she cried suddenly, and I stared at her in surprise.

Embarrassed by her outburst, she said, 'I'm so sorry – goodness knows what you're thinking. It's just that I wanted – I've been wanting to tell you something for quite some time. Would you care to sit down?'

I politely declined and instead helped her onto the seat on the bench while I remained on my feet.

'Is something troubling you?'

'I wouldn't really say it's been troubling me, but it's certainly been on my mind for weeks now. I've been debating with myself, on whether I actually reveal this to anyone.'

'It's sometimes for the better to let things out from time to time,' I advised.

'You'll often feel much better after you've let it out. There's no use in bottling it up.'

'Yes,' she said and her eyes, which had curiously been avoiding mine, gazed up at me. 'That's what I've decided too.'

'That's a good girl,' I smiled.

'Would you mind awfully if I confided in you?'

'Of course not, Janett. You know I'm always ready to listen if you want me to.'

'I'm glad to hear it...especially when what's been on my mind...it concerns you.'

'Me?' I said blankly.

Color was rapidly entering her cheeks, and she said in a rush, her voice shaking a little.

'Yes. I know – I know this probably doesn't seem to be the best time to say such things, but I've always had a fondness for you, Nicolas. Ever since I was a young girl, you've always been so attentive to me...sometimes even more so than Ella or Larry when you came along to visit them during the summer. You can imagine what it's like – a young orphan like myself entering a new strange world where everyone told you that this person or this place was related to you in some way but having never seen them before, it was difficult to feel a connection to anything.

"But you changed that. You made me feel quite welcome when you really were only a friend of the family."

"We were like brother and sister, as you so frequently said to me during those summers, and yes, I must say it was never ever more than that and I was more than happy with the fact."
She stopped, fearing that I would interrupt her, but when she saw that I had no intention of doing so, she continued.

'But I must confess that when I saw you after all these years as you entered the dining room that evening you arrived here, I felt something I've never experienced before.
I had expected to look at you as I did when I was a girl of twelve but instead – well, instead something else suddenly took over and I was no longer a girl of twelve but a woman of twenty and who I saw sitting before me was not a young man of eighteen who was like a brother to me but a man of twenty-six. I tried hard not to think of you over the next few days or so, but it was really no use.

"What – what I mean to say is…I think I love you, Nicolas."
I admit I was a little more than taken aback by Janett's words to me and was suddenly very glad that I hadn't accepted her offer to sit down, as the bench would have undoubtedly collapsed had I been sitting on it.
My prolonged silence prompted her to speak haltingly.

'Oh, I know what you must think of me. It's not quite correct, I know, for ladies to be the one bringing up these things. It must be breaking all sorts of conventions, I must say. But with all that's happened and these terrible deaths…you must understand how difficult it is to keep your feelings in when it feels like you might be killed off tomorrow. And you've always been so kind to me, Nicolas. You always have when you never had an obligation to do so –'

'Janett,' I said, finding my voice at last. I hesitated a little before continuing a little awkwardly, 'I'm deeply moved that you feel this way towards me.
Deeply moved,' I emphasized.
I was struggling to find the words to coherently describe my feelings. The shock at receiving her sudden declaration was wearing off and was being replaced with varying degrees of embarrassment, affection, and pain. Pain for causing her the heartbreak I was undoubtedly going to bring about.

'You're going to scold me, aren't you? I know this isn't the most conventional of –'

'It's not convention or social expectations I'm concerned about, Janett,' I blurted, my unusual liberality of thought surprising me. 'I'm not at all concerned about those, though I must say that this is a little irregular. I'm only concerned about whether I'm the person you really want as a husband.'
I fiddled with a piece of loose thread dangling from one of my waistcoat buttons and realizing this was making me look ridiculous, I shoved my hands into my pockets.

'Now you're only being modest.'

'Far from it. Well, I've been told I'm a fairly decent fellow by all accounts, though not the brightest chap you'd ever come across, I suppose. And I've always felt like I've been like a brother to you –'

'Only a brother?' I could hear the fear creeping into her voice.

'Truth be told, I'm more than happy being like a brother to you.'
I paused, attempting to soften the blow, which I was on the verge of giving.

'But to take on the new role of being your husband – that I'm not entirely sure about.
I'm uncertain whether I'm the fellow you really want.
You hardly know me and we've hardly seen each other in eight years...'

'I feel like I've known you all my life, Nicolas.'
I sighed inwardly. Her determination was not making my task any easier, and I chided myself for causing her pain yet at the same time, forcing myself to go on.

'I don't want you ending up marrying an illusion, Janett. And the last thing I want to do is to feel as though I've deceived you or tricked you into something which you will later regret. I've been known to disappoint sometimes...and I wouldn't want to disappoint you.'

'You probably think I'd make quite a dull wife, I suppose,' she said resignedly.

'I think you'd make a splendid wife for any man, Janett,' I countered with genuine feeling. I really did think that any man fortunate to marry Janett was very lucky indeed, but as for myself being the man in question, I wasn't entirely certain. I loved her as a sister, but I simply couldn't see myself as loving her along more romantic rather than platonic lines.

There was an unbearably long pause, and it was at times like these that I wished nothing more than for the ground to open up from beneath me and swallow me up completely.

I felt such a dreadful cad, but I didn't want to hurt her. After all, she had probably fallen in love with an ideal of me rather than myself and I was certain that in time the differences between these two men would reveal themselves rather mercilessly to such a young, naïve heart as Janett's.

'Tell you what,' I whispered, stepping closer to her.

'Why don't you think about it a little more? Marriage is quite a serious business – it wouldn't do to rush such a thing like that.' She opened her lips to say something but closed them and instead nodded slowly.

'I will if you'd like me to do so, Nicolas.'

'Indeed, I'd like that very much.'

She seemed to hesitate a little before asking: 'And will you – will you think about it as well?'

I bit my lip. I was sorely tempted to refuse outright but instead gave a small smile.

'I shall.'

She rose to her feet and surprised me by kissing me lightly on the cheek, which only deepened the sense of guilt I was already feeling.

'I really don't deserve your sympathy, really. Other people would have laughed at me, I suppose, and told me what a silly girl I am.'

'I'd be heartless if I even thought about doing that.'

'Thank you, Nicolas.'

She gave a small smile, though I could see that her smile this time did not quite reach her eyes as before. 'You've always been so kind to me.

So kind.'

'Not at all, Janett. Not at all.'

After an indeterminable length of uncomfortable silence, Janett announced her intention of returning to the house and I offered to accompany her across the grounds.

We said nothing during our walk, and it was when we had nearly reached the front door that Giallo appeared.

'Oh, I'm so sorry, Monsieur Giallo,' said Janett as she nearly walked into him.

'Pas du tout, mademoiselle.'

He gave a small bow as Janett excused herself and hurriedly entered the house. I looked after her retreating figure anxiously.

'You appear a little out of sorts, St. Louie,' noted Giallo after a while.

'I suppose you can say that,' I admitted, my former irritation at him dissipating in the face of my new dilemma. I decided it would be best to recount the whole matter to Giallo, and he listened attentively.

'Women, Giallo,' I sighed, shaking my head as I finished.

'I can't quite fathom them out.'

'I believe most men, even after years and years of marriage, never entirely do fathom them out, mon ami,' he said with a faint smile.

'So in that you are not alone.

But I am surprised, St. Louie, that you did not offer to marry Mademoiselle Janett at once. She is very close to you, is she not?'

'Oh. Well, she's a nice girl and all. And I really do love her as a brother, but I'm not entirely certain whether I'll be able to love her the way she wants me to.'

I gave a sudden laugh.

'Good Lord, but I believe Larry's advice to me the other day has somewhat rubbed off on me.'

'What advice?'

'I told him of the unusually sentimental conversation I had shared with Larry two weeks previously on the subject of Lady Wiggins and Samantha.'

'Très interessant,' commented the Paris as I finished.

'His advice on not marrying someone you didn't love, you mean?'

He smiled.

'His advice is without doubt very useful, but that was not what I was primarily interested in. I was more interested in the sad story of his mother, the late Lady Wiggins.'

'Yes, shame about that, really. But seeing that she had set her heart on a foreigner –'

I stopped abruptly, immediately berating myself for my lack of tact. What on earth had possessed me to say such a thing, especially in front of Giallo?

'You perhaps have something against foreigners?' asked Giallo, his tone suddenly losing much of its customary warmth. I swallowed nervously.

'Not at all. It's just that – well – I'm sorry to say that foreigners back home aren't treated with as much regard as Englishmen, but I, on the other hand, am all against that, you know. Extremely bad state of affairs, Giallo, but can't be helped.' He appeared to take my word on it and continued,

'It is good that you told me of this little conversation between you and Monsieur Wiggins. I feel it will allow me to make a little more sense of this crime of ours.'

'In that case, may I assume that this will also be of use, Giallo?'
I asked with a hint of accomplishment as I passed him the note I had found.
He took it from me and read it through carefully.

'So…a note warning someone of Monsieur Wiggins' temper on the night of his father's death was sent off, presumably on the same day or a little earlier. But by whom? The murderer?'

'On the other hand, it might have been a friendly note of warning.'

'That is a possibility, yes.' He read it through again, murmuring what seemed to be the line 'you of all people should know' several times under his breath and stowed it away in his waistcoat pocket.

'You have done very well, St. Louie. Already I feel the case marching on splendidly.'
I grinned.

'And since you have not already done so, I think it is now time that we pay a visit to Monsieur Mallon.'
My grin faded.

'Really, Giallo. – Do we have to see that beastly fellow?'
I cried as I tried to catch up with his surprisingly furious pace across the grounds.

'I am afraid we must.'

'But why?'
He did not endeavor to reply and, in view of his silence; I questioned him on his interview with Stanford, which I learned hadn't quite gone as smoothly as planned.

'Your Monsieur Stanford is the typical English butler,' he said reproachfully.

'Whenever I attempted to question him on a particular topic, he clammed up like an oyster.'

'That's odd. I know for a fact that Stanford isn't the type to withhold information, old chap. He's normally rather forthcoming.'

'Apparently not so forthcoming when I questioned him on Monsieur Mallon.'

I chuckled.

'Of course he wouldn't be so forthcoming about him,' I said drily.

'Haven't you seen how irritated he gets every time he sees the fellow coming into the house?'

'There is something about these two which I dislike, mon ami. One of them or both of them are withholding something about the other which I would like to find out. Stanford, as you have mentioned to me, he does not hide his irritation with the gardener. But why? Has Mallon done something to displease him? Or does he dislike him because of his character? Perhaps Stanford is old-fashioned and Mallon represents or embodies something which he does not approve of? People do not wake up one day, St. Louie, and decide that yes, today I am going to dislike so-and-so simply because I dislike them. Non, that is not logical.'

'Yes, that doesn't quite make sense,' I agreed.

'Normally if I didn't like someone, I'd stay far away from them and now that you mention it, it is a little odd to hear that Stanford was often seen near Mallon's cottage.'

'That was what Estrella mentioned in her testimony.'

I turned over the point in my mind.

'I say, you don't think that it was this which led to her death, do you?'

Giallo pressed a finger to his lips for silence. We had made our way past a thick hedgerow and just as we reached the end of it; we were confronted with the impressive sight of a sturdy-looking cottage made from grey stone. I looked at the house with some surprise, for I had expected it to be more of a hut than a real cottage with all the comforts of one.

Wordlessly, we walked up to the front door and Giallo reached out to knock on it but lowered his hand suddenly.

'What's the matter?' I whispered.

'Do you smell smoke, St. Louie?'

I sniffed the air experimentally and recognized the telltale smell at once.

'You're quite right. Curious that a fire's been lit in such hot weather. Look, Giallo!'

I had turned to my right and noticed the unmistakable sight of smoke coming from just around the corner of the house. Quietly, we crept towards the source of the fire and saw that instead of weeds or logs being used as fuel; we saw piles upon piles of books in their place. By the thick dark smoke now streaming towards us, it was clear that the fire had been burning for some time now and that most of the books had been burnt to a crisp but there was still one at the top of the pile which had not yet been consumed by the flames.

Without thinking, and not heeding Giallo's cry of warning, I darted forward and saved the book from its fiery end by tipping it out of the fire with a pair of garden shears lying on a stool nearby.

'Mon Dieu, St. Louie – what in the name of the good God possessed you to –' he breathed as he watched me stamp the flames out. A few moments later, I gingerly picked up the battered and still-smoking book and passed it apologetically to him.

'Sorry,' I said as the back cover dropped unceremoniously onto his spotless leather shoes and I hastily fought back the urge to chuckle as I saw him wince.

'May I remind you that this might be an important piece of evidence and that great care must be taken with it?' he said in utter disapproval.

I shrugged.

'If it wasn't for me, we wouldn't have an important piece of evidence.'

Deciding not to acknowledge my efforts, he delicately praised the pages open and his expression immediately changed.

'Something important, Giallo?'

Instead of giving me a reply, he marched back towards the cottage door and rapped it impatiently. It was soon thrown open by an annoyed-looking Mallon who appeared none too pleased to see the both of us standing before him.

'Now what's all this racket for, Inspector? And what the devil are you doing here?' he added, throwing me an extremely unpleasant look.

My temper flared, but Giallo spoke first, brandishing the book in front of the startled gardener's face.

'And what I would like to know, Monsieur Mallon, is what are these diaries doing burning in a fire in your garden?'

'Diaries?' repeated Mallon blankly.

'No one told me anything about diaries, Inspector. I was just told to burn a couple of unwanted books.'

'Who told you to burn them?'

'I don't know. Just found the ruddy pile of them dumped in front of my door this morning with a curt note on top asking me to burn them. No consideration at all for the likes of me, as usual. Let's just put them here, shall we? Mallon won't mind…after all, he's only the gardener,' he muttered darkly.

'And so being the dedicated and uncomplaining servant I am and following good old English tradition, I did as I was bloody well told.'

To his credit, Giallo bore the gardener's angry tirade admirably and merely demanded, 'Where is this note?'

'I'm sorry, sir, but I think I must have burnt it with the rest of the books,' he replied in his customary mocking tone and not sounding apologetic in the least. I marveled at how such an impertinent fellow such as Mallon was still able to hold a post here.

'No use in keeping such things, Inspector. Oh, you mightn't believe me – I can see the suspicion in those eyes of yours – but I couldn't care less. What I've told you is the truth and if you don't take me at my word, well, that's your loss.

Now if you don't mind, sir, I'd appreciate it if you and Dr Watson here left me alone as I've a lot of duties to attend to.' He slammed the door.

'A deeply angry and unpleasant young man, eh, St. Louie?'

I nodded. I was thinking that the gardener would give Tim Mac David a run for his money in terms of extreme unpleasantness. Having been so rudely expelled by the owner of the cottage, there was no other option but for us to return to the house.

'So the pile of books we found here were actually a pile of diaries?' I asked, in interest. 'But that doesn't sound very promising –'

'Not only any person's diaries. Read the name on the front page, St. Louie.'

I examined the remnants of the badly burnt page, but the name of the owner was clearly legible in a graceful, sloping hand.

'Lady Elizabeth Wiggins?' I read bemusedly and looked up to see Giallo nodding at me emphatically.

'Precisely. Quite promising indeed, wouldn't you say?'

Chapter 9

Diplomatic Relations

A lthough I did not realize it at the time, our discovery of one of the late Lady Wiggins's diaries seemed to mark a turning point in various ways. I saw this reflected in Giallo's sharp eyes every time he held the sorry-looking object in his hands. He appeared to be deeply curious of its contents though I thought it highly improper of us to look through not only a person's but also a lady's private diaries.

'I hardly feel comfortable with all this, Giallo,' I said as I watched him peruse the diary for what seemed to be the umpteenth time. We were sitting in his comfortable rooms in Paris, as he had thought it unwise to let anyone at the villa know that we were now in possession of it. I was quite pleased at receiving his invitation, though I admit that I thought such a precaution was unnecessary.

However, I accepted it uncomplainingly.

Giallo did not answer immediately but later said without glancing up, 'What is it you say, St. Louie?'

I said that I hardly feel comfortable about all this,' I said with emphasis and I suspected that he was deliberately trying to be difficult with me.

'Hardly feel comfortable with what, mon ami?'

'You know what I'm referring to,' I said severely.

'Reading Lady Wiggins's diaries, of course.'

'What is there to be uncomfortable about? I see no reason for being so. Besides, Lady Wiggins herself would not mind seeing that. If you will pardon my saying so, she is no longer with us.'

'Giallo!' I cried, scandalised.

'Calmez-vous, mon ami.'

It was at this moment that he looked up at me.

'And also you can comfort yourself that it is I and not you who are currently reading it.'

'That isn't the point,' I persisted, but seeing my complaints were falling on deaf ears and that his attention was wholly fixed on the book in front of him, I finished my cup of coffee in silence. I can't understand what's so important about it.
You've been reading it for the past three days now.'

'And if I can recall correctly, you have only read it once in the past three days. And even during that one time, you barely seemed to even glance at it.'

'Well, I could hardly sit about and read it with the relish you obviously have, Giallo. It's not a novel, you know.'
Casting my mind back to when I had glanced over the burnt pages out of duty rather than interest when the ever unabashed Paris detective had thrust it into my hands, I got the impression that Lady Wiggins was an avid chronicler of each passing day of her tragically short life. A description of a short fête took up at least five pages, for instance, while other entries took up twice as much room, especially regarding Larry. It was in short an ordinary diary of a lady of the gentry who moved around in high society in the usual manner and who was clearly very fond of her only son.

'You should remember, St. Louie, that I do not read it merely for the entertainment.'

'Yes, I know that. But good Lord, shouldn't we be doing something?' I said impatiently. I had realized as of late that I was becoming increasingly aware of the tedium of sitting around and interviewing the various people at the house. Perhaps it was the vague sensation that my leave from my work at Christie's was gradually running out with each passing day, which was affecting my feelings towards the investigation and adding a sense of urgency to my situation. Regardless, it was now already the middle of August and I would have returned to London by the beginning of September.

'But we are doing something, mon ami,' replied Giallo with the manner of a parent speaking to a troublesome young child.

'We are examining the evidence.'

'It seems like we've been doing that for weeks, Giallo. And not very much else,' I added gloomily.

'Evidence is all very well, but don't you feel we ought to track down the murderer by now? After all, we know he's out there and he might just be right under our noses and having a laugh at our expense!'

In time, St. Louie, in time. Important as this case is, it would certainly not do to do something too hasty which we might regret.'

I didn't reply, feeling as if further conversation would only wear me out. I was now very much aware that Giallo had his methods, incomprehensible though they might appear at times, and that any attempt on my part in forcing his hand would be futile. Like so many times later on in our partnership, it was at this moment that I put my entire trust in Giallo, knowing instinctively that he would find the truth in the end and that I would have to manage as best as I could in the role of his associate and friend.

My mind wandered aimlessly and I think I must have fallen asleep at some point afterwards that afternoon. Janett's declaration of a few days previously still weighed considerably on my mind and my refusal of her, gentle as I had wanted it to be, had not made my life much easier.

The armchair I was occupying too was exceedingly comfortable, and this only eased my descent into a peaceful slumber.

My impromptu nap, however, was prevented from becoming wholly tranquil as a strange dream took hold of my mind. I was standing in the middle of the glasshouse at the villa where I had met Janett. It was late afternoon and the brilliant gold beams of the setting sun permeated the grounds, giving the whole place a rather dramatic appearance. My current solitude was soon put an end to by the approach of someone exiting the house.

Initially, it was difficult to make the person out as they appeared to be a considerable distance off. I presumed it was Janett, but as the figure got closer, I could see that it was not Janett but Giallo.

The detective in my dazed imaginings appeared to be oblivious to my presence, and it seemed that in this world, at least, I was invisible to everyone I encountered. Appearing to be waiting for someone, I then examined his face closely and saw that he was unusually nervous.

His agitation made me uneasy, and I looked about our surroundings with an increased sense of trepidation.

The sound of the front door being pushed open alerted us of another joining our company, and I was startled to see Janett make her entrance. I was even more astonished as she greeted him unhesitatingly in the shy, warm manner she customarily had shown to me while Giallo for his part appeared to be more than happy to receive her in a way which was more associated with an admirer rather than a mere acquaintance.

'Janett and Giallo? Can it be possible?'

Confusion reigned chiefly among my feelings at this, but I did not have time to dwell on the matter as there was suddenly a hand on my shoulder, gently shaking me awake.

'St. Louie.'

I opened my eyes to see Giallo standing over me.

I thought there was a peculiar softness in his countenance which I had never seen before as he observed me extricating myself from my still half-conscious state. However, when I finally became fully awake, I noted that his expression was his usual one of utter poise and confidence, and I supposed that I had only imagined it.

'You have had the good rest, my friend?' he said in slightly ironic tones.

'What time is it?' I murmured. At that moment, I noticed his close proximity to me and that one of his legs was just brushing against my knee. I discreetly withdrew the latter a little, feeling suddenly self-conscious.

'The clock has just struck six.'

My eyes took in the darkened view outside from the window across from my chair and I could see that it was indeed early evening. The lamps were now lit, immersing the room in a warm, golden glow.

'I'm sorry, Giallo,' I apologized.

'I must have nodded off at some point. You see –' I was about to continue forth on the subject of Janett and my refusal of her, but remembering the bizarre dream I had just had of her as well as the man before me, I stopped.

'See what, St. Louie?' asked Giallo.

'Oh…it's nothing,' I murmured, distractedly. He appeared unconvinced, but to my relief, he did not pursue the topic.

'Any luck with the diary?' I asked, absentmindedly rubbing the back of my neck, which was now slightly painful.

I decided I must have been asleep for much longer than I had thought. I wondered why Giallo had made no attempt to rouse me earlier; after all, he of all people should have noted at once that I had dozed off in the middle of his sitting room at probably the most inappropriate of times.

That is one reason why I woke you,' he replied and I could see that he was indeed holding the diary, which was now open in his hands. 'I would not say that I have had any luck with it, but there is perhaps something here which might be of interest. My grasp of the English language – it is perhaps not complete, but there is something in this passage here which does not seem right.'

'How so?'

Appearing as if he could not put his thoughts into words, he handed the diary to me.

'Examine that, mon ami,' he said. 'What would you make of it?'

I looked at the entry before me, which was dated from eight years previously:

18th June 1905
My dearest boy is turning eighteen tomorrow. Has it really been eighteen years? – what happiness indeed. Stanford has, of course, seen to all the arrangements; I wonder where we all would be without him. I must make the most of tomorrow; though the Dr assures me that the illness will not return within the next year, I feel my days are growing short. I feel it in my very bones. Received a letter yesterday morning; his father writes his duties will keep him abroad until October at the very least. Only four months! But alas, four months seem almost an eternity now…

The rest of the page had unfortunately been lost to the flames, and the next legible entry was dated a week later.

'Looks rather straightforward to me. She's obviously writing about Larry,' I said. 'That's one thing which is quite clear.'

'Bon. And?'

'And it's obvious too that she was very aware that she had little time left, and that she was upset that her husband wasn't able to return to the country as quickly as she would have liked. I believe there's some truth in that. She died just a few months after Larry turned eighteen. Of some terminal illness or other, I think. Tragic really, especially seeing that she was only in her forties.'

'Magnifique. Your talent at summarizing is remarkable. But read it again, St. Louie. Isn't there something which strikes you as odd or out of place?'

I did as I was told. A second reading revealed nothing new, but now that Giallo had mentioned it, there was something rather strange about the whole passage, though I couldn't understand why.

'Actually, now that you mention it, there is something rather odd about – ,' I started, turning my gaze upwards from the diary.

It was at that exact moment that my eyes met his and words abruptly failed me as I noted those glowing brown orbs gazing back at me. How odd that I hadn't noticed until now how wonderfully gentle Giallo's eyes were. A peculiar tingling sensation seemed to travel up my spine as I sat gazing up at him, my mind blissfully void of thought and when he spoke, his voice sounded muffled and distant, as if it was coming through an old gramophone.

There is something that one cannot put one's hand on, n'est-ce pas?' he suggested.

'Something like that,' I managed, disregarding the urge to correct him. My throat was suddenly parched, and I regretted that I had finished my coffee earlier in the afternoon.

He nodded.

'That too is what I am feeling, mon ami.'

He turned to consult something on the table nearby. I believe he continued speaking, but his words floated over me and I listened in perfect incomprehension. My lack of attention was soon noted by Giallo, who chided me resoundingly, and I apologized once again.

'Your mind is elsewhere, it seems, St. Louie,' he said in obvious annoyance. 'Perhaps the case, it does not interest you any longer?'

'Of course not,' I said quickly.

'It's just that...well, would you mind awfully if I make an early night of it, Giallo?

As you've said, my mind's quite boggled this evening and I think a bit of sleep should set me right. I should be all right tomorrow morning.'

He appeared to be a little put out at this but said, turning away from me reproachfully: 'If you think it necessary, mon ami, then I appear to have no say in the matter. I shall meet you at the villa tomorrow.'

Retrieving my hat and murmuring a hasty 'goodnight' I made my exit.

I was met at the villa door by Stanford.

'Ah, Mr St. Louie,' he said as he took my hat. 'We were wondering whether you'd join the rest of the family for dinner.'

'Awfully sorry, Stanford. I'm afraid that some of Monsieur Giallo's inquiries took longer than expected. Have I missed it?'

'No, sir. Dinner will be ready in a quarter of an hour.'

I looked around and saw that the entire ground floor of the house appeared to be deserted. This state of affairs was ended, however, with the appearance of Larry who descended the stairs and upon seeing me, greeted me warmly:

'There you are, St. Louie.'

'Evening, Larry. Sorry for being late.'

'No need to apologize...you're not late at all.'

His eyes scanned the space behind me. 'Monsieur Giallo, not with you?'

'No. Should he be?'

'Oh, no reason in particular. It's just that Janett's been asking to see him, that's all.'

I started a little in surprise at this, but soon recovered my composure.

'Really?' I remarked as casually as I could manage.

'Do you know whatever for?'

'I have really no idea. She's been oddly secretive these past few days. Not like her at all. Samantha's tried talking to her, of course, but to no avail. Have you talked to her, St. Louie?'

'Not recently, no,' I lied, instantly feeling like an utter cad.

'Even Tom's concerned about her, and you know he rarely concerns himself with anybody.'

He examined the newspaper in his hand absentmindedly.

'Regardless, could you please speak to Monsieur Giallo about Janett?'

'I'll see what I can do, Larry.'

'Thanks, old chap. I could so do with a drink before dinner. Besides, we've at least ten minutes left till then. Care to join me?'

Also, needing one, I accepted the invitation, and we moved into the drawing room.

'That Paris fellow's quite a clever chap, I must admit,' said Larry suddenly as he handed me a glass of whisky. 'Though how he can make head or tails of this beastly business, I'm not sure.'

I nodded, but then a thought suddenly entered my mind.

'He has made some interesting progress these past few days, you know.'

'I'm glad to hear of it.'

He took a long draught from his glass.

'I fear I might have been a little short with him that afternoon after the inquest. No one likes to be interrogated and be at the beck and call of the police, you know.'

'Of course.'

'But after Estrella got herself killed – I'm thinking that he was right to continue with his enquiries. I'm sure that both you and I are of the same mind when it comes to the task of finding that damn devil who killed her.'

'Oh yes. Absolutely.'

We were both silent for a while before I asked tentatively.

'Would you mind me asking something rather personal, old fellow?'

'Not at all, St. Louie.'

'I know it might be a little painful for you to recall these things, but I wonder whether you had any memories of your mother before she died.'

Larry's eyes fixed upon me with uncomfortable intensity and when he spoke, I knew at once that I had not gone about the subject as well as I should have.

'I fail to see how my mother has anything to do with Monsieur Giallo's investigation, St. Louie,' he replied at length, his tone cool.

'Well, naturally, I –'

'Did Giallo put you up to this?' he continued irritably, setting down his glass. I was beginning to see why someone had sent a note informing someone else of Larry's temper, which was not violent but always in danger of flaring up without a moment's notice. At Haney, Larry's temper had sometimes gotten him into some pretty tight corners but he had always scraped through and compose himself but it was really during this visit of mine that I realized my friend was more prone to giving in even to the slightest of provocations.

'Of course not, Larry –' I started, trying to make amends.

'Well, if he did, I think I'd much prefer it if Monsieur Giallo came forward and spoke to me himself,' he said, rising to his feet and disregarding my words completely.

'I won't have all this cloak and dagger business going about, you know. I won't stand for it.'

With that, he abruptly left the room, and I fell onto the settee in defeat. I vaguely envisioned the look of immense disapproval on Giallo's face if he caught wind of how badly I handled this whole affair.

The mere thought, however, I soon realized, of the Paris detective caused me to sink even further into a state of peculiar misery and I wondered what had gotten hold of me that evening. First there was the painful subject of Janett, that fantastical dream in the afternoon related to the latter and Giallo, and now Larry. It was now quite impossible for me to join the others at dinner this evening, seeing how things had turned out.

'Fine little mess you've gotten yourself into, St. Louie,' I murmured to myself angrily, tossing back my drink.

Ignoring the sound of the gong announcing the start of dinner, I made my apologies to Stanford as I passed him in the hallway and retired hastily to my room.

It is still a marvel, even after so many years, to realize what a good night's rest can do to a person. After being fully rested, I felt completely my old self again and eager to resume work on our enquiries.

However, instead of meeting Giallo at the villa as planned, I received a note during breakfast, which read as follows: Mon ami, I apologize for the short notice, but I cannot join you at the villa this morning as planned. A recent development has shown itself to me and has meant that I will use the morning in making the enquiries instead. However, I would recommend not to let down your guard. If all goes as planned, I will have need of you later this afternoon.

Yours ever, Reeves Giallo I must admit, feeling quite relieved to learn that my abrupt departure from his rooms hadn't lowered his confidence in me. Perhaps trying not to dwell too much on the events of the previous evening, I spent most of the morning trying to piece together the clues we had so far collected but came up with nothing.

It was a quarter past two that Stanford came up to me as I sat in the library after lunch and informed me that someone wished to speak to me on the telephone.

'I believe it is Monsieur Giallo, Mr St. Louie.'

Thanking him, I made my way into the hallway.

'Giallo?' I said as I picked up the receiver.

'Good afternoon, St. Louie,' came the unmistakable voice.

'You have received my note, yes? Bon. I have little time to speak to you as I still have several enquiries to make but tell me, mon ami, are you prepared to go down to the capital?'

'What now, do you mean?'

'At this very moment, St. Louie. You have I trust what you English call the morning coat?'

'A morning coat?' I repeated, wondering if I had misheard.

'I don't think I brought one with me, but I might ask Stanford to –'

'Non, I would much prefer it if you did not ask anyone – we have not the time to lose. The morning coat would have been most suitable, but I trust you will wear something similar to compensate this, St. Louie?'

'Good Lord, Giallo, we aren't going to a wedding, are we?'

Despite my entreaties for more information, they were met with little success. Giallo was being his old mysterious self again and I could do nothing but follow his instructions, which were now hurriedly given down the telephone.

'But quickly, mon ami. Our appointment is to take place at half-past three. I will meet you in front of the Hôtel de Ville in an hour. And remember to take of the appearance, St. Louie!'
He rang off and running quickly upstairs. I was left to rummage round my belongings for a suitable change in dress. Twenty minutes later and dressed in my best suit, I was driven down to Paris by Garvious, who showed some curiosity about my unusually formal attire but to his credit said nothing.
Predictably, Giallo was already waiting for me in front of the Hôtel de Ville at the appointed time. He was immaculately dressed in a dark suit, a burgundy-colored tie, and in addition, I noticed a delicate silver boutonnière holder pinned to his lapel. Following my gaze, he said, 'You examine it with interest, St. Louie.'

'Quite. I've never seen it before, Giallo. Unusual little thing – is it a family heirloom?'

'Non,' he said a little wistfully. 'It was a gift from a young lady who a few years ago I – '
He suddenly stopped and appeared uncharacteristically unsure of himself.

'Yes?' I asked.

'Non, non,' he said, shaking his head.

'It would not do for me to lead us off the track…we must return to the matter at hand.'
He looked me up and down and his eyes fixed upon my tie with an expression of immense disapproval.

'My apologies, mon ami, but your tie…it is not symmetrical. Allow me to rearrange him.'
Reaching out, he straightened the offending object in question and smiled with obvious satisfaction at my 'improved' appearance.

'Do I look presentable now, Giallo?' I said, feeling slightly exasperated.

'You look – '
There was an odd brief pause before he glanced down at his watch and said, 'You look very presentable, St. Louie.'

'Now that I'm actually here, care to tell me what all this is about?'
I asked as I followed him down the busy streets.

'We have an important appointment.'

'I think I worked that out quite a while ago,' I replied, unable to keep a little sarcasm from entering my voice. 'Can you at least tell me who we're meeting, Giallo?'

'Monsieur Vondick vann Cliffberg.'

'Vondick vann – you don't mean we're having an appointment with the German ambassador?' I cried.

Despite not receiving a reply, it seemed that we were indeed scheduled to meet the German ambassador.

We soon entered an impressive building and which was heavily neoclassical in style. Our appointment was confirmed by a clerk as Giallo gave him his name. The man took our hats and directed us upstairs and we climbed the stairs in silence, our footsteps echoing slightly in the cavernous halls.

After being shown through an innumerable series of doors and corridors, we finally entered the spacious quarters of Vondick vann Cliffberg, who rose from his seat at his massive oak desk and greeted us pleasantly. What impressed me most was how different the German ambassador was from his English counterpart, both in terms of character and physicality. Whereas Sir Charles was the strict, unyielding disciplinarian who instilled more fear than respect or affection, Cliffberg simply radiated charisma and sophistication. An educated man too, no doubt, as Larry had mentioned, by the immense number of books stacked on a nearby side table and which academic-sounding titles were beyond my interest and understanding.

He was taller than I had thought, having just seen him once after the inquest, and his gloominess that day was certainly not an issue this afternoon.

'I have read much of you, Monsieur Giallo,' he said as we took our seats.

'You take an interest in crime, monsieur?'

'When you are a diplomat, you will often have to find yourself reading of matters which usually one wouldn't care to read,' he said a little dryly.

'That being said, I must admit that it holds a slight fascination for me.'

'Perhaps that would explain why you were at the inquest of Sir Charles Stow, Monsieur vann Cliffberg.'

If I had expected the German ambassador to be badly startled by the mention of his former and now deceased rival, I was disappointed in that respect as he showed nothing but perfect sangfroid. In fact, he appeared as if Giallo had just asked him a question about the weather or some trivial matter or other.

'Ah, I was certain from the first moment I received your letter, Monsieur Giallo, that you were to ask me about that,' he said lightly.

'Did you expect a man of my occupation to do anything else?' asked Giallo, matching his lightness of tone perfectly. Cliffberg's grey eyes narrowed a little before he said with a smile.

'No, perhaps not. That was to be expected even by the simplest of men.'

'Then you will permit me to ask you questions, monsieur, regarding the death of Sir Charles Stow?'
Cliffberg permitted my friend to do so without a word of protest. To tell the truth, I felt a little uneasy about the German's unusual cooperativeness. The more he spoke, the more I wondered about Larry's description of him as that 'wily fellow Cliffberg.'
He appeared to be the last person in the world to deal with diplomatic sabotage or to take part in the willful theft of secret state documents. In fact, when Giallo touched upon the subject of the theft at the British Embassy, Cliffberg laughed heartily in amusement.

'Sir Charles Stow was never the most organized of men, I must say. Theft indeed! I wonder if he hadn't imagined the whole thing. Security at diplomatic missions is standardized these days, Giallo, especially with all these tensions between us. I wouldn't be able to comment on whether the safes at the British Embassy are of the same make or standard as ours, but neither of us could ever simply go into the other's offices and take whatever papers we liked. That would be impossible with the number of men standing guard at night. That as well as the fact that people are walking all over the place – no one can break into a safe that way, they're bound to be seen.'

'Sir Charles told his son, M. Larry Stokes, that he suspected you to be responsible for the theft.'

'To tell you the truth, I'm not surprised. He was never original in his ideas – it was a common tactic of his to blame everything on us since he couldn't find anyone else to be the scapegoat.'

'You do not seem to have a high regard for Sir Charles, monsieur.'

'I doubt whether anyone who has met him would be capable of holding him in high regard,' replied Cliffberg darkly. 'Wiggins was never the type of man whom one could respect for long.'

'He appeared to have had a particular dislike for you. Surely such dislike is rarely unwarranted, n'est-ce pas?'

'I would say that the dislike is wholly unwarranted in this case. I suspect it had something more to do that I was the only German diplomat of high enough importance in this country whom he could set his attacks on, Monsieur Giallo, rather than a matter of personal difference. Being a former naval man, I would assume that my Kaiser's policy of naval expansion over the years would have been a source of great annoyance to him.'

He paused, then added musingly: 'I cannot say that I approve of the policy myself, but that is beside the point.'

'Quite so,' agreed Giallo. 'Quite so. However, this brings me to the question of seeing that since you never held Sir Charles in high regard, why did you decide to go to his inquest?'

I thought I detected a slight change in Cliffberg's otherwise jovial countenance.

'Surely it isn't a crime to go to an inquest, is it?' he said with a small smile.

'No, monsieur, it is not. You are perfectly free to decide whether or not to do as you please. But to go to an inquest of a man who you plainly dislike is rather curious.'

'Perhaps to most people, Monsieur Giallo. However, unlike most people, I have a keen sense of duty and dignity,' stated the German quietly. 'Let bygones be bygones, as they say. Once a man has died and especially in the most violent of ways, he has paid the price for all the sins he has committed in life.'

'A sound choice of words, monsieur. I was not aware that he committed sins towards yourself.'

'I was speaking figuratively.'

Cliffberg had spoken calmly but there was something about his manner which did not quite convince me at this point and it appeared that it hadn't convinced Giallo either.

'I do not think so,' said Giallo. 'Forgive me, monsieur, for my impudence, but Reeves Giallo does not believe you.'

For the first time in our meeting, anger seemed to flare beneath that composed face.

'Then M. Reeves Giallo,' replied the other man coldly, 'is clearly mistaken.'

There was a long uncomfortable pause where neither of the two men spoke as they glared at each other, the brown meeting the grey and which would have appeared faintly ridiculous had it not been for the unbearable tension which had erupted between them. The silence was broken, however, when Giallo suddenly slammed his hands on the desk before him, startling the rest of us in the room.

'Non! Giallo is never mistaken. You, of all people, must know that. It is useless to hide the truth from me.'

I was astounded at Giallo's abrupt descent as it was into recklessness. He was going against everything he had told me. Had he not always advised that one was to always hide one's suspicions from the enemy? Furthermore, the enemy in question was a high-ranking diplomat, and I was certain that if his wild accusation hadn't meant our instant dismissal from the man's office, we were to be expelled from the place soon. My fears were confirmed when Cliffberg rose from his chair and gazed frigidly at us from his very considerable height.

'I fear, Monsieur Giallo, that the strain of all this business has unfortunately got to your head. The Prime Minister designated you to this case, I heard. I presume it hasn't been an easy past few weeks for you and you have my fullest sympathy. However, I am afraid that this does not give you the right to accuse me of anything you so wish and therefore, our interview is at an end, gentlemen.'

He reached for a hand bell, presumably to summon his secretary to usher us out, when Giallo too rose to his feet and pulled a piece of notepaper from the inside of his coat.

'Very well. However, at least do me the courtesy of reading that if we are no longer on speaking terms.'

The German ambassador's face paled as his eyes took in the contents of the note and his manner underwent a change, which surprised me. It was a while before he appeared able to speak and even as he spoke, his heretofore confident voice shook a little.

'How did you –' he started.

'Never mind how I know, monsieur. The only question to be asked now is will you now cooperate?'

He examined my friend closely, as if attempting to gauge Giallo's thoughts. At length, he nodded and murmured.

'I will.'

'Thank you.'

'You will know all by tomorrow morning, Monsieur Giallo. I will send one of the Embassy clerks to bring a letter to you.'

Giallo offered his thanks once again, and we turned to leave.

'Monsieur Giallo.'

Turning back, we saw the ambassador was holding out the piece of notepaper Giallo had handed him, and I admit I was now extremely curious to examine its contents. I half-proffered a hand to take it from him when Giallo stopped me.

'Not at all, monsieur. I leave it with you to do what you like with it. We have reached an understanding, yes?'

'Yes. And thank you, Monsieur Giallo,' he said with obvious gratefulness.

Cliffberg 's secretary returned to the former's office at this point and we were shown politely out of the room, our exit I noted being a complete contrast to our entrance only a while before.

'What on earth did you write in that note to Cliffberg?' I asked as we stepped outside onto the front steps of the German Embassy.

'He almost seemed like a completely different man, Giallo.'

Giallo looked up at me.

'Something which he did not expect me to know. Nor any man perhaps.'

This was not entirely the sort of answer I would have liked.

'I wish you'd stop talking in riddles,' I sighed.

'I do not speak in the riddles, St. Louie. I am merely telling you the truth.'

'Well, the truth surely doesn't have to be so dashed complicated as you make it out,' I countered.

'The truth should be simple, really.'

'Ah, but what is it that one of your famous playwrights say? That the truth is rarely pure and never simple? Well, he was right…at least regarding discovering the truth in crime.'

I flushed a little, knowing all too well which playwright he was referring to and whose name still provoked outrage amongst the educated classes. I quickly changed the subject.

'So you expect a letter from him then?'

'Indeed I do.'

'You don't think he'll do a runner, do you?'

'Comment? "Do a runner"?'

'I mean, you don't think he'll flee the country or go back on his word, do you?'

'Non Vondick vann Cliffberg is not a fool, St. Louie. Besides, I am sure that after that convenient note of mine, we have reached an understanding between us.'

We were making our way back to the Hôtel de Ville when a man suddenly approached me. Turning in surprise, I saw it was Garvious who apparently had been sent back down to Paris to drive not only myself but also Giallo back to the villa.

'Mr Wiggins's request, Mr St. Louie. He'd like to invite Monsieur Giallo to dinner this evening,' explained Garvious as we got into the car in bemusement.

'Interesting,' murmured Giallo. 'You knew of Monsieur Larry's intention to invite me, St. Louie?'

'I assure you I didn't,' I replied, still completely at a loss on the cause of Larry's sudden invitation.

'It is of no matter,' said my friend with a shrug.

'Regardless, it shall give me the chance of asking him several questions which I had not the opportunity of asking before…especially regarding his late mother.'

'I wouldn't think that advisable, old fellow,' I interjected hastily. 'Larry's awfully touchy about these things, you know. Bound to shut up like an oyster if you ask him at the wrong time.'

Giallo's brown eyes scrutinized me and I averted my gaze as best I could lest I fell once again into the trap of losing myself in them.

'It is as I have said, mon ami, you cannot hide the truth from me.'

'What?' I cried, suddenly fearing that he was reading my mind.

'It is like what I have said to the German ambassador,' he said simply.

'You have already attempted to ask Monsieur Larry about our new findings, yes?'

'Oh,' I said, and I breathed a quick sigh of relief, realizing that he was actually referring to the diary.

'And you have obviously failed, yes?'

'Oh. Yes,' I replied, past caring what Giallo thought of my apparently lacklustre skills of interrogation.

He shook his head wearily.

'Let us hope then that I can try to salvage the situation, St. Louie.'

We arrived at the villa shortly before half-past five. Larry was already waiting for us at the front door and greeted Giallo with unusual warmness.

'Evening, Monsieur Giallo. Hope you don't mind me inviting you for dinner on such short notice.'

'Not at all, monsieur. Fortunately, I was not engaged this evening and was only too happy to accept your invitation.'

'Jolly good,' replied Larry. 'Now dinner isn't to be served until sometime yet, but I wonder if I could ask you to step into the library for a moment.'

Giallo agreed to the request and, feeling distinctly unwanted, I went into the drawing room and found Ella sitting on the couch and reading a periodical which she put aside when she saw me. Tim Mac David was also in the room, sitting at one of the bay windows and looking out across the garden, a copy of The Times unopened on his lap.

'Nicolas, we all wondered where you disappeared off to.'

'Evening, Ella,' I said as I took my place opposite her in one armchair. 'I was with Monsieur Giallo down in the capital –'

'Had your fun playing detective, Mr St. Louie?' came the snide comment from the window to which I paid no attention. Ella shot her fiancé a look of complete disapproval and smiled encouragingly at me.

'Never mind, Luke,' she whispered.

'He's only annoyed because Larry wanted him to vacate the library.'

'Ah, I see.'

'You're looking awfully smart though for just a visit to the capital,' she observed, glancing down at my suit.

'You'll look such a sight at dinner.'

'I suppose I should change to something more appropriate before then. I only got into this because we had an appointment at the German Embassy.'

'The German Embassy? Not the British one?'

'No, it was the German one, all right. We had to meet the German ambassador, Vondick vann Cliffberg.'

'Oh, yes. I remember Larry telling me about him. The one who's apparently behind the theft of papers at the Embassy.'

'That's right. And from what's happened this afternoon, I think Giallo's got him now. Quite marvelous how he did it, really. Cliffberg hasn't been arrested yet, but as far as I understand it, he's not going anywhere.'

'I'm glad to hear it. Well, at least that's one mystery solved,' sighed Ella. 'If only he could solve the one closer at hand, then we'd all be quite relieved.'

'I'm most certain he will,' I replied with the utmost confidence.

Larry joined us in the drawing room with Samantha following soon afterwards. To my puzzlement, Giallo was nowhere to be seen. I was tempted to ask Larry where he was, but I thought it best not to tempt fate, especially after last night's disastrous conversation. A minute later, Tom also entered with a book in his hand.

'Anyone know where Janett is?' he asked.

'She's left her book again in the conservatory.'

'She's taking a walk in the garden,' replied Larry when no one had spoken.

Tom stared at his cousin in astonishment.

'A walk in the garden? At this hour?'

'Don't worry, Tom. I've asked Monsieur Giallo to...accompany her.'

I do not recall exactly what my thoughts were upon hearing this unexpected news, apart from the fact that I had the sudden urge to throw Tim Mac David off his window seat and see the two together for myself.

This urge was fortunately countered in time by reason and remembering that I had to change for dinner, I excused myself from the room and rushed upstairs, remembering my bedroom window was directly above a bench frequently used by the family in the garden and Janett and Giallo had stopped by there. I opened the window as quietly as I could. I was in luck; familiar voices soon rose to my ears and Janett was the first to reach me, her voice full of emotion.

'You dear thing. You must know I love no one else in the entire world. My feelings – '
The next voice was Giallo's and what I heard spoken in such gentle tones rocked me to the core.

'Oui, je comprends. Je comprends absolutement…and I accept them.'
There was a sudden outpouring of joy in Janett's voice at the Paris's words, but I was oblivious to it. All I was aware of now was the horrible sinking feeling in the pit of my stomach as I shut the window, my mind in a complete and utter daze.

Chapter 10

Revelations

I confess I am not usually the sort of man who gives in easily to his emotions. However, it was upon hearing this exchange in the garden that a violent torrent of disbelief and regret washed over me and I sank heavily onto a nearby chair.

I felt numb and in a complete blue funk. Thoughts of the case were now unimportant to me. All I heard now repeated over and over in my head was the gentle endearment Janett had called Giallo and the latter's unbearably gentle response of 'Oui, je comprends. Je comprends absolutement...and I accept them.'

Had I misunderstood the whole thing completely?

Or was what I heard literally the truth of the matter?

That Janett had transferred her feelings from me to Giallo and that he had in turn accepted them? Thankful as I vaguely was because Janett appeared to be no longer interested in me, I was now thrown headlong into another situation which I had never dreamt of experiencing.

While I had sincerely wished her to find happiness with another man other than myself, the fact that she had exchanged her affections for my good friend was another matter entirely and which oddly did not sit well with me.

'Giallo...'

Was he my good friend as I heretofore regarded him as or was he something more to me? More than just a friend? After all, wasn't it the usual thing to feel delight at seeing a friend being united with a young woman who you knew was one of the best of her kind?

I imagined my current predicament being sympathetically looked upon by my friends back home as a reaction to what was called at the time, the 'Continental air'.

'You got yourself a little too much of it, old chap, they'd say. Wonderfully liberating in small doses, but positively dangerous in large ones, they would add in grave tones. Giving in to your feelings is frightfully foreign. Better get out of the place while you can and the sooner you return to good old England, the better, St. Louie…you'd soon be your old self again.'

The prospect of returning home suddenly appeared very appealing. Yes, I could simply leave the entire thing and pronounce apologetically that Christie's had need of me, and my father insisted I return to London at once. Surely no one would doubt my reasons for that score…

Deep down though, I knew it was nothing but pure cowardice to run away from this whole unpleasant and unexpected situation. And not only running away from that, but also my own feelings. It wasn't the 'air' or the people or the food or the landscape which was causing such a tumult of mental anguish; it was all due to one person and one person alone: Reeves Giallo.

Looking back on my younger self, I can now find it faintly amusing that it took so long really to realise that all I had done was to have fallen in love with him. In those days, however, such a revelation was no trivial matter – it was gravely serious and I am sorry to say still is the case now as I write this.

The very public trial, humiliation and ignominy of Oscar Wilde was still painfully fresh in all our minds and the very mention of his name even thirteen years after his death caused exclamations of contempt and disgust in all walks of society. Thus, the risk and danger of being found out by the authorities was what men of his kind – which I supposed now included myself – feared the most; even more than death itself.

I thought it ironic and another example of my bad luck to have also fallen in love with a man who was also a detective – an agent of the law. I do not know what the laws in France were regarding what people refer to now as 'queers' but seeing that a considerable amount of the nation were devout Catholics…Giallo no doubt was one of them, I hazarded a guess that a liberal and sympathetic standpoint on the matter was out of the question.

No, there was really no other way. I had to keep my feelings to myself whatever the personal cost and that meant accepting the fact that Giallo was now attached to Janett and that whatever happened in the future between them would be out of my hands completely. If I were to survive this investigation with my reputation intact, I would have to act as if nothing had happened, continuing as I was before: a faithful friend and associate of Reeves Giallo, Chief Detective Inspector of the Paris Police, and nothing more.

Though I had mulled over these depressing thoughts for at least an hour, I realised it had only been a quarter of an hour since I had left the others downstairs. What a difference did only a quarter of an hour make…

I dressed mechanically into another suit and my hand shook a little as I reached for the doorknob. Seeing Giallo suddenly seemed as daunting as it had been reassuring for the past few weeks. Could I trust myself to keep calm with all the confusion and bitterness now tossing within me?

I glanced at the mirror and saw a young man struggling to keep his emotions in check and I was astonished to see that tears were silently cascading down my now pale cheeks.

I hastily wiped them with a handkerchief. It was ridiculous really how I was reacting and I was suddenly angry with myself. Self-reprobation is always preferable to wallowing in one's grief (for it was indeed grief which I was experiencing to a certain extent) and I quickly took advantage of it, wrenching open the door and stepping out over the threshold to dinner where the others and Giallo were undoubtedly waiting for me.

Even to this day I do not know how I endured that dinner at the villa, but endure it, I did. Admittedly, I was helped because Giallo's attention was almost wholly occupied by Larry, who was querying him on this or that matter, thus meaning that I did not have to speak to him until he had to return to his flat. If I had been forced to speak to him upon my arrival in the dining room downstairs, I have no doubt that my nerve would have abandoned me and goodness knows where we would have ended up.

Though we said almost nothing at dinner, I thought I saw Giallo's gaze direct itself in my direction during the occasional lulls in Larry's conversation. His expression was one of complete puzzlement and it was along this same vein he accosted me in the entrance hall as he was about to leave.

'Is there anything the matter, mon ami?' he asked.

He reached out and put a gentle hand on my forearm, and it took all my willpower not to snatch my arm away.

'Anything the matter?' I repeated, and I was surprised that my voice sounded quite calm despite the torrent of mixed emotions I was currently feeling. 'No, I don't think so. Why do you ask?'

Giallo suddenly appeared as if he was about to reprimand me, perhaps having seen through my pathetic attempt at a lie but just as suddenly, he shook his head and removed his hand and I was left feeling half-relieved that he had released me and half-longing to feel his touch again.

'C'est pas grave,' he said. 'It is only that you looked a little pale at dinner, St. Louie. You are not getting la maladie, I hope.'

'Oh. No. I'm a little…tired, I suppose.'

'You seem to be tired very often of late,' observed Giallo gravely, and I knew he was thinking of my sudden departure from his rooms the other night. He looked up into my face and I had the distinct feeling of being scrutinized to the very core of my being, but I held his gaze, hoping desperately that I gave nothing away. After a few moments, he added quietly.

'St. Louie, if at any point that you feel you would like to take the sojourn from the investigation, you need only tell me. I comprehend very well if you think that your position as Monsieur Wiggins's friend –'

'What?' I cried.

'No! I mean – well…yes, I suppose that I haven't had an easy go of it being Larry's friend and all, especially in the past few days, but I made a promise.

To seek the truth and nothing but the truth. Don't you remember that?'

Indeed, I do. But are you sure that is what you want?'

'Quite sure. Until the very end, old fellow.'

A brief smile passed over Giallo's lips.

'Fortunate was the day when Reeves Giallo met Nicolas St. Louie. You are a good friend, mon ami.'

Whereas his words might have pleased me a few days ago, even a few hours ago, they gave me no pleasure now.

Was I only just that to him, I wondered fleetingly as Stanford appeared from behind us and handed Giallo his belongings. A "good friend?"

'Same here, Giallo,' I murmured. There was then a moment where I was mad enough to consider asking him what he had been doing in the garden before dinner, but I stopped myself in time. The memory was still too painfully fresh in my mind and I concluded that if Giallo really regarded me as the good friend as he had said I was, he would tell me in his own time.

I followed him outside onto the gravel drive before we said our goodbyes. It was a beautiful night; the sky was wonderfully clear; the moon shining high in the heavens and there was a cool breeze fluttering about in the air but I was in no mood to enjoy it. All I could think of was Giallo and as I watched him being driven away by Garvious into the darkness, I reflected with no great enthusiasm on the days to come.

In the days which followed, I was fortunate enough to have the opportunity of being distracted from my rather low spirits by the preparations for Sir Charles's funeral. Macabre as the 'distraction' might seem, I was grateful for something else to occupy my mind and seeing that the coroner had just recently given permission for the body to be returned to the family, the most urgent matter at hand was not to find the person who had brought about Sir Charles Stow's end but to see that his remains were properly buried. All of us living at the villa wordlessly took it upon ourselves to lend a hand despite the mixed feelings he inspired in us while he was alive.

Meanwhile, Giallo was, as he described it, 'advancing' with his investigation. Our interview with Cliffberg a few days previously had apparently done its trick; a letter had been received the day after our meeting, which Giallo read with great interest but refused to share its contents with anyone and on the eve of Sir Charles's funeral, he brandished a small memorandum triumphantly before me.

The past few days had also given me time to control my emotions, and I managed to bear up tolerably well whenever I found myself alone with Giallo. However, it does look like he had observed nothing in my manner towards him.

'What does he say?' I asked, putting down the pile of books I was helping Stanford move from the sitting room to the library. Giallo smiled at me enigmatically.

'The German ambassador wrote to tell me that he will be present at the service tomorrow morning to pay his respects.' There was something in those eyes of his, now shining brightly with excitement, which told me that there was something more to his announcement than met the eye.

'You're up to something, Giallo,' I said reproachfully. 'And there's something that you're not telling me.'

He admitted this but revealed precious little else.

'It is a brief experiment I have set up for tomorrow, that is all.'

'Does Cliffberg know about this?'

'Parbleu! He has given me his full cooperation, mon ami. He knows exactly what I have planned.'

'Well, who's going to be the one being 'experimented' upon, then?'

He smiled another mysterious smile.

'You shall see, St. Louie. Observe carefully tomorrow and perhaps you shall see.'

If Giallo had been planning for anything dramatic to happen at the service, I think it was safe to say that it failed to take off entirely, if indeed at all. There were few people present at Sir Charles's funeral and I could see that many of them were there simply because they had come there out of duty, while those who had been unable to come instead sent letters of condolences or wreaths.

What caused the most commotion was the presence of Cliffberg, who appeared highly discomfited at all the attention being given to him. Larry himself appeared mildly surprised at the German ambassador's appearance at his father's funeral, but greeted him courteously nonetheless when he arrived. They shared a couple of words and I could detect nothing but the utmost civility in the snatches of conversation I overheard.

Seeing that Giallo had asked me to observe carefully, I watched him closely and was more than a little astonished to see the German leaving the churchyard where Sir Charles was finally laid to rest almost immediately after the service was finished. It was my opinion that he had done nothing but converse with a couple of his fellow diplomats and watch impassively as the coffin was lowered into the ground. I wondered whether this was all part of Giallo's brief experiment. This apparently was the case, as he did nothing to prevent him from leaving even as the ambassador passed him as he got into his waiting motor.

The remaining guests returned with us to the villa for refreshments and settled into conversation in various parts of the sitting room.

'Curious that Cliffberg should come,' commented Larry as we stood about sipping from our cups of tea or coffee.

'Curious indeed.'

Out of the corner of my eye, I could see Giallo look up in interest from his spot near the mantelpiece, but he said nothing.

'Were you surprised to see him?' I asked.

'Very,' replied Larry and I could see from his face that he was in earnest. 'I've heard many horror stories about how he runs his embassy from Father, so I didn't think too highly of him when he walked through the church door this morning. Found out that all of it was a whole lot of rot, really. Cliffberg's actually quite the decent fellow. Extraordinarily well read, too. I asked him to call on me any time if he so wished – it's rare you can find decent, intelligent fellows like him, you know.'

Some of Larry's colleagues at the Embassy wished to speak to him at this point and I disengaged myself. Looking about, I saw Giallo, who had moved from his place on the mantelpiece and was now gazing musingly out of the window. For one moment, during which a twinge of my heretofore repressed jealousy briefly entered my stream of consciousness, I thought he was watching Janett in the garden before remembering that she was currently speaking with Tom on the other side of the room. Taking another sip of my tea in an attempt to perhaps steel myself, I joined him at the window.

'Your little experiment doesn't seem to have worked, Giallo,' I announced quietly after ascertaining that no one could overhear us.

He turned his gaze from the window; the sunlight illuminating his dark eyes so they seemed to blaze before me.

'You think so, St. Louie?' he asked.

'I was watching Cliffberg all through the service. Didn't seem to do anything really apart from talking to some fellows and sitting rather grimly in his seat.'

'Ah, but it was not the German Ambassador was watching.'

'What?'

'When you are Reeves Giallo, you focus not only on one thing or person, mon ami. Broaden your mind;Look all around you. I think my experiment achieved what I wanted it to achieve.'

'And what's that?' I said, rather exasperatedly.

'That some people are not as innocent as they pretend to be.'

I sighed wearily despite myself. 'Giallo, your riddles are becoming infuriating — '

'And also that Monsieur vann Cliffberg did not play any part in the death of Sir Charles Stow.'

'What?' I cried again and Giallo shushed me almost immediately, for my exclamation had not gone unnoticed by the surrounding people, some of whom had momentarily darted their gaze curiously in our direction.

'Come, St. Louie. We shall continue our conversation in the garden.'

I admit I was feeling a little reluctant to venture to a place which gave me no happy memories, but I wordlessly followed him and we slipped outside unnoticed.

'So Cliffberg didn't murder Sir Charles?' I said as soon as we were outside.

'No, he did not.'

'What about the theft at the British Embassy? Sir Charles's papers?'

'That too was not the German's work. That was Sir Charles.'

'Sir Charles stole –'

He did not steal them in any real sense of the word, but he tried to lay the blame at Cliffberg'door.'

'But why?'

'Sir Charles's character is not one which recommends him to people, St. Louie. He was a petty, narrow-minded individual, and he made life difficult for those who had the misfortune of being disliked by him. Cliffberg, alas, found himself falling into this area, and I believe this 'theft' was merely an attempt to undermine the German Ambassador as part of their long-standing 'duel.'

'Duel?' I asked.

'Surely that's taking things a little far, isn't it? They disliked each other perhaps because of all this political rivalry business between Britain and Germany, but –'

I was cut short here as we nearly cannoned into Ella, who was walking towards us. She had evidently not seen us and, in the ensuing confusion, she dropped a piece of paper she had been reading. Both Giallo and I attempted to retrieve it for her, but my friend got to it first and handed it to her.

'Thank you, Monsieur Giallo,' said Ella with a smile. As was the custom, she was adorned in black, and the contrast with her blonde hair and white skin made her appear more ethereal than ever.

'Pas du tout.' Giallo made a slight gesture towards the note in her hand.

'It is heartening to see that Monsieur Grimms writes the letters to you. He cares for you deeply, mademoiselle.'

If Giallo had thought this would please her, his words backfired completely. Ella's smile stiffened considerably, and she said coldly.

'I was under the impression that true gentlemen never read private letters, monsieur.'

The snub was painfully obvious, and I felt half-embarrassed for Giallo's sake and half-satisfied to see his outrageous habit of looking into matters which were never meant for his eyes finally being confronted. He apologized and perhaps his sincerity touched her, for Ella soon added.

'Perhaps I was being unduly harsh, Monsieur Giallo. Mr Grimms and I don't quite get along with each other and it's always difficult for me to understand what he means by these kinds of things,' she said, showing the piece of paper in her hand before tucking it neatly away.

'I think I might have to speak to him directly about this. Will you please excuse me?'

We let her pass and as soon as she was out of earshot; I said.

'Tight minor scrape you managed to get out of there, Giallo.'

Giallo ignored me and though he said nothing, I could see that he had been humbled by Ella's reaction. We walked a few minutes in silence and though the surroundings still gave me some unhappiness; I was happy to be in Giallo's company, happy to have him as it was all to myself in that quiet garden. I wondered what he was thinking. He was in a meditative mood this morning. Was he thinking of that evening a few nights previously when it was Janett and not I would had walked with upon the same grounds? Surely such thoughts wouldn't have escaped him, I mused, especially when we neared the bench beneath my bedroom window. I thought I saw his gaze fix itself briefly upon it as we approached, but he said nothing and was about to walk past it when I made a sign that I needed to sit down.

'Sorry, old fellow. Damned laces of mine keep coming undone,' I said as I leaned over to retie my shoelaces. To tell the truth, it was all just a show and my laces were not as loose as I had made them out to be. I merely wanted to see whether this would stir anything within that unfathomable mind of his and press him to share with me the details of his conversation with Janett the other evening. To my disappointment, Giallo merely nodded as I sat on the bench and turned around to gaze contemplatively at the front gate through which several cars full of diplomats were now leaving.

His behavior confused me. If I had not known of his exchange with Janett, I would have never imagined that he had entered an understanding with her. And although Giallo liked to be at times deeply mysterious, he didn't appear the type to be deceitful. Or was he simply an excellent actor? It was only years later that I learned that regardless of his unique and unmistakable appearance that Giallo was more than adequately able to 'play the comedy', as he termed it.

At this point in our friendship, I realized I knew almost nothing of him at all, apart from the fact that I had fallen in love with him.

Unable to contain my thoughts and taking advantage of the quiet which had settled between us, I ventured tentatively.

'Do you know what I think, Giallo?'

He turned his head a little in my direction but did not turn round.

'What, mon ami?'

I thought carefully, wondering how best it was to put my thoughts into words without giving too much away.

'I sometimes think this whole business is just some bizarre play of sorts with all of us playing parts like actors. People dying and disappearing…all these twists and turns. I wouldn't be surprised if one day we'd all wake up and think this some terrible dream – Giallo?'

My friend had suddenly gone still, and he was murmuring to himself.

'Un acteur,' he muttered.

'But of course, why did I not think of it before?'

I stared at him in complete bewilderment and was even more at a loss when he added mysteriously: "Tomorrow. All shall be well tomorrow. J.H."

'What's that you say, old fellow?'

He started a little out of his reverie, and he turned round to face me.

'That was written on Mademoiselle Wiggins's note, St. Louie.'

'Really? Probably Grimms's way of consoling Ella after all this dreadful business,' I suggested. 'But to tell the truth, I'm surprised to learn that Grimms's actually the consoling type.'

'Perhaps. Perhaps it, as you say.'

Giallo's face was a study, and I found it exceedingly difficult to grasp what was going through his mind.

'But if I am right…if the little grey cells are right…mon Dieu, we have not the moment to lose, St. Louie.'

Oblivious to my utter astonishment, he rushed back towards the house and I dashed after him to find him questioning a very bemused Stanford.

'The telephone, sir? I believe you may find one just down here –'

'Non, that will not do. Is there a telephone in your room, Stanford?'

'No, sir, but there is one in the corridor down near the servant's quarters.'

'Is there anyone down there at the moment?'

'No one at all, sir.'

'Bon. That will do parfaitement.'

We squeezed ourselves into the kitchen and then into the corridor leading to the servant's quarters. Giallo stopped me as we entered the corridor.

'St. Louie, you stand guard here until I have finished my telephone call.'

I nodded and took my post. I had been with Giallo long enough to understand that he was not in a mood to be contradicted.

'Allo? Oui, I would like to make a call to London, please.' Glancing over my shoulder, I saw him retrieve his small notebook from an inner pocket and give a number to the operator. A few minutes went by without a sound from my friend, but at long last the person he was attempting to reach finally spoke.

'Allo? Is that Inspector Zane? This is Reeves Giallo.' Though I was a few feet away from him, I heard muffled sounds of surprise from the receiver. 'It is good to hear your voice too, mon ami. Yes, yes. I wonder whether you could do me a small favour, Inspector. But attendez, it is a most urgent request I must make of you. I must have an answer by tomorrow morning. C'est possible?

'You are much too amiable. Bon. I would like if you please a list of all known actors who have left England for the Continent in the past three years. No, not those who only left for a tour. Those who left England and who have not yet returned.' Zane seemed to be astonished upon receiving such a request and from what I could hear from my post at the front of the corridor, Giallo was having some difficulty in persuading him to agree to his request. I was not in the least surprised; I imagined the task Giallo had given the inspector was a monumental one, and I wondered whether it would be humanly possible to complete it by tomorrow morning.

'But of course, mon ami. I know it is a task difficile which I give you but I am certain that you are ready to rise to the challenge.'

There was another pause before Giallo's expression changed and he smiled happily.

'Je vous remercie, my good Zane. A thousand thanks, my friend.

'A telegram?'

'Yes, that will be more than enough. Very well, tomorrow morning then.'

He carefully put down the receiver, and he was beaming when he joined me.

'Who's Inspector Zane?' I asked.

'Inspector Luke Zane of your country's Scotland Yard, St. Louie. I was fortunate to have worked with him nine years ago on the Frederick Mocomrand case. It was quite a well-known affair at the time. We were both just starting our careers as police officers, and it was our first case of importance.

Ever since, we have established a friendship of sorts.

He is an outstanding police officer, not very imaginative but competent, and possesses what you English might call the dogged determination.'

I took in all this new information with interest and tried very hard to imagine a much younger Giallo as not the celebrated chief inspector he was today but an ordinary police officer, though I suspected he was anything but ordinary even at such a young age.

'What's all this business about actors, Giallo? Wouldn't it be easier to ask Samantha about all this?'

'Mademoiselle Milton is the actress par excellence, mon ami. Though I am certain that she is well acquainted with many renowned actors and walks in the most illustrious of acting circles, we cannot expect her to know everyone.

I have a feeling that the person I am looking for is not to be found walking in the same circles as the good mademoiselle.'

'An amateur then?'

Giallo gave a small shrug. 'C'est possible,' he said thoughtfully.

'But now is not the time to dwell on that.

The good Zane will give me all the answers I need tomorrow morning. I only hope that it will not be too late.'

'Too late to do what?'

Giallo examined me gravely before replying.

'To prevent another murder.'

Chapter 11

The Grapple with Death

I have never seen my friend look graver as he did the next day, and I had a vague sense of foreboding as to what was lying in store for us. He had warned that the murderer was to strike again, and that it was our task to prevent another murder from happening. How he could foresee where and how the villain would strike escaped me; I felt we were vainly looking for a needle in the proverbial haystack, but once again, I put my faith in him entirely. Reeves Giallo, as I was to learn firsthand on so many countless occasions, was rarely mistaken. But before we could throw ourselves into doing anything, we had to wait for Inspector Zane's telegram and it arrived just as Giallo was on the verge of leaving his rooms for the telegram office after several hours of waiting. I must say that I was grateful for Zane's timing. I had done nothing but wait glumly in my usual chair in Giallo's sitting room ever since my arrival that morning and just as the delivery boy received his couple of francs with a polite touch to his cap, I could feel my stomach rumbling and I was suddenly eager for us to go to lunch.

'Ah, the little grey cells, St. Louie!' Giallo declared as his eyes took in the contents of the telegram. 'The little grey cells. They never fail me.'

'It is good news, I trust?'
I asked, half-rising from my chair.

'Good news? It is the best – at least regarding our investigation. Mais non, my friend, only I will read this for the moment,' he added as I reached for it. 'It is in the best interest of everyone.'

I frowned a little, wondering whether Giallo really had so little faith in me.

'All shall be revealed in time, St. Louie,' he said soothingly, observing my expression.

He tucked the telegram neatly into an inner pocket.

'Now we must go to the Wiggins villa but first, I must make all the arrangements.'

With that he disappeared into his bedroom and I had to content myself with thoughts of what Stanford and the cook had prepared for lunch that afternoon and what the others were probably already enjoying. A quarter of an hour later, Giallo reappeared, carrying a small valise in his hand.

Bon. Now all is prepared. We may depart, mon ami.'

Within a half an hour, we were at the villa.

To my disappointment, lunch had already finished only twenty minutes before our arrival, but Stanford quickly arranged for some sandwiches to be made and a plate of them was placed before me as the both of us sat in the sitting room as we waited for Larry.

Giallo did not appreciate the sandwiches as I did.

His eyes scanned them disdainfully, then widened slightly in surprise when he realized I had nearly finished half the plate in five minutes.

'They really are quite good, you know,' I said, finishing off my sixth sandwich and now feeling rather full. I offered the plate to him. 'Besides, you have had no lunch either, Giallo.'

He eyed the plate suspiciously then gingerly took one, examining the small sandwich made up of two triangular slices of thin white bread with what I guessed was shrimp paste and cucumbers.

I hadn't been really paying attention to what was inside them. He tentatively took a small bite of it and immediately made a face.

'This is what you English call a sandwich, St. Louie? Mon Dieu!'

'Well, it's nothing like what you get in France, I suppose, with all the baguettes and things,' I said, a little defensively.

'But it's a decent meal, old chap.'

'It is not a meal, mon ami?'

'It is liable to give you le mal de ventre!' he complained and shuddered a little. He finished the sandwich in what I supposed was mere politeness.

Larry entered at this point and the sandwiches were soon forgotten. I too appeared to be forgotten as Giallo led Larry into a side room and I wondered what they were up to.

It was only a few minutes later that Larry emerged, appearing slightly puzzled.

'Can't say, St. Louie,' he replied as I asked him what the matter was.

Giallo looked up at me as he re-entered the sitting room and nodded at Larry, who left rather hurriedly through the door.

'Monsieur Wiggins has just received his instructions, monami,' he said in reply to my quizzical gaze, a hint of humor in his eyes.

'He is at this moment going off to fulfil them.'

'Instructions? What instructions?'

'Calm yourself, St. Louie.'

His expression became serious.

'In fact, if you choose to accept them, I will be also giving some instructions to you.'

'I knew at once that these were going to be rather important. Of course, I'll accept them, Giallo. Just say the word and I'll do it.'

At my words, he smiled at me and nodded.

'Always the good and dependable St. Louie. But are you certain, my friend? The task I give you is not an easy one and there is much danger ahead.'

'Most certainly,' I replied. Giallo cast one long look at me before retrieving his valise from near the couch. He opened it and pulled out what was unmistakably my revolver.

'I believe this is belongs to you.'

I shuddered a little despite myself as I cast my eyes on it. Memories of finding it next to Sir Charles's body that dreadful morning came unbidden to my mind.

Though I had been told that it hadn't been used to murder him, it still sent me an unpleasant shiver down my spine.

'It is unpleasant to behold, is it not, mon ami?'

'I have to admit, I'm not entirely pleased to see it again.'

'Je comprends. However, you might have to use it this evening.'

'Not to kill, I trust,' I said grimly as he placed it in my hand. It had been meticulously cleaned since I last saw it, and I supposed that Giallo had taken pains to do so after the police had finished with it.

'Non, I pray to the bon Dieu that it will not come to that. But one must always be prepared, especially when we are dealing with someone who has killed twice already.'

'And who's planning to strike again as well?'

'Precisely.'

I ruminated on this point momentarily.

'Has it been only one person all along, Giallo?' I asked. 'This villain we're after?'

Giallo nodded.

'Yes,' he said gravely.'

And tonight I hope we shall finally bring an end to all this madness. The killing of the innocent Estrella in particular was a murder most terrible.'

I agreed wordlessly, uneasiness rising once more within me as I remembered how the maid had died. Surely this villain, whoever he was, had no regard for human life whatsoever – and to think that he was planning to take another's repulsed me entirely. The murderer would have to face the consequences of such acts and I couldn't help feeling delighted that the walls were slowly closing on our so far faceless adversary.

Despite this, and apart from being told to prepare myself, Giallo gave no hint of what he was intending to do and left the villa soon after his interview with Larry.

'What, are you leaving so soon, Giallo?' I asked as he made to leave.

'Staying here until the late evening would only arouse the suspicion, St. Louie,' he replied, a hint of weariness in his voice and I immediately felt a little abashed at not thinking of this.

'But fear not, mon ami, I shall return at nine o'clock when I hope you will quietly let me through the back door.'

'The back door?'

'Exactment. It is vital that I am not seen by anyone entering this house this evening. I trust that the good imagination of my friend St. Louie will decide how best this will be done.'

'Well, of course –' I started, feeling slightly confused at Giallo's course of action, but my friend soon dashed off, leaving me wondering what the evening would bring.

Nine o'clock that evening could not have come slower. Each hour which elapsed seemed ludicrously long, a fact which did not help at all with my growing sense of trepidation.

I scrutinized each face and every face of my companions as we sat down for dinner, even Stanford, who served our various courses with his usual stoic expression.

I ate without paying much attention to what was being served; my thoughts were instead focused on how to get to the back door without arousing too much suspicion.

Much to my relief, everyone retired early, but I could not get to the back of the house at the agreed time as Stanford and Camie kept ongoing back and forth from their rooms. At last, I made my way there without incident at a quarter past nine.

'Good evening, St. Louie,' said Giallo coolly as I let him in.

'I wondered when you would remember that Giallo was waiting in this terrible cold outside.'

The 'terrible cold' he described was really an exaggeration, I thought. It was seventy degrees Fahrenheit; a typical summer's evening.

'Sorry, old fellow,' I replied, unwilling to start a quarrel with him.

'Stanford and Camie kept on coming in and out of the place. I just hope I haven't upset your plans.'

Giallo's expression softened.

'That fortunately, you did not do. But come, mon ami, we have not the time to waste.'

Most of the lights in the house by this time had been put out, and it was in a sort of semi-darkness that we ascended the stairs in silence. I hadn't the least idea where Giallo was going, but I followed him wordlessly, gripping the revolver in my right hand. We appeared to be heading towards the bedrooms in the east wing. We stopped in front of Larry's door. I looked at it in bemusement but before I could say anything, Giallo had opened it and entered the room before pulling me unceremoniously inside with him.

'Giallo, what on earth –?' I whispered as he quietly shut the door behind us, throwing us into darkness which was only penetrated by a slight sliver of moonlight peeking through the gap in the curtains.

'Quiet, mon ami!' he hissed.

His breath was warm near my right cheek, but at that moment, I was not in the mood to appreciate the close and rather intimate proximity of his presence.

'You realize that this is Larry's room?' I went on.

'If he realizes we're here –'

He cut me off.

'He already knows we're here, St. Louie.'

'What?'

'In the morning, I told him to vacate his room this evening. If I am not mistaken, he should now reside in the room next to yours.'

'Those were your instructions to him? To vacate his room and move to another one?'

'Exactment.'

A terrible thought entered my head.

'Good God, Giallo…you don't mean that Larry was to be the next victim?'

'Yes, St. Louie,' replied Giallo gravely.

'And I pray to the bon Dieu that our murderer has detected no change in Monsieur Larry's sleeping arrangements this evening.'

'That utter cad, whoever he is,' I growled.

'So we lie in wait, do we, in this little trap of ours?'

'Yes. I have asked Monsieur Larry to pile up the pillows on his bed beneath the sheets to replicate a human figure. Our murderer will not know the difference in this darkness until they are very close to the bed.'

'And when he tries to do the dastardly deed, we catch him red-handed,' I said, trying in vain to suppress the note of triumph in my voice.

Giallo's voice was sober.

'I hope it will be as easy as you say, St. Louie. But we must be vigilant. Hide yourself behind the door while I shall hide here in the corner.'

We moved silently into our hiding places, and then the waiting began. Minutes once again seemed to crawl by, and it felt like a hundred years had passed when I finally heard the clock downstairs strike midnight.

By this time, I felt tired and worn out; the tension of the past week having built up within me and I wanted nothing more than to go to my room and retire for the night, desiring nothing more than to sleep and for some respite from my state of suspended anxiety regarding my desire for Giallo and the long sought for conclusion of this confounded mystery.

The creaking of the floorboards outside was enough to rouse me back into alertness. I got out of my cross-legged position on the floor and gripped my revolver tightly.

Only the door beside me separated both Giallo and I from the murderer, and I felt my heartbeat faster in anticipation as it was slowly opened, inch by inch. I squeezed my frame behind the door, hoping that I wouldn't be seen, and I darted my head round cautiously to see if I could see Giallo in the darkness but could see no one. It appeared to be an empty room save for the occupant apparently sleeping in his bed, and this was obviously the case with the person who had just entered. The dim light from the corridor outside briefly illuminated their outline before the door was shut, and I could instantly see that it was a man.

Thoughts of endeavoring to select a person from our list of suspects immediately disappeared as I barely made out his figure making his way towards the bed and the unmistakable sound of a revolver being cocked.

'Now, St. Louie!'

It all happened so quickly. One moment I had been near the door and the next I was throwing myself across the room at the man, who was now swathed in moonlight as Giallo pulled the curtains open. The man howled in rage as he pulled one hand over his face, the other raising his gun in my direction.

Before he could pull the trigger, I saw Giallo attempting to disarm him by aiming a sharp blow at the man's gun hand with one of Larry's riding crops.

A loud cry and the revolver fell to the floor. I took this opportunity by reaching forward to seize the man's collar, but a fist came out of nowhere and, though it was intended for me, it hit Giallo directly across the temple and he fell onto the floor.

I cried out, and I brought up my hand holding my own gun, but the fist which had hit Giallo instead lashed out again and I got the full brunt of the blow across my face and in the confusion, I dropped my revolver.

Obviously aware that he was cornered like an animal in a cage, the man accordingly fought with all the strength of one. We were fighting to the death; that I knew for certain once the man's rough hands seized me by the shirtfront and I was thrown headlong into a nearby dressing table.

Objects of all shapes and sizes rained down upon me, shattering deafeningly as they hit the ground.

My head pounding where it had collided with the solid oak, I staggered to my feet and saw with horror that the revolver which had been so recently fixed on me was now aimed at Giallo, who still remained motionless on the floor.

'No!'

Without a second thought for my own safety, I flung myself upon the man and as I did so, a loud retort erupted from the deadly piece of metal. A sharp pain pierced my left arm, and we both fell heavily to the ground, the murderer evidently being taken by surprise.

Swearing lowly, he pushed me hard off him and I landed hard on my injured arm. I cried out in pain and a wave of sickening nausea rose in my throat.

Despite this, I scrambled to right myself to fend him off, looking desperately for my fallen revolver. But it was too late for I realized he had got to his gun before me and I could only helplessly watch as he aimed it at my defenseless chest.

'It all ends here, Mr St. Louie,' said the man, and I recognized the voice immediately.

'Mallon!' I cried.

'You've hit the nail right on the head, old fellow,' the man replied mockingly, and stepped calmly into the space where the moonlight pooled on the carpet.

'This time you've outsmarted your friend here for once.' He smirked derisively.

'Though I think you've little time to savior the accomplishment.'

'You devil,' I managed, my voice surprisingly betraying none of the fear which was clawing away at my heart.

'You won't get away with this, you know.'
Even as the words left my lips, I knew they sounded foolish. I was all alone now and if help was to be obtained, it would be much too late and the rage and fear I had felt on seeing Giallo collapse onto the floor, either alive or dead, I did not know, returned once more.

'Always the typical English gentleman to the last. Brave, but unbelievably stupid. I knew you wouldn't disappoint.'

I braced myself and shut my eyes.
This was the end…
The gun went off.

But to my astonishment, the fatal bullet I had been expecting never struck. Instead, there was only a faint gasp of pain, followed seconds later by the unmistakable sound of someone crashing heavily onto the floor.

It was at least a few heart-pounding moments before I even dared to open my eyes, unable to believe that I was still alive. Breathing hard, I opened them to see the gardener in a crumpled heap before me. He lay still and not moving, and it was clear that he was stone dead, a small patch of blood seeping through the back of his shirt.

It was not this sight, however, which overwhelmed me with relief; it was the sight of the man standing unsteadily behind him, my revolver gripped tightly in his right hand.
Giallo.

Uncharacteristically ruffled and clearly still shaken but very much alive – as was I it seemed.

His attention appeared to be focused entirely on the dead man, but when my sigh of relief filled that now silent room, his gaze fixed upon me instead.

'St. Louie,' he said, moving towards me, his face quite pale in the half-light. There was an odd expression on his face as he looked at me, his brown eyes shining even in the darkness.

'We did it, Giallo,' I said breathlessly.
'We did it.'

'St. Louie,' Giallo said again. There was something odd in his voice too, which was rough with some strange emotion which I had never heard before.

But I did not have time to dwell on it, for it was at the moment that I fell back fainting, pain and exhaustion overwhelming me at last.

Chapter 12

The Missing Link

I came back to the world painfully and slowly; it was half a day before I finally regained consciousness. When I awoke, I found myself in my bed, my left arm bandaged up and aching badly, but fortunately it seemed I had survived my confrontation with Mallon relatively unscathed. The entire house apparently had rushed to Larry's room the moment they heard the gunshots. There was much consternation over the sight of the dead gardener, but I was touched to learn from Larry that Giallo had resolutely ignored the body until a doctor was called for to tend to my injury.

'You're lucky, Monsieur St. Louie,' said Flexthure as the gruff sergeant made a surprise visit to my room. 'The doctor says that the bullet went clean through your arm, hitting nothing important. Monsieur Giallo sent me up to see how you are progressing,' he added, as he took in my bemused expression. His manner towards me was much improved since our last meeting and he was genuinely concerned about my well-being. His last words, however, emphasized the absence of my friend, which I felt quite keenly.

'Where is Giallo?'

'He is in Paris, tending to the paperwork of this case. For us, it is much easier if our criminal is captured rather than killed, but seeing that Monsieur Mallon was on the point of killing the both of you, Monsieur Giallo had to do what was necessary.'

I remembered Giallo mentioning that he had had to shoot a man down once before, describing it as one of the low points of his career. I could clearly see how desperate the situation was and wondered what my friend must have gone through before pulling the trigger to save my life. Regardless, I had to admit that I felt my heart sink a little at the thought of paperwork apparently being more important in his eyes than myself. I am not the most demanding of invalids – and I can assure people I am not in the habit of usually making myself one – but I had rather hoped that it was Giallo instead of the sergeant paying me a visit.

'But do not think that the good Chief Detective Inspector has disappeared, Monsieur St. Louie,' added Flexthure suddenly, and I looked up at him in surprise.

'He plans to call upon the villa the day after tomorrow. It is not over yet.'

And indeed, it was not as I was to learn later during the many cases in which I was to take part in the following years. Giallo is not the type of person to leave cases lying about without a denouement. No, that is not his way. Regardless of him protesting the contrary, he has a flair for the dramatic and the conclusion of this particular case is indeed one of the few which truly shocked me.

Despite protestations from all sides, I was determined to see the case through to the end. With my arm placed carefully into a sling, I joined the others who had already been assembled in the sitting room on that bright summer afternoon. The family, Stanford, Camie and even Cliffberg, was present along with Sergeant Flexthure and a couple of constables who stood near the doorway.

All eyes turned to examine me and Giallo's face was grave as he watched me take my place. I gave him a small smile, which he returned, albeit appearing slightly strained.

I had no time to dwell on this, however, as he soon spoke.

'Mesdames and messieurs,' he said, his manner not unlike a professor about to give a lecture. 'It has now been nearly a month since I was called upon by my country to investigate the death of Sir Charles Stow. At the beginning, it appeared simple enough. A case of suicide, they said. After all, suicides are not uncommon among those in the diplomatic corps, are they not?'

The man had been found locked in his study, the key was found under his desk, and a revolver lay by his left hand, which made sense as he was left-handed. There seemed to be no sign of a struggle.

'All seemed perfectly clear and logical and there seemed no need to contest the idea of suicide.'

He paused, looking about his audience, which was listening with rapt attention.

'I then examined the room where the body had been found and realized that there were certain points, certain details there which did not seem right. For example, the bell pull which did not ring, the mysterious cup of coffee which no one remembers ever bringing to the study and St. Louie' revolver which had been found next to the body but which we later discovered was not the weapon used to inflict the wound in Sir Charles's head.'

'After another examination, more curious clues were to be found; a trace of gunpowder on the window sill, coffee spilled not only on the carpet but onto the flowerbeds outside and then the bullet found in the garden below...non, it was now clear that it was not a suicide we were investigating but a murder.

'But everybody knows that a murder needs a motive and so it was at this point that we looked around,' he said as he suited the action to his word, casting his eyes over us.'

However, before we discuss motives, we must reconstruct the events of that night and, after questioning each one of you, I believe I can more or less recount them with accuracy. At eight o'clock, an argument breaks out between Larry Stokes and his father at dinner. Sir Charles has somehow been informed of his son's secret engagement to Samantha Milton and they later move into the library.

At half-past nine, Mademoiselle Samantha retires to her room, as do Mesdemoiselles Ella and Janett and Messieurs Mc Cloud and Grimms twenty minutes later. St. Louie remains in the drawing room, waiting for his friend to come out of the library. He waits however, in vain and at half past ten, he goes up to his room. A quarter of an hour later, both Sir Charles and Monsieur Wiggins leave the library and go their separate ways.

'Monsieur Wiggins however, in dire need of someone to talk to soon enlists the company of his friend St. Louie, who lets him into his room at around eleven o'clock.'

"They talked for about an hour. Monsieur Bentely is understandably upset and angry, no doubt fueled by the drink he has recently consumed and talks of taking St. Louie' revolver to his father's room and to quote, "to blow his brains out there and then."

'Really, Monsieur Giallo,' said Ella heatedly.

'Don't you think that my brother's had enough of this?'

'I apologize, Mademoiselle Wiggins,' said Giallo with a slight bow of the head. 'But these are the facts I am presenting, and it is a fact that your brother alas selected a poor choice of words that night.'

'It's all right, Ella,' said Larry calmly.'

'Giallo's right, I have to admit. Please continue, monsieur.'

'Much alarmed by his friend's state of mind, St. Louie helps him back to his room. Returning to his own a couple of minutes later, he assures himself that his revolver is still in his possession and retires.'

He cannot go to sleep immediately and only does so after one o'clock, vaguely noting a popping noise somewhere nearby. The next morning, I am certain, you can all recall very well. Everyone awakes, Monsieur Wiggins being the first to rise at six, and all are assembled at the breakfast table by nine. Only Sir Charles is nowhere to be seen. Steps are immediately taken to find out his whereabouts, and he is soon found by St. Louie along with Messieurs Wiggins and Mc Cloud in his study.'

'Yes, we all know this,' said Tim Mac David, with obvious irritation. 'We've covered this before at the inquest. We now know that Sir Charles was done to death by that fiend Mallon at one o'clock in the morning. The crucial question we want answered, Giallo, is why on earth he did it.'

If Giallo was indignant at being so rudely interrupted, he made no sign of being so.

'Thank you, Monsieur Grimms,' came the polite and cool reply. 'I was about to come to that point. Mallon, I am certain that you all agree, would have been the last person one would have any reason to kill Sir Charles, who is, after all, his employer. Killing one's employer makes little sense other than the possibility of Sir Charles having found out something unsavory about the gardener. Perhaps Mallon had stolen something from the house, even from his employer's private possessions.'

'I wouldn't be at all surprised if that was the case,' said Grimms and looking at all the faces in the room, it was obvious that most agreed with him on this point.

'Mallon did not have the qualities to commend himself to anyone,' continued Giallo.' He was obnoxious and insolent and many of the mesdemoiselles here suffered under his boorish behavior. Yet until the moment of Sir Charles's death, and even afterwards, he was still employed at the house.

For Sir Charles, Mallon allowed him to save money and, more importantly, he was English, which always made a difference to Sir Charles's insular mind. If the gardener had indeed been caught stealing, the entire household would have immediately known of it in view of the British ambassador's personality. Sir Charles was a man of the navy, a man of discipline despite his faults, and it is doubtful that he would have allowed a thief to serve at his house longer than necessary.'

'He might have been blackmailed by Mallon to keep his peace though,' I offered, the thought leaping suddenly into my mind.

'And we caught him burning those diaries.'

'Diaries?' said Larry in bemusement. 'What diaries?'

'Your mother kept diaries, did she not, Monsieur Wiggins?' asked Giallo.

'Well, yes. Father kept them here in Paris, as he thought it wouldn't do to leave them in England while he wasn't there.

You don't mean to say that devil Mallon somehow got his hands on them and started threatening my father with them?' cried Larry, outraged.

'But what on earth was there to find in them? Mother rarely commented on anything other than the things she did with us or the friends she met. She was never interested in politics or what Father did at the Foreign Office.'

'Calm yourself, monsieur. Blackmail though, once a possibility in my mind was never considered.

However, there was something in one of those diaries which either Mallon or someone else did not want anyone to find.'

It was as if a great weight had suddenly befallen the occupants of that sitting room. Giallo never chose his words lightly, and the implication that there was still someone other than Mallon involved in this terrible affair was lost upon us.

'Yes, Mallon was not working alone. There is still among you an accomplice, mesdames and messieurs.'

'Preposterous,' muttered Grimms.

'As unlikely as it might seem, Monsieur Grimms, I would like you to spare me some more of your time in listening to what I have to say,' said Giallo sharply. This time he made his displeasure at being contradicted piercingly clear.
The barrister kept his peace.

'From the beginning, all the evidence seemed to point towards Monsieur Larry Stokes murdering his father.
He of all those present in this room, had the most reasons to kill his father. After all, he had been denied permission to marry the woman he loved and had been given the choice of either marrying her or losing his inheritance.
You wished for your father's death, did you not, monsieur?'
Larry's composure, which had remained composed throughout, slipped somewhat as Giallo pivoted towards him.

'I do not deny that I wished him dead that evening,' he said, his face paling. 'But as God's my witness, Monsieur Giallo, I swear I didn't kill him. Foolish thoughts passed through my drunken head that evening, but I swear that I had no intention of putting them into action.'
Giallo examined him closely.

'Monsieur Wiggins here speaks the truth. From the start, he pleaded his innocence and two nights ago, an attempt on his life was made. In my experience, even the most enterprising of murderers rarely put their lives at risk to prove their innocence. Therefore, Monsieur Wiggins did not murder his father. But someone in this room did desire to give the impression that he committed the crime.'

'So my belief that I was being framed was correct all along?' asked Larry.

'Oui, most certainly. Someone was determined to see you hanged for a crime you did not commit. Someone who, rather than Mallon, was the real mastermind of this terrible affair.'
Giallo was pacing the room now, looking at each of our faces intently, faces which were now full of fear and trepidation.

'Mallon was merely the puppet, the servant whom his master used to achieve their ends. But even Mallon was not entirely guiltless; he had his own accounts to settle. Especially against you, did he not, Monsieur Stanford?'

Our eyes flew to Stanford, who appeared startled at being so called out. The elderly butler's expression was still one of customary calm, but the pallor of his face told us otherwise and he suddenly appeared much older.

'Stanford? What's all this about?' asked Larry.

'I think we should let him sit down,' said Samantha in concern. A chair was duly proffered and Stanford sank gratefully into it. As I gazed into his face, I realized that the man Mallon had reminded me of in the conservatory all those weeks ago was none other than the butler himself.

'Mallon...he was your nephew, was he not Stanford?'

For the first time in my entire acquaintance with him, I believe I saw emotion welling up behind that usually expressionless façade.

'Yes. He was my nephew, sir. He was my sister's son – born out of wedlock. His father was divorced at the time of his birth, but I forbade Emma to marry him. I simply wouldn't hear of it; it was scandalous enough for a child to be born out of wedlock and our family reputation was already ruined because of it. As I was head of the family and because I had always been her favorite brother who she looked almost to as a father, she gave in to my request and broke off all connection to the gentleman.

'All seemed settled, sir. My sister and the boy moved in to live with our mother in Kent. But I didn't foresee the difficulties we would face while he was growing up.'

I asked Emma to give him the surname of Mallon, a name which had been part of our family on our mother's side, but this only alienated the boy. Once he found out that I had been the reason he had had no father to bring him up, he hated me. And when Emma died when he turned seventeen, he blamed me for her untimely death and ran away.

'I didn't hear from him until last year when he sent me a letter informing me he was out of work, had travelled to the Continent and that he required a post.'

'His work, it was in the theatre, was it not?'

The butler was startled once again and he stammered, 'But that's right, sir. How did you?'
My thoughts immediately flew to the request given to Inspector Zane and the subsequent telegram received only days before. Giallo however, only replied: 'I have my methods, Monsieur Stanford. Please continue.'

'As it was, sir, Sir Charles often explained to me the need for a new gardener and I sent John a letter asking him whether he would like to be employed here. I didn't expect a reply; he was never one for manual labor but a week later, I received a letter from him and within three weeks, he was installed here.'
He broke off.

'If I knew what would happen after he came, sir, I would never have answered him.'

'Do not derange yourself. You are not to blame for your nephew's actions. And did your relations improve with your estranged nephew?'

'I regret to say that they didn't improve in the least.
I see now that my choices were not the wisest, and perhaps I had been too unyielding. Perhaps it was this which persuaded me to help him in his time of need, but even after his arrival here, it was clear that he still resented me.'

'Thank you, Stanford,' said Giallo, clearly appreciating the butler's honesty.

'So we have here a nephew and uncle; the former who cannot overcome his hatred for his elderly uncle and the latter who realizing his past misjudgments tries to make amends. Attempts at reconciliation fail and Mallon, still full of resentment, decides to put his considerable dramatic talents to work during this whole affair.'

'I'm sorry, Monsieur Giallo, but I don't quite follow,' said Larry. 'How does Mallon, being an actor, have anything to do with my father's death?'

'It has everything to do with it, Monsieur Wiggins. One question which has been constantly asked these past few weeks is how did the murderer, or in this case, Mallon, ever enter the room without causing alarm to Sir Charles?'

'One possibility was through the window behind the desk, but seeing that the study was at least seventy feet from the ground, I doubt that any man would have been able to climb up the walls unseen. No, the only possible way was simply through the study door.'

'But my father would have thrown him out of the room the moment he walked through that door.'

'Yes,' agreed Giallo. 'Without a doubt, Mallon would have immediately been turned out of the room had he come as himself. But in this instance, he did not come as himself. He instead appeared in the garb of his elderly uncle with his face made up and aged, a grey wig perhaps concealing his fair hair and carrying a cup of coffee for his master while the real Stanford was asleep at his desk, his evening cocoa having been quietly drugged by his nephew after dinner.'

'Impossible!' exclaimed Tom.

'In a bright room and a victim with perfect eyesight, yes, it would have been nearly impossible to deceive anyone for long with such an outfit. But Mallon had studied Sir Charles' arrangements well; the study lit only by candlelight, the thick spectacles which the middle-aged man had to wear in order to see anything properly. And being the consummate actor that he is, to mimic his uncle's voice – it was simply too easy for him. It was a merely a game. What a wonderful joke it would be to incriminate his hated uncle in such a way while fulfilling the orders he had been given.'

'The risk the man took!' I gasped.

'Yes, a risk it was indeed. But he was confident that his disguise would work. It had worked after all on the poor maid, Estrella, who had been taken in by it even when she encountered this Stanford in the house at two in the morning a month before the murder took place.'

'My poor sister!' cried Camie suddenly when Flexthure had finished translating Giallo's last sentence to her.

'She saw through his disguise in the end. That was the reason that monster of a man killed her!' She broke off here, and the sergeant looked half torn between pity and discomfort as she sobbed noisily on his shoulder.

'C'est vrai. Estrella saw through his disguise and was later silenced in the most terrible of ways after the inquest,' said Giallo sadly.

'But on this particular evening, everything, by contrast, progresses smoothly. Mallon enters the room without incident. Sir Charles is perhaps too deep in thought regarding his recent argument with his son and absent-mindedly gestures for his coffee to be put on his desk, not detecting any change in his butler's appearance. Mallon obediently comes forward, leans behind Sir Charles, extracts the silenced gun he has been hiding behind his back and shoots him in the head. Sir Charles falls forward dead and the key to his study, which has been on his desk, falls onto the floor. His goal accomplished, Mallon carefully wipes off his fingerprints and places the gun next to Sir Charles's body.'

Wishing to make it indisputable that his uncle was the last person in the room before Sir Charles's death but unwilling to drink the coffee himself, he instead throws it out of the window – some of which spills onto the windowsill – before replacing the cup onto its saucer. He then exits the study, locking it behind him so that the body is not to be discovered until much later.'

'But what about my revolver, Giallo?' I asked. It was only one of the many questions now swirling about my head. 'How did Mallon get hold of it?'

'Ah, we come now to the role played by our yet unknown accomplice, or rather, the true architect of this entire scheme. It was this person, not Mallon, who obtained your revolver and left it to be found the next morning.'

'But Sir Charles was dead. Their goal was accomplished. Why was there any need to change revolvers?'

'Because the death of Sir Charles was only their secondary goal. His death was of course, necessary, but it was secondary compared to the overriding need to implicate Monsieur Wiggins in this crime.'

'But why?'

'Because Larry Stokes was never Sir Charles Stow's son.'

The silence in the room was appalling. Shock permeated our very beings at this fantastical statement. Our combined stares directed themselves to Giallo, judging perhaps that the little man had taken leave of his senses. I was tempted to share this opinion but held back, for I knew he was rarely ever mistaken despite the sheer audacity of this declaration.

Larry was the first to speak.

'What do you mean, Monsieur Giallo?' he asked, his voice trembling as he rose from his seat.'
Giallo gazed at him intently before turning his attention to the German ambassador, who looked as pale as Larry now.
'Monsieur?' said Giallo simply.
Cliffberg's grey eyes darted nervously between Giallo and Larry as he sat there almost petrified in his chair. As with belatedly recognizing Stanford in Mallon's face, I suddenly saw another face reflected in Cliffberg's. Realization dawned upon me once again and my astonished thoughts were confirmed when he spoke.

'I was engaged to be married to Lady Elizabeth nearly thirty years ago. She was Elizabeth Colville at the time and I loved her as deeply as she did me,' he said slowly.

'However, I could never compare to a Commander of the Royal Navy in her father's eyes and I was thus ordered to break off our engagement. I refused and so did Elizabeth, who I believe was prepared to follow me wherever I went, but when Sir Garnet Wolseley threatened to break off all contact with his daughter, I knew I had to let her go. It is true that I had a degree from Cambridge, but I was only beginning my diplomatic career then and I had no guarantee that I would be able to offer her a life which I knew she deserved. It was one of the most painful experiences of my life, but we went our separate ways and I heard she married six months after we parted.'

'I rose steadily through the ranks of my profession, regretting more than ever that I had let her go. I read and heard from various sources that she was not happy in her marriage to Sir Charles. Despite this, I never dared to contact her. About three years after her marriage, I found myself posted in London for a temporary stay for about four weeks. Then –'

'Yes, Monsieur vann Cliffberg?'
Cliffberg inhaled deeply, then continued.

'Then one evening Elizabeth came to visit me at my quarters. She had heard of my arrival from her husband's friends at the British Embassy and discovered where I was staying.'
As Sir Charles was not in town, I accompanied her to the opera and then to dinner. I was determined not to let myself be taken away with my still very considerable feelings for her and endeavored to keep our relationship strictly platonic.

But it all fell to pieces when she became hysterical when I offered to escort her back home.

'She said that she would rather die than spend one more night at her husband's house and, reluctantly, I took her to my quarters. I sometimes wish I never did. We talked of many things; she of her lonely existence with a husband who could never appreciate or understand her and I of my work and travels. One thing led to another and then...'
He trailed off, appearing lost in memories.

'It only happened once; that I promise you. We were both equally aghast after we realized what we had done.
The rest of my stay in London was mostly filled with social gatherings where I met her as Lady Wiggins and not as Elizabeth Wolseley. But that was not to be the end of our discretion. A week later my arrival in Paris, she wrote to me saying that she was with child. I knew the child was mine and not Sir Charles's.'
He looked tentatively at Larry, who appeared absolutely dumbfounded. 'And I still know now.'

'But being posted to other countries did not stop you from visiting Lady Wiggins, Monsieur vann Cliffberg?'

'No. Love does not let go of the heart so easily, Monsieur Giallo. I visited her every year, secretly, of course...except the year in which she died. I was a month too late,' he said with great regret.'

'My God,' managed Larry as he lowered himself into his chair again, staring at Cliffberg.

'That's why you were at the inquest. It wasn't for him...it was for me.'

'You never doubted your parentage, Monsieur Wiggins?' said Giallo gently.

'Of course I didn't. I never did.'
It was painfully clear that Larry was speaking the truth, and Giallo's face was wholly sympathetic. His expression hardened rapidly however, when he said.

'Yes, you never doubted your parentage, Monsieur Wiggins. But unfortunately, there was someone who did and lost no time in taking advantage of it once they had discovered the truth.'

'Oh, for heaven's sake, Monsieur Giallo,' cried Ella, rising to her feet. She was evidently taking the latest news regarding Larry as hard as her brother was doing.'

'Haven't we had enough of this shilly-shallying about? Can't you tell us once and for all who the "mastermind" of this entire thing is?'

Giallo turned sharply towards her.

'With pleasure, mademoiselle,' he said coldly. 'It was you.'

Ella's face was expressionless.

'Me?' she enquired. She gave a short laugh.

'How ludicrous.'

'Indeed, Mademoiselle Wiggins? Is it ludicrous that while you were valiantly "putting on the brave face" as the English call it, you were actually longing to have your father's fortune passed on to yourself? Non, for despite all your declarations, it is actually quite the contrary.

You lead the bohemian life, mademoiselle, and with the little annuity that your father provides, it is not enough to fund your habits. Soon you are accumulating debts, both here on the Continent and in London and on which I have received reports from my colleagues across Europe.

'You are desperate to find a solution and hence you agree to marry Monsieur Grimms who being a barrister, will of course provide you the money that you need.'

'Really, monsieur. I believe you're quite out of your mind,' said Ella. Her voice was deceptively light, but there was an edge to it which made one extremely uncomfortable. Grimms too, had risen from his chair now and was striding towards Giallo in the most aggressive manner imaginable.

'Look here, Giallo. We've heard quite a lot of nonsense being passed about this afternoon, but this is simply the limit. It's libel, you understand, sir?

One more word and –'

'I believe not,' said Giallo and he continued as if he had never been interrupted.'

'But then it becomes increasingly clear that Monsieur Grimms is a man that you cannot stand. You grow impatient, you need to find a way to make money which can wholly be yours to keep and spend as you wish. You look through your mother's belongings, no doubt wondering whether she will have anything else of value which you have not already sold or pawned.'

You find nothing but stumble across a certain entry in your mother's diary. The implication of one particular sentence, one particular choice of words catches your eye...'

Giallo brandished the diary in question from an inner pocket and read.

'My dearest boy is turning eighteen tomorrow. Has it really been eighteen years? – What happiness indeed. Stanford has, of course, seen to all the arrangements; I wonder where we all would be without him. I must make the most of tomorrow; though Dr Varrus assures me that the illness will not return within the next year or so, I feel my days are growing short. I feel it in my very bones. Received a letter yesterday morning; his father writes that his duties will keep him abroad until October at the very least.

Only four months! But alas, four months seem almost an eternity now...

'There is perhaps nothing of note to observe here. The late Lady Wiggins is referring to Sir Charles. But it is unusual, is it not, to call her own husband as "his father"? Surely it would have been simpler to call him by his Christian name, as Charles or as perhaps "W."

'No, it was not Sir Charles Stow whom she was referring to here. It was the man who she loved nearly all her life and the true father of her son, Vondick vann Cliffberg.'

Most would not see the implication, but it cannot deceive you, mademoiselle, for you know, as I do now, that the whole family, including Sir Charles, was present at Monsieur Larry's eighteenth birthday.

'Now armed with the knowledge of your half-brother's illegitimacy and all sisterly affection vanishing from your heart, you devise a plan for not only your father's demise but also your half-brother's eventual one by the gallows. But first you need an accomplice to help you in your terrible scheme. This is not difficult; it is easy to seduce the new gamekeeper who is clearly attracted to you, and he willingly joins you, especially when it means that he can implicate his hated uncle. Everyone is taken in by the apparent conflict between you and Mallon, failing to see two actors behind the façade. Mallon's experiment with Estrella proves a success and soon you put your plan into action, first with the sending of an anonymous note to Sir Charles of Monsieur Larry's secret engagement.'

Sir Charles expectedly breaks into a fury and threatens openly to cut off his son without a penny. No better motive could have been concocted than this for his wanting to kill his father. The scene too, with the broken vase the night of your father's death, was simply a sham and planned in advance.'

'What complete nonsense.'

'At ten to eleven, you knock over the vase, the sound of which is certain to wake Janett in the other room and Mallon just returned from killing your father arrives to play his part. You have the mock quarrel which Janett naturally overhears.'

'Thus doing so you provide yourselves with alibis for no one is ever to doubt that you spent the rest of the night in your room with the door locked or that Mallon was at his cottage at one o'clock in the morning when the "real" moment of Sir Charles's death is to take place...when the last unwitting witness of this whole affair makes his appearance.'

'She sent that note to me?' cried Cliffberg, and I swiftly recalled the crumpled up note I had found near the front gate.

'But why?'

'Because she discovered your connection to your son, monsieur. No one heard what was said in that library that night. Sir Charles and Monsieur Larry's argument might have easily been over the latter's illegitimacy and Sir Charles using it as another reason to take away his inheritance. As it was, the ambassador never doubted that he was his father and died believing this was the case. Regardless, Mademoiselle Wiggins needed assurance that Larry's guilt would never be questioned and warned you of the event to take place at the villa that night. She predicted your response perfectly, and you arrived at the appointed time when both you and St. Louie heard the shot of the revolver.'

Giallo paused here, and I saw that the entire room's attention was concentrated on Ella, who merely was smiling at him in detached amusement. 'And it was the revolver which proved your undoing, mademoiselle. Your idea was undoubtedly clever, but alas, too ambitious. No doubt you wished to take advantage of Monsieur Larry's careless remark of wanting to kill your father with St. Louie' revolver when you overheard it by chance in the corridor. It was of course, an opportunity not to be missed and it would be evidence of the most damning kind.

'You take the revolver in their temporary absence, replacing it with the one you have already obtained from your father's study before returning to your own room.'

St. Louie returns, mistakes the gun in his drawer as his own and retires for the night. When it is one o'clock and you see the German Ambassador, appear at the front gate, you fire the Webley out of the window, the bullet of which is later found in the garden.

'Yes, your little spontaneous afterthought would have indeed worked – had it not been for that fact that the Nagant and the Webley are of two completely different calibres.'

'Well done, Monsieur Giallo,' said Ella frigidly after a long silence. 'I must admit you figured out this little plan of mine very well indeed. What may I ask, was it that finally gave me away?'

'The note you dropped in the garden, mademoiselle.'

She scoffed, tossing her head back contemptuously.

'So late, monsieur? I thought you would have suspected me sooner. I should have destroyed Mallon's note the moment I read it. Trust him to have gone and got himself killed.'

She stepped closer towards him.

'But you're no better than him or I, Monsieur Giallo. For I think this is the second time you've taken away someone's life, isn't it?'

Giallo's face paled with anger.

'I cannot think how you can even begin to compare my actions with yours or Monsieur Mallon's, Mademoiselle Wiggins.'

'Indeed? I think it is only natural to compare them.'

'Surely the thought must have occurred to those little grey cells of yours,' replied Ella as she put up no resistance as Sergeant Flexthure clasped a pair of handcuffs to her wrists.

'You're a murderer, sir. Just like so many of the criminals you've arrested and by God, I hope you burn in hell like the rest of them.'

Giallo remained silent and nodded at the sergeant who led her out, followed by the constables.

Ella's departure from the room allowed my attention to return to those who still remained in their seats. Shock was the single expression shared by all of those present in the room though in varying degrees and Larry appeared to be the most stricken of them all and I felt nothing but pity for my friend who had the misfortune of having to endure such a variety of developments in dizzying succession.

The next unexpected development however came as a gunshot from outside and as Flexthure rushed hastily back into the room, Giallo was ready for him.

'It is Mademoiselle Wiggins, yes?' he said simply.

The sergeant nodded, and he pulled out the missing Nagant revolver.

'She hid it under her clothing, Monsieur Giallo. We tried to stop her, but it was too late.'

Giallo gazed at the gun humorlessly and lowered his head.

'It is over.'

Chapter 13

To Part and to Love

It is over. Those were the very words Giallo had said. It was not only the case which had preoccupied our minds and energy for the past month, which was over, but so was my time here. Soon, I would have to return to my job at Christie's and leave the city. I did not mind leaving Paris; the business which had occurred here had left a bitter taste in my mouth and though Sir Charles had not been a generous, kind-hearted man, his death had been undeserved…especially at the hands of his own daughter and her lover.
A shiver ran down my spine at the very thought of my own sisters taking part in such a horrendous scheme.
Half of me though wanted to remain here in the hope of a desire which, alas I could only dream of being fulfilled. The hope that Giallo might come to regard me as the way I did him, but memories of that overheard exchange in the garden kept returning and I knew it was foolish to continue in this manner. However, I could not help remembering some lines I had come across in a novel some years previously:
It isn't possible to love and part. You will wishthat it was. You can transmute love, ignore it, muddle it, however, can never pull it out of you.
'I know by experience that the poets are right: love is eternal.' I thought it summarized my feelings entirely.
It appeared very much that I would have no choice but to love and part and I looked in my mind's eye upon the forthcoming

weeks, possibly even years of transmuting, ignoring and muddling my feelings, which lay ahead of me with no great satisfaction. There were other ways, of course, of satisfying one's desire for another's embrace – many men of my kind have done so before – but it would be no replacement for the embrace of the man who I wanted most of all.

Setting aside my own disappointment, I hoped that something good would at least arise after the tumultuous events of the past month.

And such an event occurred for three days after the case had been concluded that Larry came up to me and said in subdued tones that he and Samantha were finally to marry. He had thought long and hard on the matter, wondering whether it would be tasteless to marry so soon after a long string of tragedies.

'But I do so want to get it over and done with, for all our sakes,' he said.

'I don't think I can stand another week in Paris, St. Louie; too many awful memories. But neither can I bear the thought of leaving without being finally married to dear Samantha.'

'I don't think it is tasteless at all Larry. It's admittedly a little against the norm, but after such an awful month, no one would blame you for wanting some good to come out of all this.'

Nodding, he then spoke of both his and Samantha's plans. Gone were the wishes for a lavish celebration and it was evident that Larry was very much inclined to have a quiet ceremony at the town hall, an idea which I supported wholeheartedly.

'St. Louie, I wonder too if you'd be the best man. It's the least I could do after –' He gestured a little guiltily at my injured arm.

'My dear fellow, you needn't put the blame on yourself about this,' I said.

'If there's anyone to blame, it would be myself.'

He passed me a grateful smile.

'You needn't do anything in particular,' said Larry.

'Just keeping the ring for safekeeping till the ceremony and all that. Of course, I'm certain that it will be far from what you'd normally expect – '

I cut him off, smiling kindly at him.

'There is nothing in the world which would delight me more.

'I'd be honored to be the best man.'

The wedding took place the following week, three days before I was about to return to London. The ceremony was modest and subdued according to the newlyweds' wishes, and the group of invitees amassed that morning was indeed a small one. There was Stanford dressed in his usual black, a distraught-looking Grimms who looked as if he barely knew where he was, Vondick vann Cliffberg who initially wanted to sit apart from the others but was persuaded by Larry to sit with the rest of the family, Tom in his naval uniform, a radiant Janett and next to her, Giallo who watched the proceedings with obvious satisfaction.

A dozen or more so other guests were also in attendance, and I recognized some of them as Larry's relatives, but I ignored them; my attention instead was fixed wholly on Giallo and the small smile he gave each time Janett leaned forward and murmured something into his ear.

So engrossed was I that as I stood in my place by Larry during the ceremony, I nearly missed my cue when it was time for me to produce the ring. The nerves which assailed me along with the lingering uncertainty and depression whenever I had seen Giallo and Janett in each other's company returned with a vengeance, and it took all my willpower not to leave immediately after the ceremony.

However, I had made a promise to see both Larry and Samantha off as they prepared to leave Paris for Paris by train that same evening and I kept to my word.

'It is an event most wonderful, is it not, Monami?' asked Giallo as he stood beside me at the station, observing the newlyweds as they got into their train.

'Even more so when it comes to all these awful happenings.'

'Yes.' There was a thoughtful pause.

'Have you ever considered marriage, my friend?'

I turned to him a little more sharply than I had intended.

'Marriage, Giallo? Why no – I haven't.'

An immense fear was rushing through my veins, and my heart rate quickened. Could it be that Giallo and Janett had come to some arrangement in the light of Larry and Samantha's nuptials? I glanced at my friend's face and saw that he was watching me with a curious expression on his face.

'Your family, they do not arrange a marriage for you?'

'Well, they tried in the past,' I admitted.

Being the only son in the family had its share of disadvantages and I recalled the various ways in which my father had tried to cajole me into marrying ladies of what he called 'good stock'. Suffice it to say, it all ended in disappointment for him, and I told Giallo so.

'Ah,' said Giallo, nodding. I had the sudden impression that he was considering his words very carefully, as if treading on delicate ground.

'And you, Giallo?' I asked quickly, eager to turn the question back on him.

'Is there anyone you'd like to be betrothed to?'

If he was going to be married, I judged that it would be better to learn of it sooner rather than later.

He looked up at me at this and as our eyes made contact; I was taken aback by the intensity in his dark brown eyes.

The entire world suddenly seemed to fall away as we held each other's gaze. That look in his eyes I had seen it before in the aftermath of my fight with Mallon and despite my doubts over his relationship with Janett, surely the look Giallo was bestowing on me could certainly not be mistaken for anything else but –

The shrill blast of the station master's whistle was enough to destroy the moment, and Giallo turned away from me.

He appeared to recollect himself and without another word; he made his way to the front of the train where Larry and Samantha were saying their farewells.

That look stayed in my thoughts in the days prior to my departure for London, and I ruminated long and hard over the meaning of it. I was a novice in the ways of love but that expression of such intensity and yet such tenderness…surely, unless I was very much mistaken, that was a look of love if I ever

I saw one and I endeavored to convince myself, futile as it was, that it was not one that mere friends bestowed on each other but one given to a lover.

However, I dared not to delude myself with false hopes and I deliberately kept to myself, for it was just as well since I had many things to attend to before returning home.

Larry had extended his hospitality to me regardless of his absence and I enjoyed the solitude, taking time to read the letters my sisters had sent me and which I had neglected over the past month. Their letters reminded me of a country I had left only weeks before and yet it seemed far off, as if it had been another life. Returning to my work at Christie's seemed strange and unappealing. France had changed me – for better or worse, I still did not know.

The day before I was to leave Paris, I received a note from Giallo declaring his intention of inviting me to dinner later that evening. I held the piece of notepaper with Giallo's neat and precise handwriting for a full minute, deliberating whether I should give an excuse and forgo the added torture of seeing him. I must admit outright that the option was extremely tempting. The train was leaving at eleven the next morning, after all – and I could easily say that my schedule was much too tight and that I could hardly find any time to meet him.

However, I knew deep down that this was unfair to the little man who had, after all, taught me so much and had borne my somewhat naïve brand of character throughout the whole affair. He had given me a great deal of freedom where criminal investigation was concerned; an opportunity which was rare to come by, particularly for an amateur like myself. Also, I could hardly blame him for having made me fall in love with him. That was my doing, entirely my own and therefore my problem. Writing a hasty but friendly acceptance of his invitation, I gave my note to the waiting message boy before returning to my room. There I continued my packing and waited for the next day and the things to come.

I arrived at his rooms just on time and Giallo nodded in approval as he opened the door.

'Your timing is impeccable, St. Louie. Half past seven exactly,' he announced, glancing at his pocket watch.

I smiled and stepped inside Giallo's flat, wondering at the back of my mind if this was to be the last time I would see the place.

'Thank you,' I said as he handed me a glass of pastis which I knew the French and possibly the French were very fond of, but I had never really taken to the drink.

However, I sipped it out of politeness.

I imagined he was inviting to me to dinner in a restaurant of some sort and I said, 'It's very kind of you, you know, but there's really no need to invite me...I'll foot my share of the bill.'

'Non, non. There is no need of the footing of the bill, for everything has already been prepared.'

'Prepared?'

'Just so. Of course, there are still a couple of things I need to attend to, but that should not take more than a quarter of an hour. I hope that you like coq au vin, mon ami.'

'Good Lord, Giallo. I never expected you to cook dinner.'

'You sound surprised.'

'Well, yes,' I admitted.

'It's just that when you said that you were inviting me for dinner, I thought you were, well, going to do just that.' Giallo was looking at me rather perplexedly and I believe that this was one of the extremely rare occasions where I ever saw him appearing so.

'But I am inviting you for dinner, St. Louie. It just so happens that I am also cooking it. You do not approve?'

'Oh, I approve of it very much. It'll be a new experience, to say the least. It's just that you really didn't have to go through all this trouble...'

Giallo shushed me in a manner reminiscent of a mother hen dealing with its brood. 'It was no trouble at all.' Despite my efforts to help with dinner, I was forced out of the kitchen on account of my arm and to while away the time, I took out a book from Giallo's bookshelf but found myself unable to focus on the words before me.

Ten minutes later, we were seated at the table, and I was given the opportunity to savor my friend's wonderful cooking. As we ate and conversed over the last puzzling details of the case, an odd feeling of longing struck me, and I mused quietly to myself on how wonderful it would be if I were to stay at Giallo's side for the rest of my life.

At this point in time, I didn't even mind if we were to continue on merely a friendly basis – to converse, to share ideas, to have meals such as this one and even to be on the receiving end of those harsh critiques from that occasionally sharp tongue would be enough to satisfy me.

It would appear to be an existence to some, but with Giallo, nothing could be further from the truth.

Perhaps my unusual quietness caught Giallo's attention for when we were seated in our usual chairs in the sitting room after dinner. He asked, 'Is there something on your mind, St. Louie?'

'What? Oh, no,' I said, rather untruthfully.

'You have been avoiding me, mon ami,' he said without preamble. It was not a question; it was an obvious statement of fact and I coughed rather awkwardly.

'Really? Oh, well – I certainly didn't mean to, Giallo,' I managed, slowly setting my glass of whisky down, biding for time.

'You see, I've been so tied up with writing letters back home these past few days. Got side-tracked because of the investigation and my letter writing got backlogged quite a bit.'

'Ah, yes. I comprehend. Always the diligent and loyal son and brother. I too have had my fair share of that familial duty. It is difficult perhaps, but the family, it is all important.'

'Yes,' I said, not entirely in agreement, seeing that I hardly considered myself to be the model son personified.

'Your family, I trust, will be happy to see you?'

'I suppose so.' I wondered what my father's reaction would be upon seeing me back home and with my arm in a sling. Probably not the warmest of homecomings would await me from that quarter.

'I'll certainly have a lot to tell them. That's one thing,' I said.

'Imagine that Giallo – two murders and a wedding and all in just a few weeks!'

'Make that two weddings, monami,' announced Giallo quietly.

'I beg your pardon?' I asked, not believing my ears.

'Two murders and two weddings, St. Louie. There is to be another wedding.'

My heart sank; the dreaded moment of confirmation had finally come and there was no use in beating about the truth any longer. Observing that those keen brown eyes were watching me carefully, I took the plunge.

'Oh?' I managed as casually as I could.

'Between whom?'

I mentally braced myself, and then was completely dumbfounded when Giallo calmly replied, a faint smile appearing on his lips.

'Between Mademoiselle Janett and Lieutenant Mc Cloud.'

'What?' The word burst from my lips, and I leapt from my seat in astonishment. I immediately regretted doing so, as this only caused him to look up at me in intense curiosity.

'This surprises you, St. Louie?' asked Giallo, his dark brows raised.

My face flushed with embarrassment.

'Well, yes. To tell the truth, I – I didn't expect –'

'You didn't expect –?'

I inhaled deeply and sat back down. I hesitated before saying slowly, 'Well, I expected you were to marry Janett Giallo. The possibility of Tom ever proposing to her never entered my head at all.'

'Really? And what gave you that idea?'

'Why, the conversation you had with her, Giallo? That time you walked with her in the garden after we came back from – '

I stopped, knowing that I had said much more than I had intended.

'I did not know we were being observed,' responded Giallo drily, and I flushed even redder still, if it was possible, with further embarrassment.

'I gather then you also overheard some of our conversation, yes?'

'Seeing that you were both talking below my window, it was unavoidable, really,' I confessed.

'And what exactly did you hear?'

I shifted uncomfortably, knowing it was in extremely bad taste to recount eavesdropped exchanges, but I agreed to his enquiry and related exactly what I had heard.

There was silence with the ticking of the clock on the mantelpiece the only source of noise in the room. Giallo's expression was serious, his fingers steepled together and raised towards his chin. I wondered if I had outraged his professional sensibilities by admitting that I had eavesdropped on what was obviously a private tête-a-tête between two people, which had included none other than himself. Then a small smile appeared slowly on his face, and he startled me when he started chuckling amusedly to himself.

'Ah, St. Louie. You are always the same and never will you change. The leaping of the logic and to the conclusion.'

'Yes, Mademoiselle Janett was quite right.'

'Right about what?' I queried and not finding the whole affair amusing in the least.

'About your nature, St. Louie. Your beautiful and so honest nature. And really, mon ami, your skills at eavesdropping should be improved. Yes, she called me a 'dear thing' but the rest of that sentence you heard was referring entirely to you.'

'What?' I cried once again.

'But why? Why on earth would she want to talk to you about me?' I asked, completely perplexed.

'After your conversation with her in the garden and receiving your less than enthusiastic reaction, Mademoiselle Janett was, as you say, out of sorts. So much so that Monsieur Larry was concerned for his cousin's well-being and thus asked me to talk to her that evening. She told me all what she was feeling and also talked much about you in particular. I allowed her to do so – for I find it is easier to let the ladies say what is in their minds or their hearts than to stifle their feelings; it is unhealthy that.'

'I merely asked whether marriage was what she truly wanted.'

'So what did she ask you to do?'

'She asked me whether she would be allowed to confide in me from time to time. I accepted, and it was probably at that moment, St. Louie, that you overheard us.'

'And when I said that I understood and accepted her feelings for you, I meant just that. No more and no less,' he added as he predicted the question I was about to ask.

My mind which had been stubbornly endeavoring not to believe he gave in at this point.

'What made her choose Tom then?' I asked.

'Monsieur Mc Cloud has always harbored the affection for her from the start. He hides it well underneath that disciplined exterior, but I suspect that he was always ready to leap at the first opportunity to offer himself as a suitor to the young woman. Fortunately for him, the young woman in question finally noted his feelings and returned them in kind.'

'Good Lord, do you mean to say that you saw Tom's feelings for her right from the beginning?'

He passed a weary glance in my direction. 'And you did not? St. Louie, I would have thought the young man's feelings for her would have been obvious to anyone with eyes. I have even overheard Larry Stokes murmuring one afternoon to himself that 'poor Tom' was helplessly in love with the girl.'

'I coughed again, feeling like an absolute fool for not seeing things clearly. I had let my mind run away with itself when I should have been following Giallo's gods of order and method.

'This news displeases you, my friend?'

'Not in the least,' I said, and I felt more relieved more than anything at this moment.

'Janett's found the better man, I'm certain of that. To tell the truth, Giallo, I think I'd make a rather dull husband.'

A curious expression entered Giallo's face at this and he said,

'On the contrary, St. Louie, I think you would make an admirable husband. You have the courage and the sense of honor that so many men nowadays lack.'

I felt my face flush again, though this time from pleasure. Distractedly and looking for an excuse to do something, I stood up to straighten some objects on the mantelpiece, despite knowing that they were in no need of rearranging.

'Tell me, St. Louie,' said Giallo after a while, 'why were you so startled when I told you of Mademoiselle Janett's engagement just now?'

'Oh. Well, it's as I said. I always thought that it was you she was intent on marrying after I – er – overheard you both that night.'

'But surely if she had any intention of doing so, either she or I would have immediately told you of the fact.'

'Yes, I realize that now,' I sighed. 'I apologize, Giallo. I've been rather foolish, haven't I?'

'I think that is not all, St. Louie,' he said quietly, and he rose from his chair to join me by the mantelpiece.

'Whatever do you mean?' I said, my uninjured hand now frantically reshuffling the objects before me in heightened anxiety.'

'I mean it is not only the foolishness which made you to think as you did.'

Although this was precisely the case, I denied this when Giallo suddenly reached out and covered my hand with his own, stilling my movements. I turned to look at him, my breath catching, as this time I was in no doubt of what he meant by the look in those brown eyes of his.

'Not only foolishness, Giallo?' I managed to breathe, aware that his face was only inches away from me.

I watched enthralled as his gaze travelled down to my lips, then back up again.

'No, I think not,' murmured Giallo and slowly he leaned forward and pressed his lips to mine.

For a few moments, I did not know how to react – such was the depth of my utter disbelief – until I felt Giallo's hand burrow itself in my hair, pulling me closer into his embrace and then I was lost. All the accumulated frustration and longing I had suppressed seemed to manifest itself at this point, and I returned his kiss passionately, something which I was delighted to learn that Giallo welcomed.

At length, we broke apart.

'How did you know?' I asked, slightly breathless.

'How did you know that I was in love with you?'

Giallo smiled.

'Because I felt the same way towards you, mon ami. Ever since we met that day in Paris.'

'Good Lord,' I whispered, surprised that he had been in love with me for so long and I hadn't learned of it until now.

Taking in my astonishment, he added softly.

'Do not think me heartless, St. Louie. I only did not reveal my feelings for fear that you might not reciprocate them.' He brushed his hand against my cheek, and I instinctively leaned into his touch.

'Well, you picked an extremely inconvenient time to reveal them,' I said in mock annoyance, and we laughed despite ourselves, but my face grew grave as I glanced at the clock between us. It was nearly eleven; only twelve hours until my train was due to depart.'

Our gazes caught, and I said impulsively, 'Come with me to England, Giallo.'

Giallo's face fell.

'As much as I would like to …I cannot.'

Disappointment filled me to the core. I had been a fool in expecting him to abandon everything he had here just for my sake. Here he had fame and a respectable position in his chosen profession. It would be madness for him to uproot himself and try to establish himself abroad. And though he had never told me, I suspected that his family depended upon him to support them and that therefore he had to take them into consideration before making such a move to a foreign country.

'St. Louie –'

'I'm sorry, Giallo. That was thoughtless of me to even suggest such a thing.'

Silence enveloped the room, and I said tonelessly, 'There's a war coming.'

He looked up sharply at me at that, but said nothing.

'There's talk among most of the chaps in my family about joining the army if war ever breaks out and, to tell the truth, I've always intended to follow them.'

'I paused, then said rather desperately, 'Giallo, if I end up being killed –'

A swiftly placed a finger on my lips prevented me from continuing.

'Do not speak of it, mon cher,' he said, his eyes filled with a powerful emotion which caused my heart to ache.

I gently removed his hand from my lips and clenched it.'

'Then if you can't come with me to England…can't you give me this night instead?'

An inexplicable expression came across his face at my words, but I could see the desire in my eyes reflected in his.

'You have wanted this, St. Louie? You have wanted Giallo?'

Instead of replying, I merely leaned forward and kissed him.

'Mon ami, we should not…your arm…'

'Damn my arm,' I murmured, frustration entering my voice.

'I've wanted this moment to happen for weeks and I will not let it stop me from having you.'

Actually, I had probably wanted him from the very beginning, but didn't realize it until much later.

My thoughts were evidently written all over my face, he said softly.

'Then it shall be so, St. Louie.'

And he took me gently by the hand and led me to his bed

Chapter 14

Epilogue

I t was not until July 1917 that I could see Giallo again after
my departure from Paris. Four years had gone by and so too
it seemed the peaceful world we had inhabited in 1913. The
war took its toll on both of us; Giallo was injured in the opening
stages of the German invasion of his beloved country before his
flight to England, while I was to be invalided out of the army
after the Somme. Despite this, we were fortunate because we
survived the war. Tom Mc Cloud was not as fortunate; he was
killed at the Battle of Jutland though not before he and Janett
spent some happy years together and seeing the birth of their
only son, John.

Larry and Samantha are now living their lives peacefully in
Australia, where Larry is now Official Secretary to the Governor-
General. After lying low for some years after the death of Sir
Charles, my friend became a diplomat in his own right and
every Christmas, we send him and Samantha a card. For without
them really, where would Giallo and I have been? Luke Grimms,
I understand, never married, and now lives alone at his family's
country estate.

As for Giallo and I – older and greyer as we now are – time
has been relatively kind to us and, despite our rather contrasting
characters; the years have forged an even closer bond than the
one we had in 1913.

All the things I had only hoped of attaining as a young man of twenty-six were made reality when we finally were given the chance to share rooms after Giallo's success regarding the Birmingham case allowed him to set up business in London.

Undoubtedly, such an arrangement has caused people's tongues to wag, but this does not bother us in the least, and Giallo's reputation as a renowned detective admittedly has some influence over the press, which affords us some privacy.

For the past few hours, Giallo has been reading the finished draft of this case at his desk. Despite having written countless accounts of our past cases over the last decade or so, this one is the most personal of them all and I observe him nervously from my place on the couch, awaiting his reaction. I marvel at the fact that even after more than two decades; I am no closer to deciphering that great mind of his than I was twenty-three years ago.

Giallo has now reached the last page. A smile slowly creeps over his face, and he looks up at me with that expression I am well-acquainted with and I know exactly what his intentions are as he neatly puts the book aside and makes his way towards me. And like the Nicolas St. Louie in Paris all those years ago, I give in to him without protest.

For, there are things that even twenty-three years cannot change.

The End

Milton Keynes UK
Ingram Content Group UK Ltd.
UKHW020701040324
438885UK00018B/1169